The
Winthrop
Covenant

LOUIS AUCHINCLOSS

The Winthrop Covenant

Houghton Mifflin Company Boston

A limited edition of this book has been privately printed.

FOR MY SON
Blake Leay Auchincloss

Foreword

These stories, thematically related, are arranged chronologically from 1630 to the present day and are designed to trace, by the use of fiction and dramatized history, the rise and fall of the Puritan ethic in New York and New England. By Puritan ethic I mean that preoccupying sense, found in certain individuals, of a mission, presumably divinely inspired, toward their fellow men. To show how different puritans have accepted, converted, stood aside from or rejected the burden of this mission, I have chosen members of the Winthrop family. Only John and Wait Still are modeled on actual persons.

Contents

(1)

The Covenant

THAT MISTRESS ANNE HUTCHINSON should have desired to transport
her large family across a wilderness of ocean waves to settle in Massachusetts in what was called the "Bay Colony" occasioned little
enough surprise in Alford. The woman was renowned, after all, for
her restlessness, for her boldness of imagination and her willingness
to pull up stakes and try new ideas. And everyone knew how sorely
she had missed her minister, John Cotton, of the silver tongue and
winning ways, to whose church in the neighboring town, before his
emigration to the New World, she had journeyed every Sunday for
several years. Anne's eyes and heart had been in the west ever since
his departure, and she had a great faith in the Almighty's predisposi-
tion to smooth any difficulties in a path that she chose. Why should
she fear rats or rattlesnakes, pirate sails or pillaging savages?

But that William, her William, Alford's William, comfortable,
solid, well-to-do William, at whose prosperous linen shop one was assured of a consoling banality for every change of weather, every piece
of neighborhood gossip, every bit of domestic news, that William, at
the overripe age of forty-seven, when he might already with some
justification be looking forward to greater leisure with his pipe and
bowl as able sons took over his business, should be willing to hazard
his fortune to the untried mercies of Governor Winthrop's unproved
foreign settlement, seemed more amazing than the birth to a poor
woman in nearby Lincoln of a babe with two heads. People could
only agree with a shrug that it must be true, after all, what William's
father had said when his son had married Anne Marbury: that peace
in *that* household would only be bought at the price of an exchange
of trousers for apron strings.

They would have been surprised had they heard a conversation between William and his clerical brother-in-law, John Wheelwright, just prior to the latter's own departure for Massachusetts. The interview took place on a Sunday morning after the service in the little whitewashed room in the rear of the chapel where Wheelwright was wont to read his Bible before dinner.

"I want to ask you a theological question, John," William began soberly. "I know you expect such questions from Anne and not from me, but it's my own sister you're married to, not hers, and I think you should hear me once in a while."

"But, William, I'm glad to, very glad!"

"Thank you, John. I shall take little enough of your time. What I want to ask concerns the doctrine of the elect. You and Anne and Mr. Cotton, who has already gone over the sea, hold that only those shall be saved whom God has elected. And that the only sign of election is the presence of the Holy Ghost in the saved one's soul. Is that correct?"

"That is correct."

"So one cannot tell that a man has been elected because he leads a righteous and sober life? Or because he goes to church, or because he is a respected magistrate?"

"That is also true, William."

"Then it must follow, must it not, that some lewd fellow who leads a disorderly life may be elected, while some holy, church-going matron may be damned?"

"If you push me to it, yes. But allow me to doubt if the lewd fellow be one of the elect."

"But he *might* be?"

"It is so. He might be."

"And a man who tries to be a good Christian may be damned while one who doesn't try at all may be saved?"

"Who is to say that the sinner has not tried? I had no idea that you considered these matters so closely, William."

William's countenance bore its usual impassivity as he contemplated the light and shadow passing over his brother-in-law's big features. Wheelwright's pointed nose and long, pointed chin and large, flashing eyes might have been assets in the pulpit, but they simply emphasized his condescension outside of it. William knew perfectly that his brother-in-law regarded him as an amiable dunce to be tolerated only on account of his handsome property and brilliant wife. Yet he also knew that he had some points of superiority over the minister. Wheelwright, for example, had no notion that his wife's affable brother disliked and distrusted him.

"And if a man is not elected, it does him no good to lead a godly life?"

"None."

"Then why should he do so?"

"Because he cannot know that he is not elected."

"I see. He can only know if he is. And not always then. For there are some who are elected who don't know it. So there always appears to be a chance. But what it still boils down to is that one is or one isn't. Why, then, do we need *you*, John?"

Wheelwright smiled broadly. "So that's what you're after. I see it! Do away with the wretched clergyman and save your tithe. We are needed, dear William, so that those who hope to be elected may gather together to anticipate their blessedness."

William did not betray what his reaction to *this* was. He simply proceeded with his argument, having already anticipated that the minister would say what he had said.

"Let me return for a moment to the non-elect. Their case is hopeless, and there is nothing they can do about it. Must they be damned?"

"What else? A soul must be saved or damned."

"And burned in eternal fire?"

"I do not presume to know what form their tortures may take."

"But there will be tortures?"

"Indubitably."

"I saw two women burned alive in London once. It is a fearsome death. Yet I wonder if it's not more painful to light the faggot than feel the fire. I'd rather be the burned than the burner. Think of it, John. Having on your conscience that you had set fire to a living woman!"

The idea seemed less horrific to Wheelwright. "Surely, that would depend on what she'd done."

"Would it?" William continued to follow aloud the thread of his speculation. "But I suppose, in an eternity of torture, the particular nature of the pain might not signify. One would get used to anything: the feeling of the flames or the feeling of guilt at having lit the faggot. Eventually there would not have to be any heat at all, or any cold. One's simple existence, without end, without hope, would be as horrible as anything the Spanish Inquisition could devise."

"Indeed, it has been said that hell is simply the separation from God."

"And that heaven is union with him," William rejoined, more eagerly now. "Just so! Now that is what I am coming to. In the Bay Colony, where John Cotton has gone and where John Winthrop governs, there is a city of the elect. Or let us say of many elect. The fact that they have gone to seek a new relation with God in the wilderness may signify the making of a new covenant with God, may it not?"

"So Governor Winthrop is said to believe."

"If the settlers of the Bay Colony shall establish a godly community, the Lord will protect it—would not that be the covenant?"

"Some such matter."

"Now here is my question, John: might it not be possible, if this great spiritual experiment were to succeed, and the Almighty to fulfill His covenant, that He could, like a sovereign on the day of his coronation, declare an amnesty and elect the non-elect?"

Wheelwright's face seemed even longer and whiter in his slowly evolving astonishment. A long moment passed. "You mean open the Gates of Hell?"

"Or close them shut. For no one is there yet, surely? Until Judgment Day?"

Wheelwright concealed his confusion in a smile and a quick glance of mock apprehension towards the door. "Do you mean that even Archbishop Laud would be saved? Don't strain my credulity!"

William was careful to risk no answering smile. "That is my question. Might not all be elected? At least all in the new colony?"

"Even those who fell away from the faith?" Wheelwright was as grave now as a member of the Holy Office. "Even blasphemers and idolators?"

"It was the question, John."

"Then here is the answer, William! No, no. There is no way of denying hell. How many will be in it we cannot know, but that it will outnumber the hosts of heaven I have little doubt. But tell me, William Hutchinson, you have not, I hope, been spreading any such heresy as this among the good Christians of Alford?"

How well William knew the gleam of authority in those focused, staring eyes! He had seen it in the orbs of far greater persons than his sister's husband. But he had learned, like a partridge squatting among brown leaves, how to make himself indistinguishable to the hawk soaring above. He was not afraid; there was no danger that a tremble might cause a betraying rustle.

"Only to Anne."

"And did she agree with you?"

"She was good enough to say so. But then she wants me to take her to the New World. Do not fear for us, John. I have simply exercised my right to speak to my pastor in private and to ask for his instruction. I have received it, and I shall be guided accordingly."

"God bless you, William."

The fool suspected nothing, and William departed. What he had wanted was to hear his own theory of the covenant enunciated aloud. It gave it reality to move it out of his brain into the air around him. A monologue would not have sufficed. That John Wheelwright would reject his theory and hug hell to his chest to warm an icy heart William had fully anticipated. As he walked to his home now, past the neat brick fronts and neat green lawns with sundials, he reflected that he might, after all, be able to fill a place in the new colony of Anne's spiritual adventure. For he might at last have found the way to shut the padlock on hell.

2

William from childhood had learned to keep himself a secret from others. This had been made easier by the fact that the others had no idea that he had any self to keep a secret. He appeared to the world as the personification of the healthy, strapping English boy who wore his heart on his sleeve and his mind in his grin, who yearned to grow up and fight on the Spanish Main like Drake or Raleigh. William found that his long blond hair and sky blue eyes, his straight, broad nose and square chin, his rugged, lanky build, did most of the work in human relations and that in the presence of his elders he had only to smile sheepishly and shift his feet bashfully to make the old men tell stories about their youth and the old women cackle about the hearts that he was bound to break. He could retire peaceably behind the stage front of his incipient masculinity, safe in his own thoughts, his own privacy. The herd was always content to let a young bull be just a young bull. One day, after all, they might depend on his horns. Let him be strong!

While William was still a boy, an incident occurred that made a grave difference in his life. His mother, who could not leave her family of young children on the Sabbath, used to send William, when his father was away buying wholecloth in London, to church with his grandmother. This dear old woman was very talkative and confidential, but a bit senile, for she treated children just as she did adults. She confided in William her nostalgia for the "old church" and told him on their walk how beautiful the vanished stained-glass windows of yesteryear had been, full of brilliantly colored Biblical and historical scenes, and how superior to the slatey white ones of their own day through which you could not even see out to the spring glories of Lincolnshire. William, during the two hours of the sermon, would imagine the old windows aglow with fiery reds, emerald greens and sapphire blues; he would visualize the Armada, storm-tossed, hurled on black, dripping rocks, and the Queen riding to Tilbury on a white horse, and Christ with the children, and Christ walking on the blue water, and Christ crucified, his bleeding side pierced with the spear. But he also had another picture, which his grandmother had inspired, and that was of the Virgin, all love and loveliness, in a blue cape, reaching down from heaven with white, milky arms, to take Granny and William and help them up to her side.

It was at Granny's house after church one Sunday that the ugly thing happened. William asked his grandmother if he could pray to the Virgin at night. He was explaining that there were things in a boy's life that Mary might understand better than Jesus, who had never married or had a family, when suddenly his withered, mumbling old grandfather, who never joined in any conversation and never went to church, but simply sat all day by the kitchen fire, jumped up.

"Have you been filling the boy's head with popish trash? Will you never learn to hold your tongue, you mad old woman?"

And he struck her rudely across the mouth with his bony, dark fist. William's grandmother quickly bowed her head, but she said nothing, she did not even cry out, and the dreadful ancestor resumed his seat by the fire from where he glared balefully at his wife and at William.

"You don't believe her, do you, William?"

"I don't understand what she said that was wrong!"

His grandfather grunted and snapped: "Take care you never understand. Things will go better for you if you don't."

William proceeded to redeem himself for what now seemed to him his cowardly response by crossing the room to put his arms around his grandmother. For several minutes he sat there, staring defiantly at the old man as he kept his arms around the tiny, trembling frame of the poor creature who had so mysteriously offended her mate. But his grandfather simply shrugged and turned back to the fire. And William thus dimly derived this early lesson: that there were two forces in the world, authority and the resistance which authority generated. His grandfather was authority: swift, arbitrary, inexorable, clear. His poor old grandmother was the other force, if force was the word for it, a natural opposition, a vine growing about a tree, an emotional voice raised only to be stifled and raised again. There was no real sense in either force, but a man might preserve his manhood by putting his arms, now and again, around the latter.

Further and more terrible confirmation of this lesson came two years later when William was old enough to accompany his father on one of his trips to London. Left to himself for a morning, he wandered about the streets in the vicinity of Smithfield, where his father's business meetings were. When he saw a crowd assembled in an open field around two stakes, his curiosity impelled him to join it, and before he realized what was happening, he found himself undergoing the initiation of his first public execution.

What he always remembered afterwards was the silence. The crowd, numbering perhaps two hundred persons, vagrants, street venders, passers-by, was quiet, attentive, but only passively interested. A man with a monkey or a bear might have attracted as much attention. Bound to the iron stakes by chains were two women, one middle-aged, one still young. The younger woman's eyes were wide and round and filled with a dumb, uncomprehending animal fear. William had seen that expression on a deer cornered by hounds. The older woman's lips were moving rapidly but inaudibly. Presumably she was muttering a prayer. William heard a man behind him explaining to his neighbor that they were Anabaptists. The two men attending to the execution were piling up faggots around the women's feet. Nearby stood the cart which had brought them from prison. The horse was grazing. There was a ghastly usualness about the scene, a sense of faint boredom. What most came through to William was a horrible feeling of participation. In some curious way the onlookers, the executioners, the two women, the cart-driver sitting with the reins in hand, William himself, were all integral parts of the picture. He, William, was setting the fire; he, William, was lighting the faggots; he, William, was being burned. That was what an execution was. Everyone was part of it.

This dire sense did not leave him even when the bundles of wood were lit. The fire around both stakes blazed up very rapidly, and there was a quick pall of dark smoke. But even here the crackle of flames was the only noise. The women did not cry out. Had they been mercifully strangled? One of the executioners was seen moving out of the smoke from behind a stake. Smoke now enveloped the women, and when it cleared for a moment William could see that their heads had slumped. Then he ran away as fast as he could.

When he told his father about it, the latter was humane, but casual. "I never could see why they have to fry the poor creatures. Why won't the noose do the trick? It's a quick death, and there's an end to it. But I'll tell you one thing, son. They talk too much about the old Queen's mercifulness. She's got a good bit of her sister Mary in her. There's something in the Tudors that likes a burning. Did you know her own mother was sentenced to the stake? But King Hal saved her. He had her head whacked off instead. I guess even he didn't want his wife roasted in public."

William's mind groped amid all these horrors. "But I thought the executioners strangled them before they were burned," he protested, returning to the silent victims. "That's just like hanging, isn't it? Those women didn't cry out."

"Well, maybe they strangled them, but I doubt it. Those fellows don't get paid for standing that close to the fire. Sometimes a lucky victim is smothered in the smoke before the fire gets to him. And sometimes he faints or dies of sheer terror. So they tell me, anyway. But not all are so fortunate. I saw a poor devil fried in Lincoln—he was a witch, they said. It was a wet day, and the fire kept going out. You could hear his bellows halfway across the town."

William put his hands to his ears.

"Well, we'll talk no more about it," his father concluded, with a callous adult grin. "Anyway, there's something more important. I have a treat in store for you. The Queen is going to Blackfriars this afternoon. We'll see her pass. If you live to be an old man, you can tell your grandchildren you saw Gloriana in the flesh."

"Gloriana?"

"That's what the poets call her. Because she beat the Spaniards and brought us peace."

"But the burnings, Father! You said she was responsible for them!"

"The burnings? What does the burning of a couple of heretics have to do with the greatness of the Queen of England? When you see her go by, my boy, take off your cap and cheer as loudly as ever you can. And pray that she lives forever! For there's trouble enough about who's to succeed her."

Two hours later William stood in awe by his father as the royal procession emerged from Whitehall. All were on foot, the halberdiers, the priests and bishops, the gentlemen of the court, the bearers of the golden palanquin with the sovereign's chair. Elizabeth alone in the cortege was carried, and she was borne, as befitted so great an empress, on the shoulders of the finest young nobles of her court. Under the gorgeous canopy she sat in placid majesty, wearing the orbed crown, the great ruff collar, the many necklaces of huge jewels that William had seen in a dozen prints. Behind her, in pairs, walked her ladies-in-waiting, all young and beautiful, all with ruff collars. William felt that his image of royalty had come to a splendid life.

But as the procession passed, and the great palanquin drew closer, he sustained a profound shock. The sovereign, motionless, glaring, might have been some hideous wax dummy borne by mute, superstitious heathens as part of a pagan ceremonial. Under the crisply curled, shining red hair of the wig, which seemed no more part of the head than the pearled crown, the white powdered mask of the face with its high cheekbones and small mouth and great aquiline nose had the rigidity of a death mask. William was beginning to wonder if it really might be an effigy when the head turned, and he sensed the hard black glitter of the queen's stare directly upon him. The palanquin was only a few yards away now, and William, feeling his father's sharp pinch, shouted out in a voice that was strange to him:

"God save the Queen's Grace!"

And majesty smiled, majesty actually smiled and nodded as the procession passed on! William's father patted him on the back, and strangers standing in the crowd congratulated the lad on being the recipient of the royal nod. William was thrilled. He had actually been, or had seemed at least, what majesty expected: he had huzzaed with the lustiness of a youth who wanted to fight in the Spanish Main for Good Queen Bess! Oh, yes, so long as he could do *that*, he was safe. He had learned the shape of the mask that would keep him immune even from the black, prying eyes of old royalty herself. For William, in that very moment when his own image had been stamped on Gloriana's eyeballs, had recognized her stare. It was the same stare that he had seen in his grandfather's eyes when the old man had struck the poor crazy woman on the mouth.

3

William's life had consisted of tracts of comfortable brown and green punctuated by a few moments of lightning. After that day in London a dozen years had passed without another such flash. He grew into a man; he became his father's prime assistant; he prospered. Everyone spoke of William Hutchinson as a model young man—when they spoke of him at all. He did not drink so much as to be called dissolute or so little as to be laughed at for a Puritan. He never started a quarrel, but he was not slow with his powerful fists if someone took advantage of him. He worked hard, but he was always ready for a jig on Saturday night. If he had a fault, it was silence. People suspected that there could be no great brain behind such mildness of manner. And the older women criticized him because he did not marry. But that fault was remedied by the time he was twenty-seven.

Anne Marbury was seven years younger than William, but people were already beginning to say she might never marry. She was a fine, healthy girl, tall, straight and strong, with a brown complexion, but she was plain, and the Marburys, though well connected and well-to-do, had a reputation for religious disputatiousness that contributed little to their popularity. But Anne had eyes that fascinated William. They were brown with a shiny yellow gleam, and they fixed him with an earnestness and a candor that seemed to promise good fellowship. William was normally averse to eyes that so penetrated a man, but from the beginning he made an exception for Anne.

The Marburys and the Hutchinsons had always been acquaintances, but Anne and William did not become close friends until shortly before their marriage. He afterwards learned that Anne had been observing him from a distance and that she would not become his friend until she was convinced that she wanted to become his wife. She had a way of speaking of her soul as if she were speaking of a child confided to her care. She showed a cheerfulness on the subject that William had never associated with religious matters. At first it rather scandalized him, but he found himself a rapid convert.

"I *know* my soul is saved," Anne told him one Sunday morning after church, with smiling confidence. "I know it because I feel it here." She tapped her chest. "There is something in there, telling me. I believe it is the Holy Ghost inside of me. Do you ever feel that?"

"I'm afraid I don't. Perhaps it's because I am less used to listening."

"That could be it! Oh, William, when I look into your eyes, I know you're saved!"

As she looked now into his eyes, and he returned her stare, a strange feeling of exultation shook him. It was extraordinary the way the girl could do this without even a hint of coyness or flirtation. And yet her look was still sexual. What she was obviously doing, then and there, was electing him to be her mate. There did not even have to be consent on his part. Somehow the decision had already been boldly, even beautifully made.

"I suppose I lead a fairly straight kind of life," he muttered, "if that's any sign of salvation."

"No, that's not it. It's something that comes out of you to me."

"Can you always tell who is saved and who is not, Anne?"

"Oh, my, no. I have no such gift. Nor should I even seek it. Imagine knowing that someone was not saved! How could I ever look the poor soul in the face? Seeing the darkness and terror that lay before him?"

William scratched his brow.

"What are you thinking, William?"

"I was thinking . . . well, I was wondering if I could ask you something."

"Why on earth not?"

"It's about souls being saved. Do you suppose it might be possible . . . I'm only asking, mind you . . . that *all* souls are saved?"

Her large bright eyes closed in a surprised blink. It was not the question that she had anticipated. "All?" she repeated.

"Yes. You see if heaven is perfect joy, it cannot be marred. Even by the tiniest thing. Because in eternity the least bad thing would eventually have to become unbearable. Like a noise of dripping when you're trying to sleep. And so the knowledge that there were souls burning while you were in bliss would in time spoil the bliss."

"I had no idea that you thought of such things, William."

"I do sometimes. If I wake up in the early morning. It's nothing, of course." He shrugged, embarrassed, and turned away.

"Oh, William, I wasn't criticizing you. Don't turn away from me like that." Anne went eagerly over and caught his arm to turn him back. "I think it's wonderful that you're so deep."

"It doesn't do for a man to jabber about heaven and hell."

"But I think it's just what a man should jabber about! Most of you talk only about your shops and your ale and how many birds you've killed. What more concerns us than our own souls? Indeed, I wonder that we discuss anything else. Let us go into this. You ask if all might be saved? Not even one soul damned?"

"Yes." William glanced hastily behind them. The rest of the congregation were still emerging from church after the service, but none were within hearing. "Because, you see, even one damned soul would be just as upsetting in eternity—after a million years, say—as a thousand. It would take a long time for such a speck of misery to soil all the happiness of heaven, but that's just my point. We'd *have* a long time. We'd have forever!"

He expected even Anne to be shocked by this, but she was not. She actually clapped her hands together. "Do you know something, William? That's a very beautiful idea of yours. A hell emptied of sinners! I like it. Oh, I think I like it very much!"

This statement made William so happy that he proposed to Anne the very next day and was accepted. But he was not a man to push his luck. He was perfectly contented with her theology and saw no need to give her an opportunity to change her mind—or to tell him that she had. More than a decade and a half were to elapse before he again asked her opinion of hell.

These years passed in tranquility, each one bringing another baby, borne with great ease by the efficient Anne, and an increase of income to accompany the increased family responsibility. William's father died, and he was now head of the linen shop, head of the Hutchinson clan and one of the more esteemed burghers of Alford. But although William was considered with respect and affection by his fellow citizens, he never assumed a voice in the affairs of the community. He preferred to stand aside, a silent if friendly observer, always ready to listen to anyone's problem and even, if pressed, to offer a piece of laconic advice, more noted for its common sense than its brilliance. Anne remained his only confidante, but their large and always expanding family provided an ever-present audience that diminished the occasions for intimate interchange. William tried to content himself with her general approval, however rarely expressed now in particulars. But deep in his heart he knew that she had moved beyond him. Anne seemed to be trying her spiritual wings for a longer flight than any offered by Alford.

William dated a new era in Anne's religious life from the arrival of John Cotton in the next town. Cotton as a divine was much admired by William's brother-in-law, Wheelwright, who was very close to Anne, and the drive over to hear the great man preach soon became a weekly excursion for the Hutchinsons. Even William, who was slow to wax enthusiastic, had to admit that Cotton's tongue was silver-coated. Also, it pleased him that the new divine was less harsh and dogmatic in his views than other ministers. In gracious, winning, mellifluous tones he sought to pitch his message to every member of his congregation. He never, like Wheelwright, assumed to set himself above his parishioners. Cotton always assured them that worship was an act in which all participated equally.

There was a mystical quality in his sermons that appealed particularly to the women. For Cotton grace was cardinal. Prayer, fasting, humility of heart and demeanor, a charitable disposition, a loving heart, all of these things were very fine in themselves, but they were mere hints, possibly misleading, as to the individual's salvation. The only way that a man could have any real assurance that he was saved was from within, and Cotton, waving his long robed arms gracefully before his communicants, sought to move them to constant self-examination in search for the one true seal, a faith emanating directly from God.

Anne's intensity during these sermons was such as ultimately to arouse her husband's alarm. She would sit like a statue except for her shining, dilating eyes, and when the service was over he sometimes had to nudge her gently to remind her that it was time to leave. He could not but suspect, with so much emphasis from the pulpit on being saved, that Anne had ceased to agree with her old position on that subject.

"I do not suppose Mr. Cotton would care much for my theory of paradise," he observed, on a drive back to Alford.

Anne, still rapt in a mystical communication with her parson, was staring ahead at the road. She did not answer for so long that he thought she had not heard him. But Anne always heard—even things she considered unworthy of her attention. "What is your theory of paradise, William?" she asked now, in the quiet tone of simple good manners.

"Don't you remember, Anne? That it was paradise precisely because everyone was in it."

She turned to give him a blank look. "Everyone?"

"I mean that there are no damned."

"No damned, William? How can that be when our Lord said that many are called but few are chosen?"

"But you said yourself it was a beautiful idea! Just before we were engaged!"

"Did I?" Anne seemed at last to be interested. The familiar strong line on her usually clear brow was a sure signal that the question was receiving her total attention. "And so it is a beautiful idea. An empty hell!" She clasped her hands. "I like it. But is it true, do you think, William?"

"Might it not be true in the new world? Might there not be a fresh start there for everybody?"

Anne's eyes were very grave now, but behind the gravity there seemed to lurk something like a cautious hope. "Are you interested in the new world, William? You've never told me so."

"I wanted to think it all out first."

"Mr. Cotton is planning to go there. He says that John Winthrop is creating a city of God in the American wilderness."

"It would be a hard existence."

"Aye, William, but a good one!" There was a sudden note of passion in her tone. "What sort of life is there here for our children? What is the English church doing for their spirits? When Wheelwright goes, and Cotton goes, who will be left?"

"You want to go, Anne. You want it desperately. I see that."

"Oh, William, I haven't dared to ask you!" Her eyes beseeched him, for the first time in their marriage. "Would you consider it? Really and truly? I know in my heart that the Lord means us to go. I have heard him in my soul say that the church here is not his church any more. And the fact that you have been thinking what you have been thinking . . . oh, my dear, don't you see? The Lord is speaking to you, too!" Anne clasped her hands in supplication.

William was still thinking. "But the covenant, Anne," he insisted.

"The covenant?"

"The new covenant that all might be saved in that new colony. Could you believe that?"

She hesitated, but only for a moment. Her eyes were shining. "Yes!" she cried. "Yes, William, I could believe it!"

He turned his attention back to the reins as a queer thought struck him. Had she just told him the only lie of her lifetime?

4

In later years William was always to associate their time in Boston with cold. Even the torrid summers left no impression on his mind;

they seemed to have melted away in memory before the grim picture of a hundred thatched huts, huddled together in muddy alleyways on the black hilly point in the Bay between a wintry Atlantic and an infinity of black forest. The houses were cold; the meeting house was cold, the people were cold; even the dogs and cows seemed cold. Alford became idealized in retrospect. William now saw England as smiling in a perpetual English spring.

Yet there were compensations—in the beginning, at least. When there *was* anything to buy, William's ample savings went a long way. His small capital made him at once one of the prominent citizens of the colony, and as his able-bodied sons did most of the physical labor on the farm, he had more time to read and to converse with new friends than he had ever had at home. The house that the Hutchinsons built, though bare enough by Alford standards, was the second largest in Boston and stood across the alley from that of John Winthrop, who, having been succeeded in the governor's chair by Sir Harry Vane, had himself now time enough, in clement weather, for little strolls of inspection of the settlement, in which he sometimes asked William to join him. William had learned to admire the ex-governor who had ruled the little colony with patience and wisdom, and who seemed to find in his new neighbor a respectful ambulatory audience for his political reminiscences and future projects. For everyone knew that Winthrop's retirement was only temporary. Vane was young and foolish, and his predecessor was still the first man of the settlement.

Anne, of course, was much more active. She found everything in the new world exhilarating. The days were not long enough for all she seemed to have to do. The growing Hutchinson girls had taken the housework off her hands, as the boys had taken farm work off William's, and now she was free to make calls and to receive them, to visit the sick and to go to sermons, not only in Boston but in Newtown. She said that it was her plan to know every woman in the Bay Colony, and she began to hold meetings at the house on Wednesday and Sunday afternoons, when John Cotton or John Wheelwright would lead the discussions. The new world seemed to represent to her a last chance to make something of a life that had been hitherto necessarily domestic. Anne had found her mission.

But just what was it? William began to have nervous forebodings when he came home, at the break-up of these meetings, to find her in deep and earnest conversation with Wheelwright, which they would at once interrupt on seeing him. One Sunday evening, as he and Winthrop approached the house, they noted that the women emerging from the meeting were jabbering with unusual excitement. Winthrop paused and placed his large, dark, grave gaze on the retreating females with unconcealed disapproval.

"Your wife likes meetings, Master Hutchinson," he observed in his somber tone. "Has she no housework to occupy her?"

"My daughters help her, sir. It all gets done."

"Perhaps when they are married, Mistress Hutchinson will have less time for such frivolities."

"I assure your honor that my wife's meetings are not in the least frivolous. The women speak only of church matters."

"It might be better if they gossiped," Winthrop retorted in a harsher voice. "In my opinion, Master Hutchinson, no good comes from cackling women. The female of our race has a naturally destructive nature which must be kept down. Doing housework, attending to her children, on her knees before God, she may be an admirable creature and a blessing to us men. But when she pits her brains against ours, it is only to bring misery to all. I counsel you to offer your wife the example of Mistress Winthrop. Tell her that we have not crossed the ocean and fought the savages to lose our peace of mind in idle disputes. Look to it, friend! I bid you good night."

Winthrop strode off in his most stately fashion, and William watched him disappear into his house. Then he sighed and entered his own doorway. One of the women was still there, Mary Dyer, a fervid, rolling-eyed enthusiast. She was talking excitedly to Wheelwright and Anne.

"I've heard them *all*, I tell you! I've been as far as Salem, and there's not one of them that preaches a true covenant of grace but you and Mr. Cotton. I can vouch for it. And you can tell the Worshipful Winthrop and his friend Dudley that a hundred women will vouch for it! A hundred women, led by Sir Harry Vane!"

When Anne saw William she did not actually put her finger to her lips, but the way she placed Mary Dyer's cloak about her shoulders constituted a definite injunction to be quiet and to go. Wheelwright followed the departing guest after a too hearty greeting to William and a too perfunctory remark about the chances of snow.

"Anne," William asked quietly when they were alone, "is it John Winthrop whom you'll be instructing next?"

"And why not, if he needs instruction?"

"Because even if he is not the governor, he is still the father of the colony. The magistrates will follow him. Even Dudley will follow him—if it's a choice between Winthrop and Wheelwright."

"You forget about Mr. Cotton."

"I do *not* forget about Mr. Cotton. But Mr. Cotton has a silver tongue. You can never tell which side it will persuade him to take."

Anne flared. "For shame, William!"

But William was determined to see this through. "For shame yourself, woman," he retorted with unwonted vigor. "Do you know what they do with dissenters in these settlements? They banish them! And do you know what banishment can mean in a land of snow and savages?"

"Death? Didn't Jesus tell his disciples that death would be their reward? Who am I to ask for privilege?"

"Perhaps nobody. But let me point out that you owe a debt to a husband and children who left the comfort of the old country for this barren wilderness at your behest!"

"None of you would have to share my banishment." Anne held her head up proudly. "I should go alone."

"We would share your banishment, whether or not we shared your sentence." William announced this very firmly. "We came to this land together, and we shall stay together."

Anne was made humbler by this. She nodded silently and then, closing her eyes, let her brow rest for a moment on his shoulder. "Thank you, William."

"Will you tell me now what instructions you will be giving to Mr. Winthrop?"

"Governor Vane is with us!"

"Governor Vane is nothing. A mere silly stripling of an aristocrat whom Winthrop will send back to England on the first boat that suits him. Place not your faith in Vane. Tell me, what is it you have against Winthrop?"

"He believes in works, William," Anne said earnestly now, seeing that it was useless to ignore him further. "He believes in a covenant of works. They *all* do, except Cotton and Wheelwright. The magistrates, the ministers, all of them. They believe that if you wear long faces and go to church in white ruffs and black suits and utter all sorts of pious nothings and sing psalms and hang thieves and blasphemers, you can be saved!"

"They don't say that."

"But they act it."

"And do you accuse them of this at your women's meetings?"

"Oh, no, William! Never. All I say is that Cotton and Wheelwright preach a covenant of grace *better* than they do."

William looked into those earnest eyes and knew that they could now speak only truth. But he still shrugged. "I suppose it's not so much what you actually say as what they say you say. Be careful, Anne. I have a sick feeling in my bones that we're on the verge of terrible trouble."

"Pray, then, William. Pray."

For once he permitted himself to be bitter. "Why? Isn't it a work? Can a man be saved by works?"

"William!" she reproved him, but he would talk no more, and told her gruffly that he wanted his supper.

Governor Winthrop must have expected that William would act on his hint and put a stop to Anne's meetings, for when the meetings continued there were no further invitations to walk. After three weeks of silence between the two houses William thought it advisable to cross the street to find out how matters stood. But there was nothing at first in the bland grave stare of his exalted friend that betrayed hostility as he looked up from his journal. Winthrop's large dark eyes fixed William with an air of incurious inquiry. The thin lips under the thin, aquiline nose moved in a mild greeting.

"How be you, Master Hutchinson?"

"Well, sir. I came to see if you were in a mind to answer a theological question."

"Are you joining now in your wife's meetings?" There was no threat in the tone, but the hush that followed was of the ominous sort that precedes tempests.

"That I am not."

"I am glad to hear it, Master Hutchinson. I am glad to hear it."

William scanned those sober, watery eyes for a hint of fire beneath, but he saw none. "I wanted to ask you a question about a covenant of works."

"Did you want to? Then ask it."

"There are some in the colony who believe that divers of our ministers preach such a covenant. They argue that if these ministers find evidence of salvation in godly deportment and religious demeanor, there is an implication that the cultivation of godly deportment and religious demeanor may *help* a man to salvation. Is there not such an implication, Governor?"

"No, Master Hutchinson, there is not."

"Will you allow me to say that I find that disheartening? For if there is nothing I can do to save myself—if that decision has been made, irrevocably, before my birth—what does it matter what I do or do not do in this fleshly life—or in Boston?"

"I will tell you, Master Hutchinson," the grave voice replied. "I will tell you and ask at the same time that you repeat my words to your wife. It will be especially for her good and for the good of those unfortunate, empty-headed women whom I fear she is sadly deluding." Here Winthrop paused to let his interlocutor take in the sudden change in their relationship. "The reason that it matters how a man behaves himself, even in this remote and isolated community, is that God will help him *here*. Here, Master Hutchinson, in this fleshly life in the Massachusetts Bay Colony!" Winthrop suddenly struck the table with the palm of his hand. It was like the sudden strike of the great blue heron. "Concern yourself not with the hereafter! Leave that to God. He made a covenant with this colony that if we should follow His precepts, He would protect us *here*, in the wilderness. And He has! The colony has prospered like no other in these climes. And I warn you now, Master Hutchinson, that I have not led my little band across the roaring Atlantic and established them safely here, in the very midst of wolves and savages, in order to have them confused and disheartened by raving, ecstatic women who despise our magistrates and ministers because of inner churnings which they have the audacity to call divine inspiration! The week after I arrived on these shores my son Henry was drowned. My first prayer was: 'O, God, wherein have I erred?' In the months that followed, by His good grace, I was taught better to conceive my mission. There is a time to be lenient and a time to be strong. Tell your wife, Master Hutchinson, and tell your brother Wheelwright to learn respect for the leaders of our colony and to *show* it. Or else, sir, let me assure you that they will be banished. Banished for sedition!"

Ah, there it was, William reflected grimly, there it was, the same hard little light in the eyes, the same fixed, sinister gleam that he had perceived in his grandfather's and in old Gloriana's! He rose, but Winthrop did not. The ex-governor simply returned his attention to his journal. William Hutchinson had been dismissed. The audience was over.

When he returned home, he found that Anne had left to visit friends in Salem. She had written him a note to say that she would be away for several days because she had much to "ponder on." She expressed the resolution to be "discreet," as he had requested, in her public language, but she still insisted that she must continue her women's meetings. She wrote:

"We are living, my Will, like the good Christians in the years immediately following the crucifixion. We are finding again the old truths in their simple form. You have read in the *Acts of the Apostles* of the part that women played in those days. That is all that I am trying to do. You will tell me to render unto Caesar those things which are Caesar's, and so I shall do. But *only* those things which are Caesar's."

William felt his heart invested with a sense of calm and resignation as the sureness of his defeat stole over him. Despair could be a kind of release. The days of Anne's absence passed quickly and uneventfully, at least at his home. But in the colony much was astir. By the time Anne returned, Winthrop had resumed the governorship, and Wheelwright had been banished.

5

The meeting house at Newtown was a rude frame building, made of rough-hewn boards, the crevices of which were sealed with mud. Inside, the wooden benches were filled with silent listeners. The pale winter morning sunlight fell on the craggy, solemn faces of the black-garbed ministers and magistrates seated on the long pews on the dais facing the audience. To one side was the table and chair of the governor.

The general hush deepened as Winthrop walked in and took his seat. He turned at once to William and Anne, in the first row, and nodded. Anne rose swiftly, with the composure and dignity that never failed her, and strode to the empty floor space directly in front of the dais. She might have been a great artist, a singer or mime about to offer to the distant provinces the same best efforts which had so aroused London the season before. Winthrop addressed her:

"You are called here, Anne Hutchinson, as one of those who have troubled the peace of the Commonwealth and the churches. You are known to have had a great share in spreading the opinions that are the cause of our trouble. You have said things prejudicial to the honor of the churches and the ministers, and you have held meetings at your house that have been condemned by our general assembly. Though these meetings have been censured as not tolerable or comely, or fitting for your sex, you have kept on with them. Therefore we have summoned you so that we may either rescue you and make you a profitable member among us, or if you be obstinate, so that we may take such action that you may trouble us no longer."

After a brief pause, Anne's voice, clear and cutting, rejected his assumptions. "I am called here to answer before you, but I hear no crime laid to my charge."

And so it started. William in the next noisy hour tried to follow the questions and answers, but he was hampered by his own incredulity. He had the hallucination of being outside the courtroom, somehow above it and looking down, as from a high gallery. It was a play, a very bad play, where a stunning actress suffered from the drawback of a wretched cast. There were times when they seemed even to forget their lines.

"Did you not encourage people to sign a petition for the repeal of Wheelwright's banishment?" Winthrop demanded.

"And if I did, where was the crime?" Anne retorted.

"Did you not know that such a petition would be offensive to the magistrates?"

"How could I not? Ye were the ones who banished him."

"But did you not know that the magistrates are your parents under the law? And if you offend your parents, have you not violated the Fifth Commandment?"

"Are you my father, Governor?"

"We do not mean to talk to one of your sex about this."

William's sense of remoteness had become so acute that he could now hardly distinguish the words of Anne's biting comment. Was Winthrop serious? But when had Winthrop been anything but serious? Yet a man and a woman might be sent to the cold woods, to dig under the snow for roots, to chew bark, to pass motionless hours in the vain hope of catching a squirrel with their bare hands; a man and a woman might starve, tearing at each other with ravenous teeth, or be hacked to pieces by grunting Indians, and all for such casuistry? At least, after the Indians, there might be quiet. There might be peace.

Not yet, however. William started with a shiver of cold as the babble of voices waxed shrill again. Anne had just scored a point. Now she requested a recess.

"May I sit?" she asked the Governor. "I am weary."

As William stepped forward to escort her to her chair he scanned the grim faces of the men on the dais for the least hint of sympathy for a pregnant woman. There was none. No doubt they believed that she received her support from the Devil.

"Have I not put them down?" Anne whispered eagerly to him when they were seated.

"Aye, but they haven't started yet. The ministers come next. But if you continue to do as well, my girl, you *will* put them down!"

"Pray, William! Pray!"

When she arose again and took her place before the court, the Governor called, in slow, tortuous succession, the accusing ministers. Each of them, obviously rehearsed, testified in identical words that Anne had told him that only Cotton and Wheelwright of all the clergy in the Bay Colony preached a true covenant of grace. But William, watching the black-robed figures with their white, lying faces, had an odd reaction of disloyalty to his wife. It was as if some little imp or devil had plucked his elbow and whispered in his ear the possibility of taking a different view of the drama before him. Might one not see these ministers, even these black wiggling beetles, as pleaders for humanity? They *knew* they could not preach a covenant of works. Of course, they knew it. They had to admit that man was saved by grace alone, that the list of paradise and the list of hell had been drawn up, irrevocably, before their own births, that the damned were damned already and beyond redemption. But by introducing just a hint of "works" into their preaching, by insinuating that if a man was good and just and proper and respectful and law abiding—well, perhaps it might, after all, do him a bit of good. Perhaps the Almighty might take it into consideration and, at the last moment, pluck a brand from the burning. What were the ministers smuggling into their discourses but a bottle of that forbidden liquor, hope? And when Winthrop had said that God would help the good colonists in *this* life, if not in the next, what was he doing but trying to squeeze an ounce of comfort out of a cold doctrine? Whereas Anne, fine, proud, imperious Anne, simply slammed the door in the faces of the congregation. No, she cried to the heavens! You are saved or you are damned, and there is nothing you can do about it, and you know it, and God wants it that way, and that is right. This life is without hope, as is the next. So let us, saved and damned, glorify the author of our salvation and damnation! Amen.

Anne's last answer now rang out clearly: "I swear before God and this Court that I have never told one of these holy men that he preached a covenant of works!"

The governor looked up at the double row of judge-prosecutors with a small thin smile, and William sighed. Everyone knew Anne had not said it to them; everyone knew that she believed it. What was truth?

John Cotton was called, and William's heart dropped as he saw the way Anne's old friend smiled at the court. Cotton shrugged and smiled and shook his head; he seemed to imply that learned gentlemen were learned gentlemen and charming ladies, charming ladies, and that surely there could be an accommodation between all parties more in keeping with the Boston spirit, the New England spirit, the Christian spirit, than banishment to the cruel wilderness. Ah, yes, he had been at Mistress Hutchinson's, often, and much to his pleasure, and, yes, to his edification, and indeed he had seen the other ministers there and had heard good talk about holy topics and many interesting things, and perhaps all sides should learn to temper their arguments and passions in the future, and concentrate more on their own souls and less on those of their neighbors, for after all, none of us is perfect, and we should learn to cast out the mote that is in our own eye . . .

"Mister Cotton," cried Deputy-Governor Dudley impatiently at last, "did Mistress Hutchinson, or did she not, say that the ministers who have testified in this court preached a covenant of works?"

The pause seemed to William to contain the silence of the eternal void. But Cotton's reply, when it came at last, was a trumpet of unexpected victory. "No, sir, she did not. Or at least I fail to recall that she did."

All through the explosion of heated questioning that followed this shocking admission William enjoyed a baffled, delectable, dizzy sense of tumbling about in free, fresh air far above Newtown, far above all the Bay Colony. For what was he facing but the incredible truth that Anne had won her case? And that he, William, had been *wrong*, wrong for a lifetime, wrong in his conviction that such a thing could never be, that authority could never give way before its hated offspring of mad dissent? Look now at Winthrop, look at Dudley, look at Endicott! It was only too apparent that they were losing and knew they were losing—and holy of holies!—accepting their loss. And then, like a bell ringing over his windy, airy tumbles, a bell ringing in his childhood, a bell ringing for school, for awakening, for life, for pain, for truth, a bell to drag him, reluctant and sobbing, from his yearned-for dream, he heard Anne's voice, high and strained, raised over the tumult:

"In England, before I came out here, I was troubled by a feeling that all was not well in the church where I worshiped. I fasted and I prayed, waiting for the sure guidance of God's word. And then, at last, it came to me. It came in the voice of Moses, in the voice of John the Baptist, in the voice of Christ himself! It was revealed to me, Anne, that the ministers of England were antichrists. It was revealed to me by the Lord himself, sitting upon a throne of justice, and all the world appearing before Him, that I must come to New England and must not be afraid. And I could not rest until I came hither, even though it was revealed to me that all kinds of plots should be made against me. For could not He that delivered Daniel and the children of Israel, deliver me, a poor woman, from mine enemies?"

As William came slowly to his senses and realized that it was Anne who was actually speaking, in that high, grave, would-be-inspired tone, and to a room that was now deathly silent, the ache in his heart was almost too great to be borne. He closed his eyes and moistened his lips. How should he be surprised? How should he have thought he could have been so wrong? As a bleak dry heat seemed to wither his last illusions, he began to feel something like hate for the woman who was so willfully destroying her family. Even Winthrop sought to interrupt the suicidal flow, but nothing could stop the lunatic now:

"And behold! the Scripture is fulfilled this day. Therefore take heed, ye judges, what you do unto me! You have power over my body, but the Lord Jesus hath power over my body and soul. I fear none but the great Jehovah, who hath foretold me of these things, and I do verily believe that He will deliver me out of your hands. Beware how you proceed against me, for you will bring a curse upon yourselves and your posterity, and the mouth of the Lord hath spoken it!"

"How do you know it was God that did reveal these things and not Satan?" cried Winthrop.

"How did Abraham know it was God that bid him offer his son?" Anne retorted. "By the voice of His own spirit to my soul!"

William at this seemed to lose consciousness. He did not know how long it was before he again attended the clamor, and he heard Winthrop's magisterial tone:

"The Court hath already declared themselves satisfied concerning the troublesomeness of her spirit, and the danger of her course amongst us, which is not to be suffered. Therefore, it be the mind of this Court that Mrs. Hutchinson is unfit for our society—and if it be the mind of this Court that she shall be banished out of our liberties, and imprisoned until she be sent away, let them hold up their hands."

There were only three who abstained. William went over now to his wife who stood with her head bowed in silent prayer and put his arm around her trembling shoulders to lead her away. She seemed hardly aware of him, but all his anger had gone, and his heart was filled with a great pity.

6

The cottage on Aquidneck Island faced toward the east over the ocean at land's end. William, on summer days, when his chest was not too painful, had his big chair carried outside by the boys and sat looking over the lapping waves and the gulls, over the blue sea, to a point on the horizon where he imagined he would see—if his eye, that is, could fly far enough in a straight line—the coast of Ireland. Or would it be Scotland? It did not matter. Soon enough now his soul would be released from its carnal chamber, and it could take the flight to see for itself. That is, if it still cared to. And if it existed to care.

For William had become indifferent to such matters. They seemed, oddly enough with death in sight, no longer to matter. They were problems that concerned the living; that was their function: to torture. It had been a relief to him to be able to drop the whole affair, with its angry priests, its angry rulers, its angry Anne, its angry Jesus, and accept a soothing identity with the trembling little billows of the Rhode Island coast.

Anne had not changed. She was more inspired, more disputatious than ever. She irritated even the sweet-tempered Roger Williams. She was now in Portsmouth disputing with the ministers, threatening already to leave the colony and move further south, across the great sound to New Amsterdam. William suspected that she was only awaiting his demise to do so. Well, let her wait. A wait would not hurt her; it might even save her. For she was bound to keep moving until she met the martyrdom she yearned for. Perhaps the Indians would supply it in the end. The longer she lingered on Aquidneck the better. There was something like peace on the island, a rare thing in this new world.

His daughter Bridget came out to bring him his noontime cup of warm milk. Bridget was married, but had come from Providence to look after her father. There was no mention between them of the fact that her mother was too busy to do this properly. Bridget was like him, silent, thoughtful, resigned, observant, a Martha, not a Mary.

"Will you promise me something?" he asked as he took the cup from her.

"You must tell me what first."

"If your mother goes to another colony, do not you and John go with her."

Bridget smiled. "You want some of your posterity to survive?"

"I want to disassociate you from your mother. I want you to have your own life and your own chance. It's a sorry thing to spend the one existence one has, troubling oneself about the faith of others."

"Well, I shan't do that, never fear. And most of your life you haven't, either."

"Ah, but in the intensest parts of my life I have. The rest was passivity. I have wasted, Bridget, the beautiful moments."

"Now, Father . . ."

"Don't fret yourself, my dear," he interrupted her. "I am perfectly at ease now. I have no regrets, for there is no point to regrets. Whatever I should have done instead would be over now. If I had tried to stop your mother, years ago, would I have succeeded? Wasn't she a natural force?"

Bridget contemplated him for a moment with her pleasant smile. Then the smile suddenly vanished. "Tell me, Father. I've often wondered about it. Was Mr. Winthrop right, do you suppose? Did he do what he had to do for the peace of Boston? I know that only you and I can discuss these things. I'll never report what you say to John or the children."

William was not in the least perturbed. He even smiled at her to bring back the smile that she had seen fit to banish. "I've wondered about it, too. As you know, in the early days of our life in Boston I admired Winthrop. I even liked him a little. But when we came here in 'thirty-eight and your mother gave birth for the last time, do you remember what happened?"

"Certainly. It was a stillborn child. Small wonder, after what she had been through."

"Yes, the child was born dead. But that was a blessing. The poor fetus was hideously deformed."

Bridget made a face. "I didn't know. But, again, what wonder? The trip from Boston was terrible."

"Quite so. But here is what I am getting at. I wrote to John Cotton to tell him what had happened. After all, he would have saved Anne if anyone could have. I thought he might care to hear our news. But now that we were gone, he had no further duty to us. John Cotton is a practical man. He announced from his pulpit that your mother had given birth to a monster, which proved her in error."

"How horrible!"

"Like Winthrop, he was seeking unity. The Hutchinsons were gone, so why not restore harmony? Nothing could hurt them now. And to make his point more vivid, he described the poor fetus to his congregation. With details. But Winthrop questioned the accuracy of his description. It wasn't gruesome enough for him. So he sent a commission here to investigate the condition of the fetus. When the commission returned to Boston, Winthrop obliged Cotton to publish its findings in a second public address!"

Bridget and William exchanged a long look. "Can such things be?" she murmured.

"Oh, yes, dear Bridget, such things are. And when I learned about it, I felt—after the first natural impulse of horror and disgust—an odd feeling of relief. They were simply children, all of them, Cotton, Winthrop, even your mother. Nasty little children. They played with life." He looked into Bridget's troubled eyes now and saw that he had said enough. After all, mothers were mothers. "Thank you for my milk, dear heart. I think I may have a snooze. Your mother thinks she has found peace. But there's a peace under her very nose that she knows nothing about."

Bridget nodded and went back into the cottage, and William resumed his quiet study of the sparkling sea.

(II)

The Fall

Letter from the Reverend Theodosius Leigh of Boston to the
Reverend Donaldson Leigh of New Haven, Nov. 14, 1717

MY REVERED PARENT:

This morning I assisted Mr. Mather and the other ministers and
dignitaries at the obsequies of your old friend, Major General Wait
Still Winthrop. The governor was present and former Governor
Dudley, as were half the magistrates of the Commonwealth and representatives of all the great families of Beacon Hill. It will not
surprise you that there should have been so large and mighty a congregation present. It was warranted as much by the distinction of the
decedent's birth as by his manifold services to the state. His late father, the saintly governor of Connecticut, and his grandfather, the
noble founder of our Bay Colony, will no doubt be angels to inter-
cede for the translation of his soul to a better sphere.

I say this in all humility with my head now bowed over my writing
table in silent prayer. But, oh, dear parent, I confess that my heart is
heavy with apprehension. For what will you think of your son when
you read what my filial duty obliges me herein to relate?

I know that General Winthrop was your friend from boyhood.
Since I came to the Second Church here, he and Mistress Winthrop
have been very kind to me. I have dined at their sumptuous board
some dozen times, and they have introduced me into the select circle
of their friends and relations. But there has never been a question of
any need of my spiritual counsel. It was perfectly understood between us that Mr. Cotton Mather himself, or at the very least Mr.
Stair, would attend to the General's religious wants. It came, therefore, as a source of astonishment to me when Mistress Winthrop,
who came to Sunday services a week ago without her husband,
waited for *me* outside the Meeting House. You can imagine how

grand a person she is, and how her children and step-children and servants are always gathered like a little court about her. But they all stood back while she looked me up and down, half, it would seem, in mock sternness, half in candid curiosity.

"My husband wishes to speak with you, Mr. Leigh," she said in her pleasant but commanding tone. "He is very ill. You must come to the house. Will you come now?"

Of course, there was nothing else I could do, though I suppose it was only to be expected that I should regret the anger of my superiors which so signal a preferment would be bound to bring down upon me. But who knows how God may seek to try us? I had already incurred the jealousy of other preachers for what the ladies of this town are kind enough, or misguided enough, to call my honeyed tongue. Yet I have prayed long and earnestly to the Almighty that he may keep my spirit low and that I may always recognize that any small gift of oratory that I enjoy is *His* gift, given for *His* purpose, to be withdrawn at a moment's notice. If I be puffed up—even the tiniest bit—then my gift is misused and becomes the Devil's instrument. Amen!

At the mansion I passed directly upstairs to the general's bedchamber where he received me alone. It is a very somber room, with a glint of silver from heavy sideboards and just a hint of color from indistinguishable tapestries, but I did not perceive much other than my host, who was sitting up in a huge bed under a red velvet canopy. He was wearing a silk scarlet robe tucked tight about his round body, and, even in bed, that immense white *perruque* with which you are no doubt familiar. Perhaps he had donned it in honor of my visit—in respect, I mean, to my cloth. His small black eyes penetrated me with an odd suspiciousness as he bade me sit.

"Let me assure you, Mr. Leigh, that I anticipate a full recovery. But we never know, do we? And there are things on my mind—perhaps even on my soul—that I wish to communicate to a priest. You look surprised. Why do I not send for Cotton Mather? Well, there is a good and sufficient reason for that. But it requires a bit of background concerning events which occurred before your birth, or at least when you must have been a very small child. Can you cast your mind back a quarter of a century, Mr. Leigh? Exactly twenty-five years. Have you heard of the witch trials at Salem?"

I replied that everyone had heard of them.

"And did you know that I was a judge at those trials, Mr. Leigh?"

"I did," I murmured.

"Nineteen men and women were hanged," he continued gravely, "and one man, Giles Corey, was pressed to death. Is it not natural to suppose that these should be on my conscience? Particularly when it was later found that some of them were innocent?"

I studied the man before me. Great as he was, he was only another soul before God. Every time I had gone to his house in the past I had wondered what inner torments he must suffer at having been part of so terrible a persecution. Yet I had never detected in him the smallest sign of spiritual discomfort. Nor did I detect any now.

"It is not for me to judge such matters, sir," I said. "I believe Mr. Mather has never ceased to defend what was done in Salem."

"Which is precisely why he cannot help me now. Mather can justify me legally, perhaps even before the church militant, but is that what I need? We do not, I suppose, have lawyers at the last trump. We awaken as the graves split; we rub our eyes, and there, in a radiant, blinding light stands He who knows all. Not just more than what Cotton Mather knows. But *all!*"

I agreed that it was an awesome thought.

"And then it is too late for pleas," my host continued. "There can only be judgment. Ah, Mr. Leigh, there are moments in the early morning, lying awake in this very bed, when I should be willing to barter the total extinction of my person in exchange for the simple assurance that I should not be damned! Does that seem wicked to you?"

"I understand it." I could not repress a visible shudder. "I, too, awaken in the early morning. But, as Christians, we should endeavor to see death as a desirable state."

"Do you see yours as such?"

I hesitated, for I feared that the truth might sound fatuous. "Yes."

"And mine?"

"Well, only to yourself, sir. Surely not to the community or to your poor family."

The general's expression was pensive. "Ah, yes, my family. But there are consolations, I suppose, in a large inheritance. I must seek *my* consolation in you. I hope that you are of the liberal persuasion that no longer believes in hell. Some young preachers don't, I hear."

"I *must* believe in hell, sir."

"Yes, but do you?" Those small, agate eyes had little points of fire in them. They looked at me with seeming avidity.

"I believe in hell, but I also believe that with God *all* things are

possible. And so it must be possible that He has power to redeem
us."

"Very neat." The general nodded in what struck me as rather
sarcastic approval. "Tell me, what does a casuistical young preacher
like yourself think of the Salem trials? You say you've heard of them.
I suppose you may have formed some opinion."

"I believe it was a period of great public excitement," I replied,
embarrassed. "Perhaps one might go so far as to say public . . . hysteria?"

"You imply that I was hysterical?"

"Oh, not you, sir. But isn't it true that the atmosphere of the
colony at the time was not conducive to judicial reflection? Your
task must have been a very difficult one. Only thus, I am sure, could
you have fallen into error."

"Error?"

"Well, were not some of the convictions reversed?"

He cut me short contemptuously. "A great consolation to the
dead, I'm sure." But then, all of a sudden, a look of anguish passed
over that round countenance. It took me quite by surprise. "When I
think," he continued, in a quavering tone, "of those wretched men
and women standing up there on the platform with ropes around
their necks—for it was one of my painful duties to witness the executions—I can hardly believe that it really happened!"

It was then that what I considered an inspiration struck me. "I
know what you could do, General!" I exclaimed. "You could make a
public penitence in church, as Judge Sewall did. Oh, what a grand
example! That a gentleman of such eminence, of such undoubted
probity and lofty thinking, should stand up before the congregation
and bare his soul to the public gaze . . ."

"Sam Sewall!" the general interrupted me in a startling explosion
of wrath. "You want me to make a monkey of myself like Sam Sewall? No, thank you very much, Mr. Leigh. I have more respect for
the government which I have represented in so many capacities. Sewall is in many ways a fine man, and he has been a good friend of
mine, but he has no conception of the dignity of the state. Do you
know what some of those Salem defendants were, sirrah? They were
the vilest old crones, the most dog-like peasants, who messed about
with mud and spit and the entrails of small animals to implement
their obscene incantations. They smeared their hands and faces with
excrement. They jabbered in strange dialects to stranger devils. And
you expect a judge of the Bay Colony, a major-general, a land-

owner, a grandson of the founder of this commonwealth, to rise up in public and apologize for his treatment of such scum?"

"Scum, sir? Were they not poor, ignorant souls?"

"They were malevolent souls, I tell you! They sought to harm innocent people, to *kill* innocent people, with their devilish tricks. It was not their fault if they failed. Are we not told that we are judged by our thoughts as well as our deeds? Well, their thoughts were evil, Leigh!"

As you may imagine, my dear father, I was taken aback by this. Here was my proposed penitent arrogating to himself the prerogative of the Almighty! Surely, no judge on earth is authorized to reach into a man's mind and try him for evil intent alone.

"If a man wishes his enemy dead, is he a murderer?" I put to him.

"Now, don't try to trap me, young man. The point is that a man of my rank cannot afford the luxury of public penitence. To stand up and cry, 'Peccavi' is to make havoc of the necessary degrees of society. It is to put me on a level with some malignant old hag rooting in the offal pile for lucky bones. You say she is poor and ignorant. Do not underestimate her, my friend! You may think we have come a long way from our Druid ancestors with their painted faces and human sacrifices. But all that is still boiling and hissing only an inch below our surface. Once the lower orders have seen their judges confessing to errors, what is to keep them down?"

I sorely wondered why your old friend had summoned me. Was it to lecture me on the importance of degree? I confess here to an irreverence. I thought of the speech in *Coriolanus* where Menenius makes his plea to the mob in defense of the Roman state, likening the nobility to the belly of a body which, though it seems only to receive from the other members, in truth operates as the central storehouse and distributor. General Winthrop, sitting up, round and solid on that vast soft bed, seemed amply qualified to play the belly. I began to overcome my timorousness.

"I seem to recall, sir, that not all of the accused in Salem were of the lower class. Nor were they all would-be witches. Were there not honest men and women who were falsely accused and wrongly convicted? Has this not been conceded?"

Winthrop's expression immediately changed again. He cast his little eyes down on the blanket and shook his head with short regretful nods. "Yes, that is quite true. That is undeniable. And one poor soul was pressed to death. Ugh! What a horrible end! They kept piling on stones . . . but I must not think of that. Doesn't it sometimes seem to you, Leigh, that there should be an evening up after death? Why should Giles Corey be subjected to such anguish and not you and I?"

"Our lives are not yet over."

"Ah, yes, and there may still be time for adjustments on this side of the grave. For you, perhaps, but I think in my case it is very late. What can I do, Mr. Leigh, to cleanse my soul of the guilt for Giles Corey?"

"Let us pray, sir."

"It is no longer public penitence that you require?"

"Oh, no. Let us pray here, just you and I." I knelt down beside the bed. The general simply clasped his hands together and raised his eyes to the canopy. I began:

"O, Lamb of God, who takest away the sins of the world, look down upon thy humble servant, Wait Still Winthrop, and ease his heart of the burden of false judgments. Because he truly repents of all that was contrary to Thy holy laws in Salem, because he is sorely afflicted by the grief that he caused to be inflicted on the innocent . . ."

"Stop!"

I looked up again at those small, dilating eyes. The general's mood had changed again.

"Rise, sirrah!" he cried. I rose. "It has just occurred to me," he continued wrathfully, "that we had a jury. It is a great tribute to your moral blandishments that I should have overlooked so basic a fact. But juries are juries. They must find innocence or guilt. It is the duty of the court to award penalties to those found guilty. Are we responsible for miscarriages of justice?"

"I do not say so," I responded with some weariness. "But I had thought the responsibility for what happened in Salem was shared by all concerned."

"Justice is not always obtained. Does that mean there should be no courts?" Winthrop was becoming very excited now, and his cheeks had turned red. "Every judge has a few blunders in his record. If we were so terrified of hanging an innocent man, every rascal would go free. Maybe it is necessary for a few innocents to die as a warning to the wicked! Consider our sovereign and our governors who are obliged to live in daily risk of assassination. What would their lives be worth were it not for the healthy respect which their enemies feel for the tortures meted out for treason?"

"Very well, sir," I said, picking up my prayer book from the bed. "I shall try to think of Giles Corey as a martyr to the statistical necessity of judicial error."

"Do you jest with me, sirrah?"

"On the contrary, I have never been more earnest."

"Old Corey deserved every rock that was laid on his rebellious carcass. Do you realize, Mr. Leigh, that he refused even to *plead*? That he denied the jurisdiction of the court to try him for witchcraft? We were not competent, bless my soul, to pass on the revered case of Giles Corey! He defied the court, the commonwealth, the King's majesty, the Queen's majesty, too, for good William and Mary then reigned. What did he expect? A tribunal of angels?"

I turned to the door. "I had best leave you, sir. I shall pray for your soul."

"Let us pray together, Mr. Leigh."

"I fear that it will simply weary you."

"On the contrary, it will rest my spirits. Do not seek to quarrel with me. It is your duty to stay. I may be dying, after all."

"God will have mercy."

"Do you abandon me, my friend?"

There was something suddenly so broken, so frightened in his reduced voice that I came back to his bedside and knelt down again.

"Teach us the truth, O Lord," I prayed aloud. "Teach us to learn the truth and to speak it, as you taught the martyrs of Salem. When asked to confess their alleged guilt, they steadfastly and courageously refused, even though they knew that their lives would have been spared for such false witnessing . . ."

"Mr. Leigh, Mr. Leigh!"

I looked up to see the General glaring down at me again. His panic had gone as quickly as it had come.

"Do you know that is sacrilege you are speaking?"

"Why so?"

"You imply that the Almighty *approved* of those accused who stubbornly refused to obtain their liberty by a purely formal plea of guilty."

"And that is wrong?"

"Most wrong, Mr. Leigh! They were not men; they were mules! Consider the position of the court. Already a note of uncertainty had permeated the air. There was witchcraft in Salem—no doubt of that —but how much of it? Accusations proliferated. Obviously, we knew that some of these were inspired by malice. But how to disprove them? It was a tricky business—touch and go for the very safety of the state. But if we could induce the accused to confess, we could then declare that the witches had been apprehended and forgiven, and all would be at peace in Salem. But no! Those fools had to pick that moment for literal honesty. We were *forced* to condemn them. They died, Leigh, to spite us! Can you call such conduct Christian? Can you condone it?"

"You wanted them to confess to abominations. You wanted them to lie under oath."

"Oh, come, come. I wanted them to say they had fiddled about with a little black magic. Who hasn't, at one time or other? But no, they had their pride. They stank with pride! They wouldn't sacrifice it for the good of the whole state!"

"Why would it have helped the state?"

Winthrop at this drew himself up on the bed, as if he were a judge again, delivering sentence. "When my grandfather came to Boston, Mr. Leigh, he brought only a vague charter as to his powers. There was no king on this side of the Atlantic, no peerage, no bishop. But every man in that first settlement knew that he lived under a divine light as bright as any that shone in Europe. Brighter even. It was that shared spirit that saved the Bay Colony from wolves and Indians, from frost and hunger. We were *united,* Mr. Leigh! And because our union had no king or pope to protect it, it was vital that we should learn to maintain that consensus. It was not easy. We were soon threatened by separatists. The witch Hutchinson was the first. Then came the Quakers. But the community was never threatened as perilously as in 1692. God alone knows the full extent of the deviltries with which our colony then seethed. But when the accused in Salem were given the chance to help the magistrates to reassert the indispensable cohesion of a colony in covenant with God, they refused. By God, I say they deserved their deaths! They had denied their Puritan heritage!"

At this point, God forgive me, I lost all restraint. I became utterly unconscious of a fact that no minister should ever have lost sight of: that I had to do with a man gravely ill.

"I beg to differ with you, General!" I cried out. "Those brave souls were the true Puritans! You asked them to tell an infamous lie—that they had trafficked with Satan—and they refused, even though they knew that death would be the consequence. How splendid, how holy, to demonstrate that life is not worth a lie! I can only pray that in a similar circumstance I should have the courage to choose so glorious a martyrdom!"

Winthrop had risen in his bed to his knees, and his short, stout arms were stretched above his wig. His face had turned to an alarming scarlet.

"Get out of here, you witch!" he screamed. "How dare you come from the Devil to disturb me when I am trying to settle my accounts with God? If we were back in Salem, you should have that martyrdom you long for. Only it would be followed, not by the golden paradise you dream of, but the black hell where you belong!"

At this, he fell down in his bed, unconscious, and I hurried to the landing to call for help. Mrs. Winthrop and her daughter rushed to the bedchamber, and the physician was sent for. But the General never recovered consciousness. He had had a stroke of apoplexy. Three days later he was dead.

*

And that, my revered parent, is the whole story. No other living being has even a suspicion of what occurred between me and Wait Still Winthrop. Perhaps I should be exiled from Boston, like poor Anne Hutchinson, if they did. But that is not the point. The point is: should I not deserve it? I was called to the bedside of a dying man who had grave sins on his conscience and who was seeking the way to make his peace with God. Would it not have been possible to soothe him to a mood where confession and penitence would have relieved his anxiety? Alas, all I did was contradict him and anger him until he went to his death in a spirit of defiance and hate. What a spirit with which to face the Judgment Day!

I have prayed for hours every night. I still pray for the occasion to redeem myself. I pray that I may be sent to some even more recalcitrant case than Winthrop . . . some other judge from Salem, if any still survive . . . but no!

No, dear Father, I would say it all again. Is there hope for me? Is there not still a lurking pride, a hidden conceit, an impertinent defiance in the very way I am ending this letter? God help me!

Your loving son
THEODOSIUS

(III)

The Martyr

The Account of Philippe Geyelin

I WAS SENT OUT to the New World, to the English seaport known as New York, although it had been called New Amsterdam and New Orange under the two previous Dutch rules, in the autumn of 1755. My father, the Vicomte de Fouguères, had thought it best to have me out of France for a year because of my involvement with the production of that unfortunate comedy, *La Larmoyeuse*.

This came about as follows. Being a bastard and never formally acknowledged by the Vicomte, I had been brought up in his château in Dijon as a kind of upper servant. But when I developed into a tolerable looking fellow with an aptitude for sports, particularly the stag hunt, which the Vicomte, like all of his class, adored, he took a liking to me and decided to provide for my future. The church was the solution for the nameless; a cassock covered anonymity. I was sent to Paris to study theology, but the distractions of that city proved quite worthy of their reputation. The Vicomte's mother, the amiable and ancient Maréchale who had been in her youth one of the Regent's many mistresses, provided me with a secret allowance, to avoid the jealousy of legitimate but less favored issue. I found myself drawn not only to the gambling tables and to the fair sex, but to the fashionable literary circles of the period, and in the salon of Madame de Créqui I met that popular playwright and freethinker, Georges Demarest.

He, like the Vicomte and the Maréchale, took a fancy to me, invited me to be a regular boarder at his table and even allowed me to furnish some lines for his new comedy. As all the world knows, this had the misfortune, because of broad allusions in certain verses (ascribed to me by a malicious few), to offend the Pompadour herself. The play was withdrawn, and Demarest spent a couple of months in the Bastille under a *lettre de cachet.* The Vicomte decided to send me traveling, but as he was angry at my indiscretion, he decreed that I should support myself. It was thus that Philippe Geyelin, the future abbé, perhaps the future bishop or even cardinal, became instead Philippe Geyelin, the humble French tutor for the family of Francis Bayard, Patroon of Bayardwick, on the Hudson River. Happily, I spoke English. My unhappy mother had been an English governess.

After five miserable weeks at sea we docked at New York, a small, rather pretty town with many neat, fenced gardens, huddled at the south end of a skinny island called Manhattan where there is nothing whatever to do. I was put up for a couple of days at the family's handsome brick house on Wall Street with a charming view of the harbor before being transported north to Bayardwick by stage. One of the estate managers traveled with me, and he expatiated at length on the glories of the Bayards. Titles, I gathered, were rarely conferred upon colonials by the British Crown, but if they had been, Mr. Bayard should have been a duke, or at least a marquess. His domain consisted of more than a hundred thousand acres, much of it bordering on the Hudson, including villages whose whole populations were Bayard tenants. The Patroon was a personage in politics as well as realty. He was a judge and magistrate on his own property and a prominent member of the Governor's Council. His wife, born a Winthrop, was a descendant of the founder of Massachusetts. It was as if a Noailles had married a Rohan.

From the main gate, where the stage dropped us, we rode in, leaving my baggage to follow by cart. It took us three hours to reach the house. The edifice was certainly not large by French standards, but I was told that most of the servants and slaves slept in cottages. It was a plain but graceful three-story gray stone structure with large windows opening on a terrace that commanded a stupendous view from a bend in the river. The family were all out but Mrs. Bayard who, to my pleasure and relief (for I had no idea how tutors would be treated in this country), met me very graciously in the hall.

"We are so pleased you have come, Monsieur Geyelin," she greeted me in excellent French. "We have been wondering what we could do to make your life in this wilderness not too dreary after the delights of Paris."

"A wilderness, Madame? I have never seen a country so beautiful."

"I was thinking of the life of the mind. Against nature, it is true, we have few complaints."

"But what, pray, if I may ask, will be my duties? Whom am I to instruct if your children speak French as you do?"

"Have no worries about that, Monsieur Geyelin. My children speak little French, and my daughter only so much English, I fear, as is needed for a life with horses and hounds. But you must be weary. Samuel will show you to your room."

Samuel, like the other household servants, was a stout, smiling, soft-spoken, softly-moving black slave. I could not help wondering if it was the presence of such unfortunate bondsmen that gave their mistress her charming manners. Was it a form of apology for the toleration of a system outlawed by most Christian nations? Samuel instructed me that I was to have my meals with the family and that my boxes would be unpacked by one of his boys. The New World was evidently a brave one for tutors!

I had been much struck by Mrs. Bayard's appearance. She was a beautiful woman who seemed to be trying not to be one. She was tall and graceful with broad, strong shoulders, thin hips and a quick, noble stride. Her face, heart-shaped and very pale, with large, golden-brown eyes, managed to be at once calm and vaguely tense. For all the sweetness of her tone and the charm of her manner, I did not doubt her ability to manage a large household.

I met her husband that afternoon. The two children were boating and not expected until supper, so I was free to explore the place. I chose a path that seemed to lead to the river, but it twisted instead into a dark pine forest wonderfully free of underbrush and soft to the foot. I came out after an hour's walk on a broad meadow across which I saw approaching me two cantering equestrians, Mr. Bayard, as it turned out, in resplendent red and his wife in sober black, striking at once to my fancy the note which they consistently thereafter maintained when together: that of the glorious cock and his more modest hen.

I hoped that they would pass me with only a nodded greeting, for I felt sufficiently inferior to such a great squire as Bayard without having to address him on foot while he rode a stallion, but instead they pulled up. Francis Bayard was as handsome for his age—perhaps forty-five—as his wife was for hers. He was large and strong and sat up very straight in his saddle; his brow was broad and clear, his nose very large and aquiline, his eyes blue and cheerful. Had he been a candidate for some American political office he could not have been more pleasant.

"I am so happy that my wife will now have someone to speak French with," he began, after greeting me, in a high, resonant tone. "She's an avid reader, too, Monsieur Geyelin, though I'm afraid the rest of the family are hardly that. My son Sylvester is willing enough, but the poor fellow has spent all his days in Bayardwick. You will bring a bit of Paris to us."

"A very little, I fear, sir, but I'll do my best."

"Do you ride, Monsieur Geyelin?"

"Oh, yes, sir."

"I shall see to it myself that you are properly mounted."

Mr. Bayard would have continued at my side, and I think that he might even have endeavored to discuss Paris had not his wife, perhaps sensing my discomfort, suggested a gallop. Even then he waited a few minutes before following her, though his horse, smartly reined up, was wild to go. He raised his black hat to me, smiled, gave me the precise time of dinner and then was off at a bound. My gaze followed them across the meadow, and I watched them take two fences. I wondered if many American equestrian couples were capable of so graceful an exhibition. Yet I felt a slight pang, absurdly enough, as though my new friend, Mrs. Bayard, had already been taken from me. Her black riding habit, so perfectly fitting, seemed to remove her from a tutor's world.

At dinner I met the two Bayard children. My ward, Sylvester, was a shy, blond, beautiful youth of eighteen who had yet about him an air of contained authority that showed he was no mollycoddle. Katrina, his younger sister, was very brown and strong, with a forthright, boyish manner. Such was the family. We ate and drank heartily, and the talk was spirited. Mr. Bayard warned me again that his wife was the only "literate" member of the family.

"I suggest that you spend some of your tutoring time with Mrs. Bayard. It will be a relief to you after coping with these young savages. My wife is a great reader, and she doesn't get much chance to discuss books around here. You might read some of those French plays together. The children could listen. That would help their accent, wouldn't it?"

Katrina broke in to answer before her mother could. "Now, Father, is that fair? Giving away our tutor to Mother before we've even started? Why don't you get her one of her own? If Monsieur Geyelin has that much extra time, he'd probably rather come hunting with us than read a lot of boring plays."

"How would you know they were boring?" Mr. Bayard retorted. "You've never read any."

"I've read as many as you have, Old Boy."

To my astonishment her father seemed to accept this impudence as perfectly normal. "Monsieur Geyelin is *not* your tutor. He's Sylvester's tutor. Any lessons that you receive, my lass, will be the merest indulgence on your brother's part."

"Mother, is that true?" Katrina cried vehemently. "I might as well be a slave. Sylvester gets everything. And when he inherits this place, he'll put me in a mud hut. Unless I can buy myself an Indian husband with the two sacks of potatoes which is all Father will leave me for a dowry!"

"Who said he'd leave you that?" Sylvester sneered. "I may need all the potatoes."

"Children!" Mrs. Bayard protested. "You must never talk about inheritances. It is in the worst possible taste. And in front of your father, too! Besides, Katrina, it's not fair of you to speak that way. You know perfectly well that you've been provided for. As for me, I shall not take any of Monsieur Geyelin's time, never fear. I'm far too busy running this house."

"Oh, come now, Rebecca," her husband remonstrated. "You're going to make our friend here believe that we work you to death. Of course she reads, Monsieur Geyelin. She loves that fellow—what's his name? Corneel. You and she might like to read a piece that I heard in Paris, at the Comedy French, when I was on my grand tour back in 'thirty-three. It was a bit long, but there was some wonderful ranting in it. It was about a Roman soldier who killed his sister. Do you know which one that would be?"

I noticed that Mrs. Bayard was staring down at the table surface. I suggested *Horace*.

"That's the one! Rebecca should love that one. Isn't Corneel considered your greatest playwright?"

"By some of the older people, certainly. But Racine is more the fashion today. He was a gentler poet. He wrote of love and a woman's heart. Corneille is like a flourish of trumpets. With him duty is all."

"But that's Rebecca all over!" Mr. Bayard exclaimed. "Never was a woman more dutiful or more conscious of duty."

"Mr. Bayard," his wife protested in a tone of surprising affliction, "if you continue to talk of me so personally, I shall have to leave the table."

"Sorry, my love, I did not mean to upset you." Mr. Bayard's tone was entirely casual, as if he had long discounted his wife's little nervous flurries. "Tell us, Monsieur Geyelin, of events abroad. Do you think you French will beat us in Canada? But we mustn't speak of the war, must we? Let us pass to more amusing things. Is the great Madame Pompadour as strong as ever with the King? Or is her sway disputed by some younger candidate?"

"Her sway is disputed, certainly, but it remains as strong as ever. In fact, sir, you might say that it filled the very sails which propelled me across the Atlantic."

Later in the evening, after Mrs. Bayard and the children had retired, I regaled my employer over a bottle of port with an account of how the aging Pompadour still held the King. I explained her trick of hanging on to the royal heart while consigning his senses to simple whores, chosen by herself. By the time we went to bed, very late, I prided myself that I had gained my master's confidence.

The next morning, early, my new routine started, and in two weeks' time I felt as if I had lived half my life in Bayardwick. The mornings were devoted to lessons, that is, when Sylvester was not riding out on inspection tours with his father, which was frequently the case. Culture and history, in Mr. Bayard's term, were "charming things," but he saw them as belonging to the parlor and to the evening, to candlelight and to ladies—never to be allowed to interfere with a gentleman's principal occupations. When we worked, I tutored his son in Latin and ancient history for the first two hours of each session; then Katrina joined us for conversation in French.

As I had originally surmised, Sylvester's gentleness of demeanor did not indicate a lack of character. Nor was he at all the illiterate that his father had half-jokingly dubbed him. He was polite almost to a fault and at first reserved with me, but he thawed sooner than I expected. One day, having satisfied himself that I was to be trusted, he suggested that we deviate from the assigned curriculum to pursue questions of greater interest.

"There must be so many wonderful things going on in Paris," he suggested. "I should think it a kind of heaven just to live there. All the talk and the poetry. And the wits! But then one hears, too, about the other side." He shook his head with so sudden an air of sadness that I could hardly restrain a grin. "People thrown in prison for some nobleman's whim. People tortured. Starving."

"You've been reading Voltaire! How do you get him here?"

"Oh, Mother gets lots of French books. She reads them in her room."

"You mean she's ashamed of them?"

Sylvester flushed. "Oh, no. Not that kind of books. They're very serious. It's simply that Father is . . . well, not exactly literary in his tastes."

"But he wants your mother to read. I've heard him say so."

"That's true, of course. Everyone in our family wants everyone else to be happy. But Mother is very keen to keep the atmosphere of our home entirely congenial to Father."

"So she loans you books on the sly?"

"Not at all." Sylvester paused, debating between his need to tell the absolute truth and at the same time to keep an obviously adored mother in the most favorable light. "I take them when I want, and she doesn't notice."

"You mean she looks the other way?"

"She doesn't look."

"But why should anyone object to your reading Voltaire? You're not Catholics."

"Nobody does object. It's just . . . well, it's just that Mother doesn't think I should be distracted from becoming as much like Father as I can."

I couldn't again help smiling at the idea of this gentle creature turning into a Francis Bayard. "Wouldn't it please her if you turn out to be better than your father?"

"Better?"

"Well, as great a man, say, but a scholar, too."

Sylvester appeared to muse. "I don't think Mother thinks there could be a better man than Father." Then he came back to his prior subject. "Those things are true, then, that Voltaire says? The tortures? The horrors?"

"Oh, my, yes."

"And the church is responsible? But I beg your pardon, Monsieur Geyelin. Of course, you're Catholic."

"Indeed I am. In fact I almost became a priest. But in my world a good deal of latitude is granted in these matters. I could tell you some astonishing things that go on, even in monasteries, even in convents. But I doubt that was what your father hired me for. Let me see, we had got to the Battle of Philippi . . ."

"Please, Monsieur Geyelin, not yet." His earnest bright countenance was irresistibly serious. "If everyone is so tolerant, as you imply, then why the horrors?"

"Because France lives in many centuries. In parts of Paris we live in the present, in the seventeen-fifties. Some of us, like my friend Demarest, may even live in the future. But there are plenty of towns and villages in the provinces, particularly in the *Midi*, where people still live in the dark ages. I heard of a case last year where a young man had his tongue cut out, and was then decapitated, for uttering obscenities about the Virgin. It created quite a stir in Paris—my Paris, that is."

Sylvester looked horrified, but the area of his concern came as a surprise to me. "You must never tell my mother anything like that!"

"I shouldn't be apt to. It's hardly a subject one brings up with ladies."

"Well, I don't know. Some of our neighbors like to tell ghastly stories about Indian tortures, even at table. But Mother is abnormally sensitive to any details of human suffering. No, perhaps that is not quite true." The scrupulous youth paused to orient his thoughts more precisely. "I must remember that she's very brave at sick beds. There was an old woman on the place who died last year of a terrible abdominal ailment. Her sufferings were so cruel and the odors so vile that her own daughters couldn't endure to be with her. Yet my mother stayed with her through everything to the end. No, it's not human suffering. It's . . ." He paused, undecided.

"Those Indian tortures?" I suggested.

"That may be it. The suffering man inflicts on man. She had a grandfather called Winthrop who was a judge in Massachusetts . . ."

"I know. I studied your family before I came. He was the first governor."

"I'm afraid I must correct you there, sir. The first governor was John Winthrop. He was Mother's great-great-grandfather."

"I keep forgetting how old your new world is."

"It was his grandson, Wait, who was a judge in the Salem witch trials. They caused a great scandal back in 1690. Many persons were hanged. Later, it was found that they were falsely accused. One of the judges, Sewall, even made a public repentance."

"And did Winthrop?"

"Far from it. He always maintained that the court had done a fine job. He used to tell my mother so when she was a little girl. But she was not convinced. She has always brooded about it. I think she fears that her grandfather's descendants may be pursued by the furies. Like Orestes and Electra."

"You mean she thinks that you and Miss Katrina may be?"

"Something like that. Unless she can ward it off, by taking it all on her own shoulders. It's very difficult to explain. Mother doesn't like to talk about these things. One has to deduce them."

"Deduce what?"

It was Katrina, in riding habit, who had strode in for her hour of French. Sylvester seemed unduly embarrassed.

"Oh, nothing. Let's talk French."

"No, tell me. What's it all about, Monsieur Geyelin?"

"Your brother was speaking of your mother's distress at the role of an ancestor in some old witch trial."

"Oh, that. Salem. Yes, she has an absolute obsession about it, that's perfectly true. Why, I've never been able to figure out. For you know, Monsieur Geyelin, it was entirely the fault of those people who were hanged. All they had to do was tell the court they were witches, and they'd have gone free. I'd have done it. Wouldn't you?"

"Most assuredly, Miss Katrina. Particularly as there's no such thing as a witch."

"Exactly! Those people died just to spite a bigoted old Puritan judge."

"He wasn't a Puritan, Katrina!" Sylvester cried out in sudden indignation. "Wait Winthrop was unworthy of the name. He truckled to mob hysteria. He bowed to . . ." He stopped himself, as if with a great effort, and turned abruptly away from us.

I thought that Sylvester was becoming too excited, and I tried to lighten the discussion. Besides, I could see that Katrina enjoyed provoking him. "We mustn't disagree with ladies," I reproved him mildly.

"Oh, Katrina's not as tough as she likes to make out," Sylvester retorted.

"I am so tough," his sister exclaimed. "One must be tough to survive in this world. Isn't it so, Monsieur Geyelin?"

"Well, I agree that it's better not to throw one's life away for a quibble."

Sylvester took me up boldly on this. "A quibble? Do you despise the martyrs, Monsieur Geyelin? Many of them died, I suppose, for quibbles!"

Foolishly, I betrayed my pique. "Must I learn my morals from slaveholders?"

Sylvester flushed and glanced scornfully at his sister, who had burst into a peal of laughter. "I am not a slaveholder, as it happens," he said with dignity. "And my father owns very few. Any whom I inherit will at once be freed. Katrina will probably sell hers. God help the poor devils if she gets more for separating families than keeping them together!"

Where this discussion would have led us I do not know. It might have resulted in my dismissal. But fortunately for me, Mrs. Bayard just then appeared in the doorway, and we all rose.

"Please be seated," she urged as she came in swiftly and took the nearest chair. "I don't want to interrupt the lesson." Sylvester, however, went over to greet her with a kiss, and she put a hand on his neck to hold him against her in a moment of quiet embrace. "I thought you were going to Keswick with your father today, love. Did he put you off?"

"No. I told him it was an important lesson."

"Ah." Mrs. Bayard glanced at me with what, having heard what I had heard about her, I could interpret only as an expression of mild reproach. "And you, Katrina darling, weren't you going to ride Morning Glory to the crossroads?"

"William is taking her."

"I thought she wouldn't mind anyone but you."

"Mother, don't you *want* me to learn French? Do you wish me to grow up a clod? Don't you care?"

Katrina's tone was shockingly rude. I should have liked to slap her. But Mrs. Bayard simply rose to go over to kiss her in turn. "Of course, I want you to learn French, my own girl. And to prove it, I'll take myself out of the way right now."

Katrina had none of her brother's fineness of mind or sensitivity. She reminded me of Mesdemoiselles de Fouguères in Dijon; she lived for animals and the out-of-doors. When she was not riding, she was in the kennels; when she was not there, she was feeding the birds in the aviary. Yet she was not without a certain air of distinction and a promise of beauty. She might one day be a darker, broader version of her mother. There was something engaging in the honesty of her staring brown eyes. I imagined that Katrina felt deeply and was easily hurt. It was probably her fear of pain that made her so brusque.

I took for granted that she came to her lessons to make a conquest of the French tutor. What sixteen-year-old girl, having little or no contact with boys of her own age and class, would not have? Yet she worked hard enough. She seemed determined to learn French. Perhaps she was jealous of her brother's greater competence. They were certainly competitive. When we rode in the afternoons she was always daring Sylvester to take higher fences. But when I fell off one afternoon as my horse refused a jump, Katrina was all consolation and solicitude.

"Are you sure you're all right? Can I go home and get a wagon? I should have warned you about that fence. There's a soggy patch on the landing side. I went off myself there last summer."

I laughed as I jumped back on my steed. It was an accomplishment to have made Katrina Bayard invent a fall! When Sylvester rode up, he told his sister curtly to desist from her protestations.

"Monsieur Geyelin is obviously all right. Don't kill him with fussing. It's not polite to a man."

I began to see that a struggle was starting over me. Sylvester had no intention of having *his* tutor taken over by a gushing girl.

That I had never seen a family like the Bayards should offer little surprise. I doubt that one such existed in all of France. We do not believe in that kind of intimacy between the generations. Katrina always treated her father with the same astonishing familiarity that I had observed at my first meal with them, calling him "Old Boy" and making candid fun of his personal idiosyncracies, such as his winking broadly after one of his own jokes or his almost deafening throat clearing. And Sylvester, although more outwardly respectful, had no hesitation in criticizing his father's management of the farm. He was even full of very articulate ideas for its improvement. Yet Francis Bayard's good nature with his children seemed limitless. He roared with laughter at Katrina's jokes and smiled benignly at Sylvester's suggestions, without seeming in the least affected by either. He was evidently a man of complete independence and self-sufficiency, which may have been why, for all his tolerations, he still ruled his little family as absolutely as he ruled his vast estate.

Mrs. Bayard's role in the home was more difficult to ascertain. Her husband was jovial with her, her son gently submissive, her daughter petulantly resentful. Yet all three seemed intensely aware of her. Whenever she spoke they listened, in contrast to the way in which they interrupted each other. It was as if they constituted a tribe, tightly bound by customs, fetishes, rigid habits, and that she was their priestess, or perhaps their idol, something to be protected and venerated, but at the same time to be jealously guarded. Conversation at the family board, dominated by Francis Bayard, was almost exclusively about matters pertaining to the estate, either the working side of it, the farms, orchards, dairies, or the sporting side, the fishing, riding, hunting. He and his daughter, at least, appeared to have few interests beyond the boundaries, and Mrs. Bayard always joined in their conversation with interest and enthusiasm. She was herself a skillful housekeeper and equestrian, and as great a lover of the woods and meadows as Katrina. But I wondered if I could not make out an element of discipline behind her "Bayardness." After all, she was a Winthrop from Boston. She came, I gathered, from a family who had cultivated the arts and letters. Was her husband watching her for some betrayal of her old background that would not fit in with the cheerful mindlessness of Bayardwick? I doubted it. He took her subservience too much for granted. Was Katrina? Oh, yes. Of that I had no doubt. Katrina struck me as somehow "daring" her mother to show herself in her true intellectual colors. And Sylvester? Possibly. But he was different. He would help his mother in whatever pose she adopted, provided she were still his. The Bayards may have been charming people, but they were fiercely possessive. At least about Mrs. Bayard.

When I suggested to the latter that it might help Sylvester and Katrina if she and I spoke French at table on days when the master was away, she rejected the idea, as if I had suggested something in dubious taste. And whenever she passed the schoolroom, which was filled with books and maps, she would peep in and then hurry on, as if repressing the temptation to enter some faintly disreputable mart of pleasure. But one morning, when Sylvester had accompanied his father on a trip, I entered the schoolroom and surprised her peeking into a volume of Corneille.

"Why don't you take it?" I asked, when we had exchanged a rather constrained greeting. "The Corneille, I mean. Let me move it downstairs. Sylvester is still a long way from *Le cid.*"

"Oh, do you think it would be all right?"

I couldn't help smiling. The great Mrs. Bayard might suddenly have been a little girl—younger than Katrina. "Isn't the set yours?"

"Well, I suppose so, in that way. But once I put something in the schoolroom, I consider it . . ."

"Out of bounds?" I thought I was beginning to see my way with Bayards and Winthrops. "Then why don't you read it in here? Perhaps we could read a play aloud, as Mr. Bayard suggested. In Dijon, where I grew up, we used to have amateur theatricals."

"Would you really like it?" She hesitated, obviously much

tempted. "Wouldn't it interfere with your lessons?"

"We needn't do it in lesson time."

"Well maybe then, once or twice. Just a scene or so."

"It's better to do a whole tragedy. Which one would you like to start with?"

"Oh, a whole play would be much too much. But maybe we could start one. What would you say to . . . *Polyeucte?*"

It was thus that our readings began. At first Mrs. Bayard would be constantly breaking them off, allowing the smallest household question to take priority, protesting that she was usurping the children's time, running to the door to see if her husband might not need her, but after a couple of weeks and under Mr. Bayard's hearty encouragement, Corneille began to preempt a regular hour at noon. The great tragedies, *Polyeucte, Cinna* and *Horace,* were exhausted in rapid succession, and we moved on to the lesser, *Sertorius, Nicomède, Othon.* There were other poets whom I should have preferred, at least for variety, but I could not bring myself to interrupt Mrs. Bayard's craving for this gruff seventeenth-century master. Besides, her passion for him was a curiosity in itself. Why did she never tire of the high morality, the pounding ethics, the grandly declaimed duties of these old Roman tragedies?

One morning, as she was reading in her low musical voice the speech in *Horace* where Sabine, the girl from Albe who has married into a Roman family, tells of her trouble in suppressing her native sympathies, I thought I had my clue. In marrying her Hudson squire, had not Mrs. Bayard given up the life of the spirit in favor of that of farming and sport? Not that I believed for a minute that Mr. Bayard had demanded any such sacrifice. No, it had been quite voluntary. Mrs. Bayard adored her pleasant, large-hearted Horace—that was evident to every eye—and had dedicated her life to the altar of his pleasures with a totality of submission that made the survival of any interest in things outside his circumference seem an offence to his godhead. Reading of her wifely duties in the beautiful couplets of Sabine may have given her some of the same titillation as thinking of her husband while in bed with me used to give Madame de T——in Paris. Yes, I dare affirm it, however shocking the idea. There *was* a relation between the smile of the chaste Rebecca Bayard as she read from *Horace* and the squeals of my frenzied mistress.

"You must admit that Horace is a fearful brute," I suggested once, for there were moments when her excessive enthusiasm produced a slightly weary reaction in me. "My sympathies are with Camille. I'd have cursed Rome, too, if my brother had come in boasting how he'd slaughtered my lover."

"Oh, he *is* a brute," Mrs. Bayard conceded quickly. "That is undeniable. But remember that his being a brute doesn't justify Camille in cursing her country. A triumphant hero returning from the carnage of battle is entitled to be treated with some indulgence. His wife sees that. Sabine is entirely on her husband's side. Until he kills his sister. And even then she turns against him only to the extent necessary to bring him to a knowledge of his fault. In the end she is still his faithful wife."

"One wonders how happy they will be."

"Oh, I trust Sabine." Mrs. Bayard smiled a private smile. Still, I knew who her Sabine was.

"Doesn't Corneille strike you at times as rather remote? As too far away from real life?"

"Oh, but he's life to the core!" she exclaimed in shocked surprise. "That's just the thing about Corneille!"

I was struck by her notion. I still am. Is it possibly true? Is that strange, violent world of Corneille's tragedies where brothers kill sisters, where daughters-in-law demand the heads of mothers-in-law, where children are murdered by parents, more like our own than Racine's hothouse of sexual passions? How many persons have I known who have died or killed for sexual passion?

One thing I suspected, anyway, was that if Mrs. Bayard's daughter Katrina should be motivated by love to any violent action, it would be to kill, not to die. She made no secret of her strong objections to my reading sessions with her mother. Sometimes she would sit in the room with us, looking surly and bored. If Mrs. Bayard, who never showed the least impatience with her, offered to let her read a part, she would retort that her French wasn't up to it and that she didn't understand the "stupid play" anyway. If I then asked her why she bothered to listen, she said that it was good "for her ear." She managed to convey the impression that she was acting as a kind of chaperone whose presence might have the effect of preventing all kinds of impropriety. Katrina was expert with the unuttered as well as the uttered insult. But her mother never seemed to mind her presence. No amount of ill temper would keep Mrs. Bayard from putting her arm around her sullen daughter's neck and calling her "Kitten." The mother, so reserved with friends and underlings, so passively submissive with her husband, was uninhibitedly demonstrative with her children.

Katrina at last pushed her interest in me to a point of tactlessness. One afternoon, in late fall, as we were riding along the golden-red path by the river, far behind Sylvester and the groom, she asked me about my illegitimate birth.

"Tell me at once if you had rather not speak of it," she said aggressively. "Tell me I'm an impudent minx who should know when to hold her tongue."

"My dear Miss Katrina, I don't in the least mind talking about it. But what on earth can there be to say? My father took his pleasures as he saw fit. In French society noblemen of his rank are permitted great latitude. He has since acknowledged me, which was more than I had any right to expect."

"I should think it was the least he could do!"

"There are no such situations in your family?"

"Well, not that anyone's acknowledged."

"Ah, you see, then, I was fortunate."

"You mean you think my father may have illegitimate children whom he has *not* acknowledged?"

"Please, Miss Katrina. Remember my position here. I imply nothing."

We rode on for some minutes before she returned to the subject. "How would your position affect your marrying in France?"

"Well, I could not look to a nobleman's daughter. Only a royal bastard could do that. Nor should I be welcome in the upper middle class. However, with a settlement from the Vicomte, I might look to a respectable bourgeoise."

"I think that's terrible."

"It's life, Miss Katrina."

"Over here we have no such prejudices."

"Is that so?"

"My father would allow me to marry any man of honor who loved me and whom I loved."

"Do you really believe that?"

"No!" In a sudden fit of temper, or fearing to get herself more deeply involved, she spurred her horse to catch up with Sylvester.

It behooved me now to give some thought to what I was doing to the girl—to what I was doing, for that matter, to the whole family. Certainly I was the main source of interest to the children. It was not vanity to face that. Any half-decent looking mature man from the great Gallic nation across the seas would have been bound to promote such a reaction in a boy and girl nurtured in the wilderness of Bayardwick. But suppose that interest, in the case of Katrina, were to intensify? Suppose she were to take it firmly into her head that she meant to marry me? What then?

I did not for a minute fool myself that Mr. Bayard would be enchanted to hand over his only daughter with a handsome dower to a penniless bastard. But I knew that in French society almost anything could be arranged. If the Vicomte were intrigued by his son's capturing the affections of an heiress from the American forests and chose to confer a minor family title upon me, who could tell what the reaction of the Bayards might be? Had not the Sun King himself tried to marry Mademoiselle de Blois, the fruit of his intrigue with the Vallière, to William of Orange? And had he not considered the latter's snub as almost a *casus belli?*

But I had other things to consider. I was not at all sure that I wanted ever to marry. And I was convinced already that I could never live in America. I pined for Paris and the quick give-and-take of the Demarest milieu. I yearned for the theater, the opera, the supper parties and, above all, for the girls. I had had to resort to some desperate stratagems to satisfy my sexual needs at Bayardwick. Let me draw the curtain on that! I had also to consider that Katrina might find it impossible to adapt herself to life in France. Such a possibility, I concede, would not have occurred to most of my compatriots. But then most Frenchmen are incapable of comprehending anything that is not French. That is the advantage of being a bastard. It keeps one's eyes and one's mind open.

What, at any rate, I saw very clearly was that the Bayards were fundamentally different from me. We hardly seemed to belong to the same species. It was not only in religion and morals; it was in tastes, in ideas of the good life. We got on because of our good manners, as well as of our mutual affection. But I was too Gallic, and they were too—what was it—too Puritan? too American? too hypocritical? I need not choose the term. For something now came up to convince me that none of them was the right one.

2

One afternoon when the family was assembling in the parlor before dinner I noted that Katrina seemed in a particularly aggressive mood. She walked up and down restlessly and did not even respond to her father's and brother's questions. She evidently had something that she wanted to tell somebody, and we knew whom as soon as Mrs. Bayard appeared in the doorway. Katrina almost jumped at her.

"There have been two more of those fires in Manhattan, Mother. Samuel heard it from the courier. One in Wall Street and one in Maiden Lane. I suppose you still think they're accidents?"

"Is somebody suspected?" Mrs. Bayard asked gravely.

"They say it's the Spanish slaves. The same ones who were captured by that British man-of-war and sold here."

"Katrina, that was fifteen years ago! We went through all that ghastly trouble when you were still a baby. Don't let's start that up again."

"But some of those men are still in New York, Mother! How do you know they haven't been plotting their revenge for years? Everyone knows they burn and rob wherever they can. And two Negroes have already been indicted. What do you say to *that?*"

Mrs. Bayard turned to her husband. "Is it true, Francis?"

"It is true, I'm afraid, Rebecca. Two men have been indicted, but they're in hiding and can't be tried."

"But when they're caught they'll be burned alive," Katrina said savagely. "The way they were in 'forty-one. Over a slow fire in Bowling Green."

"Katrina, shut your mouth!" Mr. Bayard shouted with a rare heat. We were all at once silent. Mrs. Bayard sat down, very white. "You know your mother doesn't like to hear such things," he continued in a lower tone.

"Well, it's true, isn't it?" Katrina cried, almost hysterically defiant now. "Isn't it, Sylvester? They *will* be burned if they're caught, won't they?"

"Don't be a disgusting pig," her brother retorted. He jumped up to go to his mother's side. "They'll never catch them, dearest. And if they do, Father will make the governor spare them."

"But if the crowd gets them first, they'll burn them, you'll see," Katrina said viciously.

"Katrina, go to your room!" her father roared, and even Katrina was constrained to obey now. Mr. Bayard turned solicitously to his wife who was leaning on her son's shoulder.

"I think I'll go to mine," she said faintly. "I don't think I could eat any dinner after that."

There were just we three men at table. Mr. Bayard explained that his wife had not been feeling herself, and we dropped the subject, using the absence of the ladies as an excuse to drink more wine than usual. But the next day, when I sought Mrs. Bayard on the terrace for our reading of *Pulchérie* I found her no better. Unwilling to read, she sat, listlessly gazing down at the river.

"May I tell you something, Mrs. Bayard?" I ventured. "May I say that I entirely share your sentiments about the torture of human beings? We pride ourselves on being civilized in France, yet our system of justice belongs to the Dark Ages."

"Thank you, Monsieur Geyelin. I am glad you are among the enlightened. But it distresses me keenly that a child of mine should be so cruel. You heard Katrina."

"Ah, but she said those things only to annoy you. A girl that age has no conception of torture and executions."

Mrs. Bayard slowly shook her head. "I wish I could be sure."

"Please believe me. I have observed many young women. She has a good heart."

Katrina's mother did not seem to resent the impertinence of my inserting my judgment before the maternal bar. She continued to look pensive, her hands folded in her lap. "You have observed us very closely, Monsieur Geyelin. And with a friendly eye. Let me tell you of a deep concern of mine. It involves a chapter of our history. A horrid chapter. My grandfather was a judge in Massachusetts . . ."

She now told me, in a low, sad voice, of the Salem trials. I knew better than to interrupt. It would have been like interrupting the reading of a lesson in a Protestant church. When she had finished, I waited a bit before commenting.

"Is it that you feel an inherited guilt for your grandfather's harshness? Or do you worry that Katrina may have inherited some of his nature?"

"I feel that it behooves me particularly to make amends wherever I can," she responded. "Certainly to correct any repetition of ancient faults in my own family."

"But all that was sixty years ago!"

"Do the years make so much matter?"

"We think so in France. My forebears did the most frightful things, but it doesn't bother me. There was an archbishop in the Fouguères family who was reputed to go to auto-da-fés the way we go to horse races and to . . ."

"Ah, don't tell me," she exclaimed with a shudder.

"I shan't, don't worry. Or any of the other horrors in the family. My only point is, why should it bother *me?* And why need Judge Winthrop's sins be your affair?"

"I try to tell myself that they weren't sins," she corrected me unexpectedly. "I try to tell myself that he sincerely believed those poor people were guilty."

"Guilty? Of witchcraft? How could they be guilty of something that doesn't exist?"

"But suppose they *believed* they could kill innocent persons by their witchcraft? And suppose my grandfather believed what they believed?"

I began to lose some of my sympathy with her at this. It seemed to me that she wanted to writhe in a guiltiness and at the same time to boast of a stainless ancestor. What perversity was it that made her wish to take on Judge Winthrop's crimes while conferring her own innocence upon his shade?

"Tell that to his victims in the flames," I retorted.

"Oh, but they weren't burned!" she cried, shocked. "They were only hanged."

"All right, tell it to them when their necks are in the noose."

"One, I admit, was pressed to death."

I could not resist a chuckle at such conscientiousness with ancient facts. "That's probably worse than burning. It takes longer."

"Ugh!" She put her hands to her ears. But once she had dismissed the image, she returned to her druidical problem of ethics. "So you think sincerity makes no difference in moral guilt?"

"I think, when you torture or kill a man, you've got to be right—not just sincere."

She did not like this, and she relapsed into silence. After a few minutes she begged to be excused from the morning reading, and I withdrew. Riding that afternoon with Sylvester I told him of our conversation.

"You must understand, Monsieur Geyelin, that my mother is a saint. I know that saints in ancient days must have been accustomed to frightful scenes in the arenas. But Mother is like a saint already in heaven. The brutal things on earth, no matter how far removed, are unbearable to her."

I had heard the argument before; it failed to impress me. "If you will pardon me, Mr. Sylvester, I do not agree that your mother is so much affected by human suffering. Or at least I do not think that it is human suffering with which she is primarily concerned. It is responsibility that horrifies her—guilt. What causes her to tremble is not the idea of some poor creature writhing in the flames but the idea that she may have had a hand in putting him there."

Sylvester's lips were set. "My mother would go to the stake herself without a cry."

"I have no doubt of it. *That* is not what she fears."

My pupil seemed divided between his evident desire to pursue the topic and his sense of the possible indelicacy of discussing his mother so intimately. For some moments we rode in silence. "Whatever my mother may fear," he said at last in a kind of compromise, "she wants all that is best for her children."

"She thinks she can stand between you and the guilt of the Winthrops."

"She thinks she can make us free," he corrected me.

"Oh, I see it, Mr. Sylvester. Even a Frenchman can make out some things in this strange new world of yours. Your mother is like one of those passionate Catholic mothers who could almost bring herself to surrender her offspring to the bony hands of death if she were convinced they were in a state of grace!"

Sylvester reined his horse over closer to mine. He saw now that we had gone too far to retreat. It was up to him to set me right by telling all. "It is not as bad as that, Monsieur Geyelin. My mother would never, if she could help it, let us die. Indeed, I may say she is very much afraid of death—for her loved ones. She wants us to have our heaven here on earth—here in Bayardwick, to be exact."

"She wants it to be a Garden of Eden for you!"

"That is right. With my father as a kind of untempted Adam."

"And any rotten apples about she'll eat herself."

"I see no reason for jesting, Monsieur Geyelin."

"My dear boy, I'm not jesting. I've never been more serious. Your mother wishes to take on her own shoulders all the sins of the world. Or at least all the sins of the Winthrops. You and Miss Katrina should then be free to live in the sunny meadows and rich green forests of Bayardwick. That is why she doesn't really see why you need concern yourselves with the vanities of the world, even with books or plays or poetry. Your native innocence will be somehow superior to those things. The one thing I don't see is why she bothered to bring over a French tutor."

"She didn't. That was entirely my father's idea."

"So in taking up some of the tutor's time with her own reading she is really not hurting his pupils? Indeed, she may be saving them?"

"Oh, Monsieur Geyelin, now you're going too far!"

"But might not your sister feel that?" I glanced sideways at the

young man. "Might not that be the reason for your sister's resentment?"

If I had expected him to be confused, my humiliation was complete. "I think that is the reason," he agreed. "Katrina and I both
love Mother, but in very different ways. Katrina is madly jealous of
anyone in whom Mother takes the least interest. In me, for example.
In you. Oh, particularly you! She resents all the pleasure that your
reading aloud gives Mother. She wants to give her the same pleasure
and can't. And she bitterly resents Mother's encouraging her to love
horses and farm things because she thinks it comes from Mother's
not believing that she's capable of anything else. And not caring!"

"Ah, I begin to see. Whereas with you . . ."

"Whereas with me, there is no resentment. I am perfectly willing
to give up heaven to sit in purgatory and share poor Mother's guilty
feelings. Absurd though they may be!"

Flushed with embarrassment, he dug his heels into his horse's
flanks and galloped away, leaving me to a sorry jumble of thoughts.
Where now was the handsome Gallic tutor with whom the whole
family was in love? Did I even *exist* for the Bayards? Speaking of
burnings, was I anything more than a faggot thrust in the bonfire of
their interfamilial passions? Surely any Frenchman worthy of the
name could only pack his bags and hurry home!

I abandoned Sylvester to his own course and rode back to the
house, brooding over my feelings towards the Bayards, and of course
in particular to Mrs. Bayard. Indeed, I have never to this day successfully analyzed them. It was something of an anomaly for a young
Frenchman to be so close to such a woman. Was I in love with her?
If I was, it was certainly very different from anything that I have felt
for any other woman. Of course, she was a dozen years older than I,
but I discounted this, as the same age difference had existed between
me and Estelle, who had for a year in Dijon proved a most delicious
mistress. And then, too, Mrs. Bayard was a magnificent specimen of
her age. Her thirty-nine years (she never made the smallest secret of
her age) had made few inroads in her beauty. Judging by what people
said who had known her in her youth, she was probably then at her
peak. I can only conclude that what may have kept my feelings in so
ambivalent a state was my sense of her utter devotion to her husband. Mrs. Bayard was of the stuff of which Lucrèces are made.

Yet love which is muffled can pop out in unexpected forms and
places. There could be no question that I had a strong desire to imprint myself somewhere in the mind or heart if not the body of

Rebecca Bayard. I was like a boy who contemplates a marble statue whose ideal beauty seems to elude or mock him and who desires to scribble his name or a message on it. Only the message that I wished to scribble was not an obscene one.

3

The family at this time moved to Manhattan for a month while Mr. Bayard attended meetings of the Governor's Council. The arsons, if arsons they were, continued, and the atmosphere in the town was tense. When I walked with Sylvester and Katrina along the Battery, we noticed that any Negroes of possible Spanish extraction, buccaneer types with gold earrings and colored silks, were the subjects of baleful glances. The atmosphere in the home, however, was one of holiday, and our lessons were suspended.

Sylvester struck me as in an odd mood. He was silent for long periods, and his attention was difficult to secure. One night, when his parents and Katrina were out at a supper party and he and I were sitting by the library fire over the port, I suggested that he was in love.

"But who can the girl be?" I demanded. "I have yet to see you with one."

"You Frenchmen think that's the answer to everything," he retorted. "You couldn't be further from the truth. What is worrying me is whether or not I can trust you."

"Trust me? My dear fellow, you're insulting."

"No, because it's a question if I can trust you to break the law."

I smiled. "Can we hang for it?"

"Possibly. But I'm not too worried about that side of it. I'm not sure how you will see it—morally."

"Why don't you tell me about it?" I asked, my interest now thoroughly aroused. "At least I can promise you my silence if I decide not to go in with you."

"Very well. On that condition. You know the men Pedella and Sells, who are under indictment for arson?"

"The ones who got away?"

"The same. Pedella is a friend of our butler, Samuel." Sylvester paused, watching me carefully. "At this very moment he is hidden in Mother's garden house."

I jumped up. "Right here? In Manhattan?"

"Well, if he were in Bayardwick, I'd have no concern. My worry is how to get him out of Manhattan. Of course, I believe him to be innocent. Samuel says he is. But in any event, his trial would be a farce. Will you help?"

I let him await my answer until I had slowly filled my pipe. He would find that he was not the only one with a flair for the dramatic. "Of course, I'll help. What's the plan?"

"There's only one way to get him off the island that is absolutely sure. He must go in Mother's carriage—with Mother in it. She can take him up to one of the Winthrop farms in the Bronx. Samuel can take care of him from then on."

"You think your mother's game?"

"I'm sure she's game. If I'm not involved. That is why it must be your scheme. Samuel will have come to you."

For the rest of the evening we worked out our plan. I was amazed at Sylvester's maturity. He had arranged every detail. The carriage would be ordered for two the following afternoon, after Mr. Bayard had gone to the governor's palace. Pedella would be in a picnic hamper which would be strapped to the back. Mrs. Bayard would be on an inspection tour. I was to tell her when she went to her garden after breakfast.

I was delighted. Never had I imagined that a tutor's life would contain this kind of excitement. "And if your father finds out?" I asked.

"He won't. But if he did, he would soon forgive. You know my father treats us with great latitude."

"But he's an officer of the Crown!"

Sylvester shrugged. "He's also a realist. If he catches us, it will be a fait accompli. My father's at his best with faits accomplis."

I could hardly wait for the morning. After breakfast I watched from the library window until I saw Mrs. Bayard step out to the garden to inspect her begonias. Then I went out on the terrace.

"Excuse me, Mrs. Bayard, but I have a matter of the greatest importance to discuss with you."

She listened gravely, without a single interruption, while I told her the story. Then she went straight to the point.

"Why did Samuel come to *you*?"

"Because he was scared. He didn't dare involve the children. He knew you'd never help him if he did. He couldn't get up the courage to break it to you directly."

"I see." She pondered the matter for a few moments as she gazed at her flowers. She seemed curiously unsurprised, even unmoved. I could only speculate that the anxieties with which she habitually lived were so real to her that actuality contained nothing to make them worse.

"It's like one of our plays," she said at last.

"Mrs. Bayard, I'm not joking."

"My dear Monsieur Geyelin, I know you're not joking. It is all deadly serious. How could it be otherwise? What I mean is, where is my duty? To the governor, of whose Council Mr. Bayard is a member, or to the poor wretch hiding in my garden?" As she looked at me now she actually smiled! "What would Monsieur Corneille say? I'm not sure. But what surprises me most is that I have no question." She drew herself up now. "Of course, we must rescue the slave. You and Samuel will arrange the hamper. I will see to the carriage. We shall leave exactly as planned."

If she had spent her whole life preparing for the moment, she could not have acted with more calmness or greater alacrity. As I stood there, awed, she reproached me.

"Come on. We must hurry!"

I spent the rest of the morning in the library. There was nothing further for me to do. At a quarter to two I went to the front hall and watched Samuel and the footman strap the picnic hamper to the back of the coach. Mrs. Bayard appeared from upstairs, splendid in blue velvet with ostrich feathers, and stepped with a fine air of detachment into the huge, embossed vehicle. I followed her. She had taken the precaution of dismissing the second coachman, taking only one, the oldest, who had come with her from Boston twenty years before. She had also dismissed the two outriders with whom Mr. Bayard always drove out.

We had not proceeded more than a few blocks when the carriage halted abruptly. I glanced at Mrs. Bayard before sticking my head out of the window to see what was wrong. She did not flinch. Looking out, I saw that we were surrounded by a crowd of men. I noted at once that it was no ordinary street gang. The men were too well dressed and were carrying rifles.

"Sorry to hold you, Mrs. Bayard." A square, impassive face under a black three-cornered hat now blocked the window. "I'm your neighbor, John Ogden. What we have to do will only take a minute."

Mrs. Bayard replied in a voice of serene authority. "I'm on my way north, and I'm pressed for time, Mr. Ogden. What will only take a minute?"

"The search of your carriage, Ma'am. We're looking for an escaped slave. An indicted criminal."

"Do you imply that I'm a party to his escape?"

"Not at all, Ma'am. But we are acting on a tip. The man may have been hidden without your knowledge."

"I assure you that he is not."

"Sorry, Ma'am. I must insist."

"Step back, sir, and let me address your friends!" Mrs. Bayard cried out. To my astonishment the man did. "I am traveling on the governor's business," she called out from the window. "I have papers in this carriage which must on no account be disturbed. Move aside please and let me pass." Nobody moved. "Go ahead, Ambrose," she called up to the coachman. The carriage did not stir.

I now jumped from the carriage and climbed up to join the terrified Ambrose on the seat. Taking the reins and the whip, I laid the latter down hard on the backs of our four steeds. They tried to leap forward, but a dozen men had seized the harness. The horses reared and stamped, and a great deal of shouting and cussing ensued. I had raised my whip to strike at the men hanging on to the harness when something hit me from behind. I whirled about to see a man who had climbed to the roof of the carriage raising a club to strike me again.

When I came to I was lying on the pavement with my head in Ambrose's lap. Mrs. Bayard was bathing my head with a damp rag.

"Where's the slave?" I cried, starting up. "Where's Pedella?"

"Never mind Pedella," Mrs. Bayard replied in a strange, flat voice. "How are *you?* That's more to the point. At least we can do something about you."

"How long have I been out?" I looked about me wildly. The carriage and horses were standing there, but the street was empty. Streets were never empty like that!

"Five minutes. Ten. Tell me, how do you feel?"

"I've got a headache, that's all. Where's Pedella?"

"They took him to Bowling Green," Mrs. Bayard said grimly, and then shrugged. "There's nothing in the world we can do. We may as well get you home."

"But what will they do to him?"

"It is probably done by now."

I stared in horror at Mrs. Bayard, but she simply stared back at me. Then she pointed to the carriage, and, silently, we got in. As we passed Wall Street I could hear shouting. Pedella was a lucky man. They had only hanged him.

Mrs. Bayard declined my arm as she walked firmly up the steps to her door which was opened wide. Inside the servants were gathered in a shivering, apprehensive knot.

"It's all over," she stated in the same flat voice. "The wretched man is dead. There is no further danger. Close the doors."

She went into the parlor where a fire was lit and stood before it, warming her hands.

"Mrs. Bayard . . ." I began.

"It's all right, Monsieur Geyelin," she interrupted, in a tone that was almost irritable. "I mean *I'm* all right. We did what we could. Had we not made our effort, they would have caught him sooner or later. What is done is done."

I heard a rush of skirts, and Katrina flung herself into the room like a wild thing. She fell on her knees before her mother.

"They killed him!" she screamed. "They strung him right up in Bowling Green!"

Mrs. Bayard fixed her grave stare on her daughter's upturned, distracted face. Katrina, in response, plunged her head in her lap. "Isn't that what you expected, dear?"

"I didn't really believe it! I didn't know what I was doing!"

Mrs. Bayard looked up at me now, as if this were my cue.

"What *were* you doing, Miss Katrina?" I asked.

The girl raised her head to face me in a fury of resentment. "Samuel told me what you and Mother were up to. He panicked. He was afraid you would be stopped, and he wanted me to warn Father so he could bring help. Well, I didn't warn Father. I told Mr. Ogden, whose barn was burned by those slaves!"

Mrs. Bayard gently stroked the back of the head that was now again plunged in her lap. "My child, we must deal with the living. You thought you were doing the right thing. You have a Roman soul. Perhaps a bit too Roman. You saw your mother delivering a fugitive from justice. You decided to correct her. Perhaps you were right. Had that man gone to trial, he would have surely hanged. You saved him the agony of waiting."

"Why do you assume, Rebecca, that the man would have surely hanged?"

We all turned at the familiar high tone. Mr. Bayard was standing in the doorway, his great blue eyes fixed enigmatically on his wife. Was it severity that I made out in them? Or sarcasm? Or was it simply pity?

Mrs. Bayard rose in confusion. "Oh, Francis!"

"The atmosphere of the town, I concede, is hysterical," her husband continued. "I have persuaded the governor to declare martial law. There will be no more hangings, you can count on that. Furthermore, it appears that the last two burnings were accidents, not arson at all. The governor is going to put a stop to the trials. What concerns him—and what concerns *me*—is that a gang of ruffians should have presumed to stop my wife's carriage."

Mrs. Bayard's detachment had abandoned her. She raised her clenched hands in supplication to her husband. "Can you forgive me, Francis, for the one and only time in our married life that I have gone against your authority?"

"If it is my forgiveness you are seeking, Rebecca, pray do me greater justice. If Mrs. Francis Bayard chooses to rescue a poor wretch from an angry mob, she does so with my blessing. But you and I, my dear, have a rougher trial to face. You and I and Katrina. *And* Sylvester. And even Monsieur Geyelin, I fear."

Katrina rose slowly now, and we all three waited for him to continue. Sylvester had just come into the room, his face oddly pinched and gray. Whatever it was, he knew.

"The man in the carriage," Mr. Bayard continued bluntly, "was a freed slave who had nothing whatever to do with the slaves who were indicted for arson. Sylvester had bribed him to take the part because he wanted you, Rebecca, to believe that you had saved a man's life. He told me he had to exorcise the Winthrop curse. Tell her, Sylvester."

I hoped that Mrs. Bayard would faint. Or even die. But she didn't. She put her arms around the frantically sobbing Katrina and hugged her as if it were somehow possible to squeeze the misery out of her daughter's trembling body.

4

Mr. Bayard had ordered us all to our rooms where our suppers were later served to us on trays, as if we were prisoners. Because of his authority, not only as a patroon and a paterfamilias, but as a member of the Governor's Council in a time of martial law, this seemed to me entirely reasonable. I had had an earlier brush at home with the *lettre de cachet*. But when my employer came himself to wait upon me in my chamber after supper, his demeanor was hardly that of a jailer. Behind him was Samuel with a decanter of port and two glasses.

"It has been a day full of incident, Monsieur Geyelin," Mr.

Bayard announced in what was actually a cheerful tone after we were seated and our glasses filled. "A day of tragedy, too, but there is no need to dwell on the past. Let us turn to happier news. The governor has decided to confer a signal honor upon the colonies. He has resolved to send his son to college here. He will go to Harvard, and Sylvester is to accompany him. Which means, of course, that we shall have no further need of your services. I suggest that you allow me to give you a year's salary and send you back to France on the *Lady Susan,* which is sailing at dawn the day after tomorrow. You shall buy what you need for the trip at my expense, and your things at Bayardwick will be sent after you. I know, my dear fellow, that this is abrupt, but I see no reason to protract these things. We have all been very fond of you, and we shall miss you sadly. But there we are. What can I do? I am told that the *Lady Susan* is the fastest and most comfortable vessel on the Atlantic run."

"Mr. Bayard," I protested. "If your offer of a year's salary has anything to do with what has just happened, let me assure you that you can count on my discretion without it."

"Your discretion, my boy? Do you think I'm a jealous husband, you rascal?" He uttered his gay peal of laughter. "No, dear fellow, I am only too happy to give you the money. I feel I owe it to you for all you've done for my children. And for reading with Rebecca. Oh, yes, that too. So there, is it all agreed? You'd better get started on your arrangements. I'm sorry to say it, but you haven't much time."

I did not see Sylvester or Katrina again, even to say good-bye. They were shipped off to Bayardwick at dawn the next day. Mrs. Bayard remained in town, and I was allowed to take my leave of her in her chamber that afternoon. She was lying on a chaise-lounge by a window that faced out on the harbor, and she looked so pale and haggard that I almost cried out.

"What have you to say for me now, Monsieur Geyelin?" she asked sadly. "Can you imagine a more desolate failure? I am glad that you are returning to France. I hope you will forget all about the bleak new world in that sunny land."

"I hate to hear you talk like that, Mrs. Bayard."

"Do you think it's unjustified? Would you try to persuade me that I've been a great success?"

"Why not? You and Sylvester have ended the arson crisis. It's over, Mrs. Bayard! Oh, I know that poor devil had to die to end it, but he died in a good cause, don't you see?"

"You mean he's an involuntary martyr?"

"You might put it that way."

Mrs. Bayard's smile was grim, but at least it was a smile. "Then let us hope he is an involuntary saint in heaven. He'll be better off, anyway. But what about my poor Sylvester who will never forgive himself, and my wretched Katrina, who will carry her guilt to the grave?"

"Ah, Mrs. Bayard, they are young. There is nothing that time will not cure for them."

"You know you don't believe that, Monsieur Geyelin. And what of Rebecca Bayard, whose obsession with bringing up her children as happy, innocent Bayards has condemned them to the very doom she sought to avoid? What of her, my friend?"

"What else could you have done?"

"I could have placed my entire faith in my husband!" she cried with sudden passion, sitting up straight in her chair. "I could have trusted *him* and not Corneille to decide what was my duty. If I had simply loved my family and left the rest to God, I should not have worried my son into causing a man's death and driven my daughter half crazy. All I had to do was love, my friend—love and accept. But no, oh, no, that was not enough for me! I had to have *my* share in creation. *My* share in hell. Well, I've earned it."

I felt the tears in my eyes, which was a rare thing for me, despite my Gallic blood. I could not speak. I took her hand and kissed it. She seemed at least moved by this. When I freed her hand, she picked up a small velvet bag from the table beside her.

"I want you to forget about the Bayards. I want you to be happy where you belong, in France. I shall always be grateful that I have known you, and I shall never forget our readings. Please accept this ring as a token of my friendship. Perhaps one day your bride may wear it."

Enclosed in the bag, which I now opened, was a ring with a splendid blood ruby. Had she told Mr. Bayard about the gift? I have no idea.

5

I had no reason to love the Pompadour, but I had to admit that Versailles was a dull place after her death. My father, like the favorite, died in 1760, and my legitimate brother, the new Vicomte, a gentleman of the new liberal views, allowed me to style myself the Chevalier de Fouguères and obtained a post for me in court in the household of the royal princesses. My duties were light but monotonous. I attended the levees of the four maiden daughters of France, Mesdames Adelaide, Victoire, Sophie and Louise, when they received diplomatic visitors in the great chamber on the *rez-de-chaussée* hung with their beautiful but highly flattering portraits by Nattier.

I often thought, in the crowded, gilded life of that hugest of palaces, of my simpler friends across the ocean. Did Mrs. Bayard still read Corneille by the river? Had Sylvester graduated from Harvard? Had Katrina married? There were times when I could hardly believe in the existence of that quiet gray manor house by the slowly flowing Hudson. Now that I had moved to the heart of the civilized world, it seemed difficult to credit the reality of a culture so much simpler at the outer circumference. And yet there were moments when that circumference appeared to me as being made of the tougher substance and the court of Louis XV seemed the fantasy.

For what did we think we were doing, twenty thousand of us, in that endless ceremonial? I had read a good deal in the lore of old pagan rites and sacrifices, and it occurred to me that we might be unconsciously celebrating the natural functions of the body. We watched the king eating; we watched him defecating. We witnessed the birth of royalty; we came very close to witnessing their conceptions. Ambassadors and distinguished visitors were led on an unvarying round of formal presentations to honor each branch of the royal tree. They bowed to the King, the father, to the Queen, the mother, to the Dauphin, the future, to the Dauphine, womb of the future, to Mesdames . . .

Where was the power in it? Where was the grace or even the majesty? Those paying homage and those receiving it were equally puppets. My poor royal mistresses, destined to old maidhood because France wanted to save their dowries, nodding and chattering, sewing and reading and praying, were as unimportant as those unwanted wives of Eastern potentates, too great to be sent home or given to other men, who lived out long, virginal lives in a harem whose pleasures were forever denied them.

On a never-to-be-forgotten morning, at a particularly crowded levee, I recognized the tall, broad-shouldered figure of Francis Bayard in a blue satin coat under a huge, splendid, if rather old-fashioned black *perruque* bowing to Madame Adelaide. His healthy, glowing presence seemed at once to fill the whole chamber. Curtseying at his side was a much younger, very beautiful woman in white. For a moment I tried to hope that it might be Katrina, grown up. But a little jab in the pit of my stomach told me it was not.

I followed them after the audience and saluted Mr. Bayard on the terrace. For a moment he seemed not to know me, but when he did, he beamed all over.

"My dear, this is Monsieur Geyelin, our old tutor of whom I have told you. How are you, dear fellow? Does everybody in France live at Versailles? What do you do here?"

I explained as briefly as possible my new duties and the generosity of my brother. He informed me that Sylvester, to his chagrin, had become a physician and had his own house and practice at Bayard-wick. Katrina still lived at home. Neither had married. When his lady turned to watch the crowd gathering around the door where the King was now expected, he added quickly, in a lower tone:

"I shall have to set Katrina up in her own establishment. Two women in the same house will never do. I'm sorry to tell you that my daughter has found it very difficult to see another in her mother's place."

"I suppose that's only natural," I replied, trembling a bit at the surprising pain that twisted my innards. "When did you lose Mrs. Bayard?"

"Winter before last. Of the cursed pox. I waited the full year." Mr. Bayard coughed away his embarrassment. "A fine woman, Rebecca. None finer. But you know the old saying, don't you? That it's a compliment to your deceased wife to marry again? Shows how much you needed her. Eh, what, Geyelin?"

The crowd thickened. The king was coming. We were separated, and I did not seek him again. I walked to the Orangerie to be alone with my memories and regrets. As I paced up and down in the cold October air, I thought of the autumnal Hudson and the little white-caps in the wind, and of poor Rebecca who had cared so desperately that her mate should not be troubled by her anxieties. She need not have worried!

(IV)

The Diplomat

A Chapter from the Privately Printed Posthumous Memoirs
of Samuel Shaw Russell: "My Life as a Diplomat."

I HAVE ALWAYS SUSPECTED that a man who is known as a great diplomat may not be one at all. Is it not of the essence of his art that it be kept concealed? How would you feel, if you were Secretary of State, and saw, sitting across the conference table, the "great diplomat" of your adversary? Would you not be very specially on your guard? Would your wits not be at their sharpest? Your adversary would have been a fool to send him. Perhaps the greatest diplomats are never known to history—if they exist at all.

I have observed most of the chancelleries of Europe since I first served under Robert Livingston in Paris in 1802, and it has not impressed me that the course of history has been essentially altered by diplomats, or even by those who send them. We are like creatures on a slowly but ineluctably moving glacier. We may skate about on its surface, but time will erase our tracks, and if our memories are preserved at all, it may be only because our corpses are frozen, quaintly costumed, in that massive ice.

My father, the Reverend Everett Winthrop Russell, a Congregational minister in Newport, Rhode Island, was of a different view. He believed that God viewed with especial favor his domain in the northern New World. He professed to see signs of divine partiality in our successful escape from ancient tyranny, in our preservation from cold winters and Indians, in our deliverance from the German mercenaries of George III. God manifested His will through individuals, divinely selected, whose impact upon history was undoubted. Where, he would ask, would Massachusetts have been without our ancestor John Winthrop? Where Rhode Island, without his own father, Governor Russell? But he gave up trying to convert me in disgust at my reaction to the news that Thomas Jefferson had been elected President in the House of Representatives by a single vote over Aaron Burr.

"It is God's hand!" my father cried.

"It was a close shave," I retorted.

Shortly thereafter my diplomatic career commenced, and in my very first post I had the curious experience that was to confirm me for good in my early conception of what shapes—or fails to shape— the destiny of nations.

I was twenty-seven when Chancellor Livingston arrived in Paris to assume charge of the American mission and to negotiate the mercantile claims and the Florida-Louisiana questions. I had already been in the French capital for a year. I found my new chief well informed and well intentioned, but also cautious and a bit on the fussy side. I should have preferred greater directness. I was like many of my generation, who had been infants in 1776. We had no clear memories of life under a monarchy, and we tended to look back upon the older time as formal, hierarchical, prejudiced, unfree. Yet Robert Livingston was in some ways a modern man. He was a scientific agriculturist, an early backer of steam, an imaginative jurist. Unfortunately, he was also an eighteenth-century landed aristocrat of great wealth who viewed democracy with a candid alarm.

"What is your opinion of Bonaparte?" he asked me as we were drinking claret after our first dinner at his *hôtel.* "Do you think they will make him emperor?"

I prided myself already on my knowledge of France. "I doubt it much matters whether they do or don't," I replied confidently. "Bonaparte is already an anachronism. He thinks he has stopped the revolution, and for the moment perhaps he has. But I cannot believe that it will not resume. It would not surprise me one day to see his head flung to the people, like Louis XVI's."

The chancellor seemed perturbed by this. He was a tall, rangy man of many nervous mannerisms. He kept crossing and uncrossing his legs; he fiddled with objects on the table. His face was full of dignity, and his great gray eyes and long nose seemed used to command, but his air of tension and the high, warbling quality of his voice tended to mitigate the rigor of one's initial impression with a distinct note of levity.

"Dear me, I don't suppose that would ease our diplomatic difficulties," he opined with a brisk shake of the head. "I don't see how one can expect to gain anything from a chief of state unless he has a firm hold on what he has to give away. But if Bonaparte is insecure, doesn't it stand to reason that he may be aware of it? And if he's aware of it, will he not prepare a refuge? He's Italian, you know, and the Italians are a practical people. Suppose we were to offer him a private suzerainty or duchy in Louisiana, in case of trouble? Might that not tickle his fancy? Might it not induce him to consider ceding us the territory?"

I could hardly repress a smile. "It might interest his brothers. And it would certainly interest his old mother, Letizia, who, one hears, is always shipping her savings abroad. But Bonaparte believes in his star. He would never provide a hedge against disaster. He would think it bad luck."

"I wonder. Those fellows are always lining their own nests. Corsicans have a criminal bias, you know. And the Latin criminal is more concerned with security than glory."

"But Bonaparte is more than a Corsican, sir. He is a genius, an artist, a romantic. He is utterly irresponsible: to mankind and to himself. He must have his fling at the sun, at the whole universe. If it all blows up in his face . . . well, *tant pis*." I shrugged.

"You amuse me, my friend," the chancellor responded with an unamused smile. "You young men have original ideas. But we older ones have had to make our terms with the real world. I must ask you to adopt my theories, at least in practice, while you serve under me. I shall need your fullest cooperation with the memoranda that I propose to submit to the foreign minister as to why it is not in the best interests of France to continue to hold Louisiana."

"Of course, sir. That is what I am here for."

It has never taken me long to adapt myself to a superior. I saw at once that the chancellor was not a man with whom it would do to differ. He was intelligent, but he was hampered by a conviction that the world was rational. If one did A, with proper planning, then B was bound to follow. This assumption would not have been so dangerous had he been more flexible. But Livingston's trouble was that he found it difficult, if not impossible, to change a plan once embarked upon. There was a right time, to his way of thinking, for everything: for working or playing, for joking or being serious, for war or peace, and a wrong time, and every rational man, even a red Indian or a Frenchman, was bound to see this—if it were only properly explained. And who could better explain it than a Livingston, a landowner, a judge, a New York gentleman in whose person the ancient wisdom of the old world and the high adventurousness of the new had been so happily combined? My new chief had a great faith in lineage. It did not take him long to discover my paternal grandmother's maiden name, and he nodded vigorously in approval.

"One of our first families," he assured me. "My great uncle, Johannes Livingston, married a Winthrop."

I was put to work, at any rate, on a series of memoranda designed to persuade the first consul and his foreign secretary, Talleyrand, that it was not to their advantage to hang on to vast, uninhabited territories in the New World and that it would be far wiser to deed these over to the young, vigorous United States, thus gaining a firm ally against England. I was fairly sure that these memoranda would not be read, or, if read, would have no effect, but it was my job to do what I was told, and, between us, Mr. Livingston and I produced some very fine briefs. The only effect of these on the world of fact was to pave the way for my odd little personal experience, which came about in an interview that I was granted with Talleyrand himself.

But I am ahead of myself. I had not yet been presented either to the first consul or to his foreign minister. Both introductions occurred at an afternoon reception at the Tuileries, a month after Livingston's arrival, to which I accompanied my chief. He and I stood in a large circle of diplomats as the great Bonaparte made his round. Needless to say, in the half-hour during which we waited I never took my eyes off the small, agile figure in the red coat and red breeches with the death pale face and straight, slick dark hair. So this was the terror of Europe! He moved like a cat.

"We hear you want war, my lord," I heard his high, metallic voice ring out. "Well, if you get it, you will know whom to blame." He was speaking to the British ambassador, but the rise in decibels was for the benefit of all. I could not catch the reply of the imperturbable British peer, and Bonaparte passed on down the line.

No, I was not impressed. I was never really impressed by Bonaparte. Granted that he had the greatest military mind and possibly the greatest administrative capacity in modern history, what was the good of his gifts? It would have been better for mankind, better even for France, had he perished in his first battle. As I looked about at that vast reception hall, thronged with genuinely admiring diplomats—for that was it: they did admire him—I had some early vision of this. It struck me then that Europe had ceased to be the "real" world, that its governing men had reverted to childhood and were playing children's games, however bloody, with plumes and swords and drums and decorations. Paris had gone mad with a bit of military success, and everyone kowtowed to this little strutting peacock.

Mr. Livingston was presented, and presented me in turn.

"You have come a long way, Mr. Livingston," Bonaparte did him the honor to observe. "I am afraid you will miss the clean air of your native clime. You will find that we are sadly corrupted in this old world of ours. Have you met Monsieur de Talleyrand? Talleyrand, tell Mr. Livingston about the sorry decline of morals!"

I examined the tall, limping figure of the foreign minister who turned now to us as the first consul moved on. Talleyrand was handsome—or had been once—an impassive young man's face frozen as in a death mask. He listened without replying to Livingston's compliments and bowed his head gravely as the latter retired. I followed my chief, but discreetly left his side again when the British ambassador approached him. To my surprise, an aide, who had come up behind me, murmured in my ear that the foreign minister wished a word with me. I returned to where Talleyrand was standing alone.

"Tell me, Mr. Russell," he drawled, "is Livingston rich?"

"I believe that he is rich in land, sir."

"Do you mean that he is land poor?"

"No, sir. But some of the great patroons, as we call them, on the Hudson River, may find it difficult to place their hands at short order on large amounts of cash."

"Do you apprehend, because of what the first consul said, that I shall demand a bribe of him?"

"Hardly, Mr. Minister. But you might think, in negotiations, that he could advance sums on behalf of his government."

"Which is not the case?"

"Which is definitely not the case."

Talleyrand nodded. My message had been conveyed. "We understand that a Mr. Monroe is on his way from Washington to join Mr. Livingston. He is a Southern gentleman, we are told. Is he rich? With thousands of slaves and so forth?"

"On the contrary, sir, I believe that Mr. Monroe's means are merely modest."

"To what, then, does he owe his station?"

"To his talents, sir. And perhaps a bit to his old friendship with our President."

"I see. So he will be the real chief of the mission?"

"I should say that the real chief of the mission will be he who most successfully prophesies what Mr. Jefferson will think of any particular event—six weeks later, when news of it, at the earliest, can reach him."

The specter of a smile creased the corners of Talleyrand's lips. "You are welcome to come and play a hand of cards, Mr. Russell," he murmured as he turned away, "any night that Madame de Talleyrand receives."

This was a command, and I presented myself at the vast *hôtel* on the Rue du Bac two evenings later at nine. The high gilded rooms were full of people, but I found my way to the corner where the great man sat at a card table with three of his aides. He was finishing a hand as I approached. He did not look up, yet I felt sure that he knew I was there. He played the final card and bowed his head to the three gentlemen, who at once arose. Everyone withdrew as he now nodded to me and indicated a vacated chair. I sat, studying the famous mask before me. Talleyrand was then only a year under fifty, and it was difficult to tell whether he looked more or less than his age. His face was the face of a pretty boy, an angel, but it was a dead boy, and, as people said, a fallen angel. Was there cruelty or indifference behind that impassivity? Perhaps an indifference amounting to cruelty.

"Mr. Livingston keeps supplying us with memoranda full of interesting reasons why we should cede to your great nation that part of Louisiana which lies north of Arkansas," he began in his faintly weary tone. "I suppose one's imagination is always fertile with motives for generosity in others. But I must admire the ingenuity which your superior demonstrates in his most recent brief. He suggests that if we convey this vast domain to you, your government would be willing to deed to members of the Bonaparte family a tract of land exceeding the size of France itself. Why, Mr. Russell, should the Bonapartes wish to settle in the wilderness?"

"It need not always be a wilderness, Mr. Minister."

"No, indeed. But one doubts if it will contain such châteaux as they now enjoy—at least in their lifetimes. I confess that the thought flickered across my mind that Mr. Livingston was considering this estate as a refuge—in case political events here should take the turn they took a decade ago. I am even afraid that the same thought flickered across the vastly superior mind of the first consul himself, when I told him of the offer."

I trusted that none of my amusement was discernible in my expression. "Can history not repeat itself?" I inquired.

"No doubt. And even the first consul might awaken one morning to find himself assassinated—or worse. But was it tactful, Mr. Russell, to suggest such a possibility to a man of General Bonaparte's great pride and considerably justified self-assurance?"

"We credit the first consul with an intellect that can take in every contingency," I replied. "We see him as being as cool and clear in the Tuileries as he is in the field of battle."

"A good answer, Russell. I see you had no hand in that foolish memorandum."

"Our mission stands behind *all* memoranda, Mr. Minister."

"An even better answer. A clever junior never exposes his superior. We can talk, then, you and I. I have been, as you may know, to America."

"It's our constant boast."

"Dear me, you needn't go that far. Even as a diplomat. I shall be franker with you. I did not much care for your country, Russell. I did not find it sympathetic. There is something in your air that . . . well, that I grasp only with difficulty. It is a kind of repudiation, not exactly of the past, but of all that I, at least, find most important in this vale of tears. The *douceur de vivre*—we might put it that way. Americans are not strong on *douceurs*. You believe more in morals. You even seem to believe that morals began with you."

"I gather that you visited New England, sir," I said with a smile.

"It's worse there, is that it?"

"Worse? Let me put it that it's more intense."

"Ah, yes. And you, of course, are a New Englander, are you not? I have observed you. You don't really quite believe that we exist over here, do you? But you will find that we do."

I bowed. "Perhaps you will exist even more substantially when you recognize that we do."

"So that's it!" He uttered a faint cackle, as if I had walked at last into his trap. "You are sensitive. You are touchy. You fear that we do not recognize the destiny of America. But we do! Some of us, anyway. We see the future of man moving westward, ever westward, across the ocean, across forests full of giant bears, and prairies full of giant . . . is it buffaloes?"

"You amuse yourself, sir. But, of course, you must see the future in the waving plumes of your famous marshals. You must see it as a *Pax Galliae*."

"Tut, tut, my friend. Don't assume we are *all* ambitious. For myself, I am three parts sloth. You imagine me to be an eagle. In truth,

I am a poor old croaking barnyard fowl. I have no yearning to follow the star of victory to the east or west or north, or wherever it may lead. The meadows and vineyards of France are quite enough for my declining years."

He was silent now, but he had silences and silences. This one seemed a cue.

"Do you imply, sir," I asked, "that you might seek a career in the West if you were twenty again?"

"If I were twenty!" A faint animation seemed to quiver in those marble cheeks. "Ah, when I was twenty, Russell, life was something that you cannot even conceive. But when one has experienced *that*, one does not speculate on other youths. Certainly not on those in barren wastes, in distant forests."

The silence that followed this I did not even try to interrupt. If the great man had something to tell me, he would have to find his own way to tell it.

"What would you say, Russell, if I were to offer you *all* of Louisiana? Not just what is north of Arkansas, but the south as well? Half a continent, at one sweep of the pen?"

I stared, not a muscle moving. "At a price?"

"Oh, at a price, of course. The first consul needs money for his wars. But what is cash in return for an empire? The ancient conquerors sacrificed whole generations, whole civilizations, for much less than we are asking. A few millions of your dollars, more or less, what is that? Might there not be a commission, too, for a foreign minister of expensive tastes? Oh, very expensive tastes, I fear. Yes, I think if the price for the cession were, say, fifty millions of your dollars, the foreign minister should ask no less than five."

It was at this moment that I had what I like to think of as my vision. It began as a solid, almost choking sensation of well-being, but the strenuous aspect passed quickly off, and then I felt a wonderful ease. I saw thick black forests and wide lakes and roaring rivers and great prairies stretching before me and below me, for I seemed to be soaring, like a great bird of prey. Now all that may seem rather banal. But the curious part of it was that I knew, in the most settled way, that there was nothing I had to do but soar, that nobody cared if I soared, swooped, or, for that matter, tumbled, a ragged bunch of claws and feathers, to the rocks below. Was the vision inspired? If so, why should I have been chosen? And for what purpose? For there was no call to any act. I could act or not act, speak or not speak. It would make no difference. I heard my own voice calmly responding to Talleyrand:

"I thought it had been made sufficiently clear, Mr. Minister, under the Directorate, that my country could not pay any such commissions."

Talleyrand was not in the least offended. He had trafficked with bigger game than I. "But that was under the Directorate. And the stakes were so small."

"Please try to understand our procedures, sir," I begged him. "It is very difficult in a republic to handle that kind of matter. One must vote the money, and that involves public debate, which is awkward. The only practical way of arranging it is by a discretionary fund which, alas, Mr. Livingston does not have."

"And yet I feel, Russell, that there have to be exceptions, even in republics. What is it that makes you so sure that this is not the case for one?"

I debated my reply so long that the gentlemen with whom Talleyrand had been playing cards and who were standing just beyond hearing distance, moved forward, under the impression that my interview was over. With a flicker of an eyelid he checked them.

"I listen, Mr. Russell."

"Because if Louisiana is to come to us," I responded boldly, "it will not fail for a commission. If the matter has been decided, even a statesman of your eminence can no longer arrest it."

"I see that I have not misjudged you, Russell. You *are* intelligent."

"From you, sir, such a compliment dazzles."

"You must have seen that I would predict your response. Why then do you suppose I put the question to you?"

"Because you had nothing to lose. And, besides, there was always the chance that . . ."

"Precisely. That was one reason. But there was another. Can you divine it?"

I hesitated. I thought I had the answer, but was it wise to utter it? And then I remembered my vision. It didn't matter. "You wanted the opportunity to explain to me that you didn't approve the cession of Louisiana."

"Bravo, Russell! The day you elect to change your citizenship, there will be a job for you in our foreign office. Claim it of me."

"It would be exciting to work for you, sir. But I love my country."

"Almost thou persuadest me to be an American. Imagine this, Russell. Because of Leclerc's defeat in Santo Domingo—a single lost campaign—Bonaparte decides to liquidate his dream of an American empire! That is what the military call quick thinking, bold resolution, cutting one's losses—the technique, in short, of battle strategy. Twenty thousand men have perished in the Caribbean; ergo: we close the books on America. If the day ever comes when our armies stand in every capital of Europe, it will be time enough to open them again. There speaks the soldier, the general. But you and I, Russell, know that life is more than a battlefield, don't we?"

"Louisiana is remote," I felt it my duty to observe. "It would be difficult even for General Bonaparte to police so wild and vast a region."

"Don't be Livingston's parrot, Russell. You know that's not true. Oh, difficult, yes. But it would be much less difficult than what you will see Bonaparte undertake in Europe. A battle in America which involves ten thousand men is a major engagement. Yet at the rate we're going over here, you can prepare yourself to see armies of a million or more locked in mortal combat. What is the defense of even distant Louisiana compared to a conquest of England, an invasion of Poland, or even of Russia?"

"Surely such things will never be!"

Talleyrand shrugged. "Not if *I* am allowed to preserve the peace. But do you think for a minute I will be, Russell? No, you don't."

He turned away abruptly now; my interview was over. I did not leave the reception for another hour, enjoying the attentions of the various diplomats on whom my long private session with the foreign minister had not been lost. I had done my job for the night; I could relax and drink champagne and talk to the women as well as the men. I was elated with a kind of spiritual intoxication. As I moved slowly across the parquet floor I felt that my slippers were balloons that might send me up crashing into the great chandeliers or the allegorical painted ceiling. I was outside time, outside space!

And then, standing for a minute alone before the buffet, I made my resolution. I resolved not to tell my chief about the conversation with Talleyrand. Of course, this was a violation of fundamental diplomatic duty, but I was not on a normal plane any more—at least for that night. I had peeked into the machinery of history: I had had a whiff of hot air from the turning wheels and clanging hammers of the forge of the gods. What would be would be. My chief was powerless. So was I. So was Talleyrand. So, for that matter, was Bonaparte, though he might have been the one man in history born with the power to change tides. Yet he wouldn't. Couldn't?

The next morning when Mr. Livingston clanged and clanged his bell to summon us all to his room and cry out in his highest, shrillest voice, with tears running down his cheeks, the great news, I was able to look as amazed as any.

*

So there you have it; my brush with the muse of history, my brief little whirl of a waltz with Clio. Perhaps without it I should have risen higher than minister to the court of Isabella II. For I am afraid that my little vision gave me a sense of human powerlessness which acted as a distinct drag on my ambition. It was not that I did not do my job as well, or even better than the next man. It was that I took less pains to establish credit for myself. I never pushed myself forward or sounded my own trumpet, as is necessary for any major advancement in government. If my accomplishment was recognized by my chief, all well and good; if not, *tant pis*, as my French friends say.

When my father heard of the Louisiana Purchase, he had no doubt that the new territory had been added to the Puritans' early covenant by a special amendment with the Almighty. And who knows? Without my vision in the great *hôtel* on the Rue du Bac I might have seen myself as another link in that chain of special human obligation which began in Boston in 1630. Perhaps God looks after the United States, or perhaps the United States is simply the type of craft able to navigate the particular rush and flow of current in the nineteenth century. Or perhaps that is saying the same thing. We shall see if the craft can survive the ugly rapids that lie ahead where the red letters "Slavery" are splashed across those wet rocks. My daughter, Sally, an abolitionist, is dubious. I am an optimist. A run of luck—or of divine favor—is not inexhaustible. But I believe that we have still some time.

A fitting episode to terminate my little drama was the falling out of Livingston and Monroe. As the Louisiana offer had been made just before Monroe's arrival in Paris, it was natural that Livingston should have claimed the credit for it. Monroe, on the other hand, insisted that it was his impending arrival that had precipitated the first consul's move. In making this argument, I believe that Monroe acted more as a party man than as a self-seeker. He wanted Jefferson and the Virginia lobby to have the glory, not New York. As under our system the man with the President behind him usually prevails, Monroe is given the major credit for Louisiana in most histories today. Poor old Livingston was very shrill and bitter about it. I should have been more sympathetic had I not possessed my own insights into the nature of laurels.

"I have learned, Russell," my old chief told me years later when I visited him at Clermont, "that there is no abiding satisfaction in any political or diplomatic achievement outside of one's own private sense of merit." We were sitting on the terrace on a mild May day, and the great Hudson was unrippled. "But I suppose that is only fair. If the world does not give us credit for what we have done, it often gives us a great deal for what we have not done, or for things that have happened through no fault of our own. I discovered just the other day that my neighbor, Mrs. Schuyler, had gone to her grave believing that it was *I* who had spread the horrid gossip about her daughter Alida's affair with their overseer, and that the reason her husband never let her have it out with me was that he thought he owed his judgeship to my intervention with Governor Clinton. Yet I was not only innocent of the gossip; I never spoke to Clinton!"

I puffed my pipe and smiled, thinking of his proposed refuge for the Bonapartes in wide Louisiana.

(v)

In the Beauty of the Lilies Christ Was Born Across the Sea

WINTHROP WARD LIKED TO HAVE his wife come downstairs for breakfast. He did not like to ask her to do so—that was not his way. He preferred to feel that she herself recognized the propriety of the mistress of the household and the mother of three sons joining with the latter in the initiation of a busy and useful day rather than—like so many women in Manhattan's "better" society of the eighteen-fifties —reclining in her bed till noon with a coffee cup and the fashion column. Rosalie and he had never brought the matter to specific debate, but he nonetheless feared that the billowing pink dressing gown in which she had recently chosen to appear, so suggestive of upper stories and closed doors, was somehow an indication of silent dissent, an "exception," as he would have put it in court. It was fortunate that none of the laxity of the gown was transmuted into its wearer's face. Rosalie's features were as bland and flat as if she had worn more formal attire, and her small lips were pinched into her usual mien of reservation. Reservation of what? Reservation, Winthrop could only infer, of any general approval of himself.

No, breakfast was never quite what he yearned it should be: the friendly, even humorous conveyance by father to sons of useful precepts for a day that would be only too full of particular problems: the confirmation of family solidarity; the pleasant reminder, before the taking up of diurnal tasks, of such manifold blessings as the comfortable house on Union Square, the cozy dining room with its bay window opening onto a tree-filled yard, the smell of sizzling sausages and bacon passed by the smiling Irish girl in her yet unspotted uniform. Alas, no. Instead, the boys were disputatious, and Rosalie seemed always to take their side against him.

James, sixteen and earnest, began. "Andy Thayer says he has an uncle who helps runaway slaves to get to Canada. He runs a station in the Underground Railroad. Isn't that brave?" A small pause followed. "Well, *I* think it's brave!"

"His uncle's a fool to talk about it," said Fred, fourteen and law-abiding. "He could go to prison, where he belongs."

"I agree with Fred," Alexander, the youngest, observed. "Slaves are private property. Father says so, and Father's a lawyer."

"Oh, Winthrop, have you been telling the boys that?" Rosalie wailed.

"My dear, they are private property. You can't deny it. I never said they *should* be. That's another issue altogether. But I happen to believe in obeying the law of the land. At least until the Congress sees fit to change it."

"You haven't lived in the South as I have, Winthrop!" she cried. "And that is why I must beg leave to differ with you, even before the children. You know, boys, I spent a winter in New Orleans with my Aunt Estelle . . ."

"We know it, Mum," came the weary chorus.

"Well, know it again. And know that no matter what the law says, God's law says that no man can own another. It is because the Southerners have tried to make that a Christian principle that their society is rotten."

"Do you mean," demanded Fred, "that if they admitted slavery was wrong, they'd be better off?"

"Much better off. At least their creed would be pure. This way, slavery is in everything they think and do."

Winthrop was impressed, in spite of himself. Rosalie undeniably had a strong mind. It was a pity that she made so little use of it. Or was it? He coughed loudly now as was his habit before making a family pronouncement.

"In times as emotional as these I find that I must constantly reiterate my central position. Otherwise I am regarded as a Simon Legree in my own house. So, boys, pay attention. When we created our Union, we had to compromise with our Southern friends. Their price was the acceptance of slavery—at least in their states. We agreed to pay that price. We wrote it into our Constitution. How can we renege on our word now?"

"It's not reneging on our word to refuse to return their slaves!" James exclaimed hotly. "The slaves should be free the moment they set foot on free soil!"

"The Supreme Court has ruled against you, James."

"The Supreme Court is packed by slaveholders!"

"If we are going to maintain the Union," Winthrop argued, trying to hold on to his temper, "we must learn to recognize the other man's point of view. Do you claim, James, that the South is not entitled to be represented on the Court?"

"What do they know of justice? You've said yourself, Father, that they're blinded by arrogance. I've heard you!"

Winthrop found himself considering the surprising little fact that —for that moment at least—he actually disliked James. "God help us to preserve our nation if the young all feel as you do," he said piously.

Rosalie sniffed. "There you go again, Winthrop, with your sacred Union. Why must we stay together? Why should we be shackled to people who beat women and children and separate families? Why not let them go? Why not let them stand up alone before the civilized world as the only nation where white men have slaves? They won't last long."

"My dear, I must ask you to be silent!" Winthrop rose solemnly to his feet. "I cannot admit the advocation of dissolution of the Union. Even from my wife. That is one heresy I will not tolerate in this house. My great-grandfather fought and died for the Union. When I hear the call, I am ready to do the same. I only pray that civil war, if it must come, may come soon enough to spare you boys. And now, having finished my breakfast, I shall proceed to my office. A good day to all of you."

There was a muffled, embarrassed murmur around the table of something that Winthrop decided to take for a general apology, but in which Rosalie obviously did not join. On the whole, however, he did not think badly of his exit. In the black, paneled hallway where Molly, the waitress, helped him into his fur coat, he listened to his heart and decided that his over-excitement was already ebbing. He chose a cane from the rack. Had he been absurdly dramatic in referring to a call to arms? Would anyone ever ask *him* to serve in the army? A lawyer, a family man, forty-three years old, with a heart murmur?

"Take the scarf, Mr. Ward. It's cold out."

"Very seasonable, Molly. It's always mild between Christmas and New Year's. May the eighteen-sixties prove as mild!"

As the door closed behind him, and he gazed down from his brownstone stoop at Union Square, fresh and glittering in the diamond morning air, he adjusted the onyx pin in his cravat. Taking a deep cold breath, he went briskly down the steps and headed south for his daily hike to Wall Street. He counted on those thirty minutes, not only for his exercise—the only kind he took—but for the opportunity to review and settle the disturbing thoughts and emotions of the early morning so that he might arrive at his desk serene and ready for the day's work.

As he headed down Broadway, however, towards the happy Gothic conception of Grace Church, he was uncomfortably aware of continued tension in his chest. Damn the South for all the trouble they caused with their slaves! Triple damn them! He paused, as he habitually did, to admire the facade of the church and to speculate on what America might have been without the slave trade. What but a paradise, what but a simple Garden of Eden! He stamped his foot. Why had the first blithering idiot to bring a black man in irons to the New World not been hanged for his pains? He recalled now the condescending words of his neighbor in Newport, Colonel Pryor of Charleston:

"My dear Ward, what in the last analysis are we talking about? An issue that could only be settled by a war in which the Northern states couldn't possibly afford to engage. For where's your military tradition? Who would be your officers? Let us face the fact, my friend, that only a few families in New York, Boston, and Philadelphia, such as your own, were reared in the aristocratic tradition. The rest are good burghers who are quite sensibly concerned with filling their pockets. All very well, my dear fellow, but you don't put burghers in a battlefield against Southern gentlemen. At least I should never advise it! Leave us our peculiar institution, and we'll leave you all of yours. It's a better way to live, I promise you."

Burghers! Winthrop snorted as he marched on downtown. It was all very well for Pryor to make a polite exception for the Wards, but Winthrop knew that it was only politeness. Pryor, of course, was sneering inwardly and lumping him with the other shysters and shopkeepers: Yankee trash, nigger lovers. Well, those slaveholders would see! They would see—that is, if they ever tried to break up the Union—how little a society of sportsmen dependent on surly blacks could prevail against millions of free men! They would be lucky if they did not live to behold their plantations burned and their sacred womenfolk raped by lusty niggers . . .

Winthrop paused, and rapped with his cane on the pavement. Really, he must control himself. What would all that adrenalin do to his heart? And, quite aside from his health, what about his eternal soul? Were those *Christian* visions? Even if the South should secede and God should then order the freeing of the slaves, would that be any reason for His holy army to indulge in scenes of rapine and murder? Never! They should go into battle like crusaders in white tunics with red crosses, singing hymns.

"Well, if it ain't Mr. Astor himself, in all his fur and feathers! Good day to ye, Mr. Astor. Have ye foreclosed any mortgages? Should I pray for a bit of snow to turn the widows and the bairns out into?"

Winthrop paused in utter astonishment before the tattered, bearded inebriate who was sitting on the curbstone squinting up at him. In the shock of the onslaught he forgot his rule of ignoring such creatures.

"I shall instruct the next policeman I meet of your insolence and whereabouts! You had better get packing!"

Accelerating his pace as the brown square tower of Trinity Church came into view, he was now a senator, addressing a gravely attentive Senate:

"It is my painful duty to bring to the attention of this august chamber the dire consequences of our rash policy of unlimited immigration. It is rank folly, merely in order to boast that we are the refuge and haven of the poor and oppressed of old Europe, to fill our land with the refuse of a cynical continent delighted to slough off its human responsibilities. How long can America be strong, how long can America be pure, how long can America be free, if we continue to dilute the blood of our Anglo-Saxon and Dutch and German settlers with that of an Irish peasantry, stupefied by ignorance and superstition, the slaves of whiskey and Rome, whose only demonstrated skill is for worming into and corrupting our municipal governments?"

He slowed his pace to slap his clenched fist against his open hand and to stare defiantly at an old woman who hurried by, afraid that he might accost her. She probably deemed him a street preacher or similar, harmless lunatic. Perhaps she was right! Smiling now at his own absurdity, refreshed by his eloquence, he proceeded in silence to

Chambers Street where he paused to consider the better view of Trinity Tower. A fit of dismay seized him. Was its sooty face reproaching him? He closed his eyes and prayed in a whisper:

"Dear God, only God, beloved father of us all, forgive thy servant, Winthrop Ward, for traducing thy other children. Help him to realize that the Irish, however misguided, are as dear to thee as he is, dearer perhaps, for they are not so puffed up. Help him to comprehend that it is no such great thing to descend from John Winthrop or to be a Ward, that his bit of money is a rag and his social position an illusion. Teach him humility, dear Lord, dear Christ, that he may come to thee and lose himself in thee."

Winthrop now shut his eyelids so tight that his eyeballs hurt and then opened them suddenly to a sky full of white stars. When his vision was adjusted, he walked on, reminding himself solemnly that every cart-pusher, every smutched-faced little boy, every black-gowned, mustachioed old Italian woman was as good as he in the eyes of God.

Passing City Hall he frowned at the sight of the tall, slim figure of Daniel Allen in striped pants and a black frock coat ascending the steps. Old Vanderbilt's broker on his way to see the Mayor, no doubt! Winthrop burst into an impassioned appeal to the membership committee of the Patroons' Club:

"Of course, gentlemen, I recognize the principle that society must continually be opening its ranks to admit new members. We are a commercial community, and new money must always have its claim. But I hope we may never lose sight of the rule that new money must be *clean* money. To an old pirate like Vanderbilt, who boasts in public that he has bought our legislature, the doors of gentlemen must be forever closed!"

This peroration took him to Sixty Wall Street, a handsome, white four-story building with freshly painted green shutters, the first two floors of which were occupied by the law chambers of Ward and Ward. Winthrop, who believed in hearty morning greetings, spoke and smiled to each of the firm clerks, to the old bookkeeper and to the office boy, before mounting the stairs to his own office in the rear and closing the door behind him. The room was clean and bare, with cream-painted walls and no accessories beyond the portrait engravings of Lords Mansfield and Cole, a bookcase of law reporters and a Sheraton table-desk on which were stacked neat piles of papers.

Ah, how quickly now his heart resumed its normal beat, how keenly his mind began to function! What a blessing was law. What were books and deeds and documents but receptacles—like pans set out in a drought—to catch the divine drops from the sky? *Here* was what distinguished men from apes. The big Celtic toughs looking to their fists to terrify the timid, the crooked financiers filling the pockets of politicians, the fire-eating Southerners with their contempt for the free world—let them look to the law books—let them beware! Let them writhe like Laocoon and his sons caught in the coils of the beneficent serpent which God had sent down to guard the meek! Winthrop jumped nervously at the sudden knock on his door.

"Mr. Charley wants to see you, sir."

"Very well," Winthrop snapped. "Tell him to come in."

"Beg pardon, sir, he asked if you could come to him. I think he's not feeling quite himself."

Winthrop at this got up and went down the corridor to the office of his partner and cousin. The moment he saw the latter's face he knew why the day had started badly. He must have had an intuition of trouble. Charley Ward looked haggard and sleepless. He might, that morning, have been forty-three, like his cousin, and not a decade younger. Winthrop had a sudden picture now of how Charley would look in a few more years, when middle age should have eroded the fragile beauty of his blond, pale type, when the still abundant smooth hair should have thinned, the round cheeks swollen to give the face a pear shape, the small blue eyes receded into dark cisterns in the skull. Winthrop loved Charley and loved his looks, and his heart was stirred even by the prospect of their evanescence. For he felt that Charley's need of him as a mentor and his own need of Charley as someone to protect might be actually intensified when Charley's appearance, puffed and etiolated, should correspond more nearly to Charley's mind and character. It was part of Charley's strange charm that weakness and mildness should so lurk behind the bright bravery of his exterior.

"This note came for my wife last night from Jane King. Or purportedly from Jane King." Charley threw down a piece of pink notepaper on the desk before Winthrop. "The sender did not know that Annie had gone to Yonkers to spend the night with her uncle. I opened it, thinking it might be something that I could take care of for her. I was wrong."

Winthrop looked at the paper without touching it. "Does your wife know you have opened it?"

"Not yet. But she shall."

"Does anyone else know?"

"What a lawyer you are, Winthrop! Read it."

Winthrop read the following message in a large, jagged masculine hand: "Beloved—can what Jane tells me be true? Are you really reconsidering? Can you deny your own soul and mine? Send me word that you are true. Save your Jules from black despair." He looked up at Charley.

"Bleecher," Charley replied to the silent question. "Jules Bleecher."

Winthrop shuddered. He saw the florid face, the French goatee, the big wet dog-like eyes, the large, fleshy nose, the heavy, tumbling hair, the great overdressed body, the effeminacy that was worse for being affected—a parvenu's idea of a cultivated manner—a brown bear with a monocle and top hat. Good God, could Annie Ward fall for *that*? A poetaster, a scribbler of sentimental drivel, a society journalist, a social climber who pranced around the ladies in every evening party, an "ooer" and "aaher" at concerts, a gossiper in the back of opera boxes, probably a Jew . . . what else?

"He's been coming to the house for a couple of months now," Charley explained. "Annie met him through Jane King. I saw no harm in it. Somebody told me he was a philanderer, but I thought he was too obvious a one to worry about. He was the kind who would lean over, when some fat old dowager was tucking her lorgnette into her bosom, and murmur: 'Happy lorgnette!' The man seemed a farce to me. He and Jane King were always giggling and snickering in corners."

"I never met him in your house," Winthrop observed.

"That was because I knew you didn't like him. Oh, you can be sure, Winthrop, that Annie and I are always very careful whom we ask when you and Rosalie are coming."

Winthrop sighed. "But do you deduce from this letter that your wife has . . . has, er . . ."

"Fallen?" Charley's laugh was a jeer. "Not necessarily. She's a cool little minx under all that gush. But what I *do* deduce from that florid epistle is that she gave Bleecher an assignation and then got cold feet. She may have even agreed to go off with him."

"And desert Miss Kate?" Winthrop cried in horror. The sole, six-year-old child of the Charley Wards was so designated because of her little-lady airs.

"It's so like you, Winthrop, to put the child before the father. But yes, I think that Annie would be capable of deserting Miss Kate. She has no real heart. Once she decides that life with me is not what she wants, nothing is going to hold her. You can talk of oaths and sacraments and family ties until the cows come home. You won't reach her."

"What does she want?"

Charley strode up and down the chamber now, clapping his hands together as he brought out his argument in sharp, jerky phrases. "What do you think she wants? What do any of them want? She wants a man who will live up to her dreams of sexual performance. I tell you, Winthrop, we men are the losers in this system of keeping girls in ignorance until they marry. It's damnably hard on the poor groom. He suddenly finds he's got to be all the impossible things that an uneducated, feverishly sentimental mind has concocted out of fantasy and dirty talk with other ignorant girls. Give me a prostitute from Mercer Street any night in the week. At least she knows what a man is! But these innocent debutantes! They smile and simper behind their fans; they blush crimson at the tiniest impropriety, and then, suddenly, after a big society wedding, that hasn't tired them one bit—behind closed doors, alone at last—they turn into fiends. 'All right, big man. This is life, isn't it? Show me life!' "

Winthrop actually shivered, so violent was his disgust. If his interlocutor had been anyone but Charley he would have walked out. But he was responsible for too many things: for the partnership, for Charley's dependence on him, for the very marriage to Annie Andros that he had so fatally sponsored. He could not help glancing back to his own wedding night. Not that Rosalie had been the tigress that Charley depicted. On the contrary, she had been silent, compliant, perhaps the least bit passive. But hadn't there been an implication of something like disappointment in the determined way in which, early the following morning, she had sat down at their hotel drawing room table to write thank-you notes for her wedding presents?

"So what do you propose?" he asked Charley.

"Immediate and final separation."

"And Miss Kate?"

"She can live with us alternately. Provided, of course, that Annie does not set up house with her paramour."

"You are determined then to advertise your shame to the world?" Winthrop stood up to give posture to the high stand that he had elected to take. "Do you want people to say that you couldn't hold your bride?" Seeing Charley bite his lip, he followed up in words from Charley's customary vocabulary. "Do you want even the debutantes, in their kittenish sessions between the dances, upstairs in their host-ess' bedroom, to whisper with high giggles that you have no balls?"

"Oh, shut up, Winty! Don't be such a bastard. What else can a man do in my situation?"

"Well, he doesn't have to throw up his marriage and ruin three lives—yours and Annie's and Miss Kate's—for what may turn out to be only a flirtation. I'm sorry, Charley. I can't believe that Annie re-ally cares for a man like Bleecher. I'm sure she has simply lost her head for the moment. Perhaps she is actually ill. If we can only get rid of this oily cad, who knows? Maybe you and Annie will find a new life. You may even discover a deeper congeniality."

Charley's impatient toss of his head showed what he thought of this. Winthrop perfectly understood what his cousin was looking for-ward to: a return to bachelor freedom, a liberation from Annie's cloyingly female, looped and tasseled interior. Cousin Winthrop must have seemed like a stiff, prissy teacher holding him after class on a summer afternoon when all the other boys had gone fishing. But Winthrop knew that he could still rely on a teacher's authority.

"Your position as a lawyer, as a father, as a member of society obliges you to do everything you can to avoid a scandal," he contin-ued sententiously. "You can't shirk this one, Charley."

"What do I do then?" Charley asked sulkily.

"Leave the next step to me. Go home and get some sleep. I'll go to Annie's uncle and ask him to keep her at Yonkers for a week. And not to allow Bleecher in the house."

"How can he do that? He can't use force, can he?"

"I don't have to tell Lewis Andros how to do anything. My confidence in him is complete. If all New York were as he, there would be no Bleechers invading the sanctity of our homes. Will you be guided by me, Charley?" There was a pause, as Winthrop stared impassively at his cousin. "Don't you think I am entitled to ask that of you?"

Charley turned away, his face puckered as if he were going to weep. "Have it your way, Winthrop. You always do. I'm going out for a drink. For several drinks."

Fifteen minutes later Winthrop entered the central hall of the Bank of Commerce and walked briskly down the aisle of yellow mar-ble past standing clerks at counters making entries to the rear where the president sat at a vast roll-top desk under a gas light in a green bowl suspended directly over his head. But Lewis Andros' apparent availability to the public was an illusion. There was an unseen wall that protected the desk and its occupant, and if a stranger dared to intrude, or even to address the silent magnate without authority, he would receive for all his answer a slow raising of the great head and a vision of the whites of eyeballs before which he could only beat a stuttering retreat. Very different, however, was Winthrop's reception.

"Ah, my dear boy, we see too little of you these days, far too little. I was asking Carrie only yesterday: when shall we have the Winthrop Wards for dinner? We cannot afford to neglect the parents of three strapping boys, can we? Certainly *I* cannot, with granddaughters their age, as well as daughters."

As the great man rose and gripped his shoulder, Winthrop reflected that Lewis Andros managed to give a sexual flavor to every topic. It was always perfectly proper, if rather heavily connubial, but there it was. The great tan eyes may have been limpid, the splendid nose arched, the lips thin and intellectual, the gray curly hair venerable, the voice rich and cultivated, but all of these aspects seemed to merge in the likeness of a velvet cloak flung over an old bull. Mr. Andros had children in their thirties and in their teens; twice a widower he was now, at sixty, the husband of a woman of twenty-five who already looked tired. He was a man, Winthrop conceded with a rueful admiration, who managed to pack the pleasures of the Renaissance into the permissible limits of brownstone New York. Nowhere did one drink finer Madeira or hear wittier talk than at bachelor dinners in his Fifth Avenue mansion when his wife and brood were packed off to Yonkers.

"Could I sit down with you for a minute, Mr. Andros? I'm afraid I have a bit of rather nasty news. It concerns your niece Annie and my cousin."

Andros' banker's countenance betrayed nothing during the dreary recital, but at the conclusion he permitted himself a windy sigh and a rueful shake of the great head.

"My dear Winthrop, you and I are men of the world. We know that Annie and Charley were mismated from the start. She is too much of a mouthful for those pearly teeth of his. Would it not be for the best if we arranged a dignified separation? Followed, in due course, by a divorce or even an annulment?"

"An annulment? With a six-year-old child?"

"Such things have been heard of, where there was a basic lack of consent at the outset. But of course I need not point out such things to a lawyer."

"I arranged all the settlements at the time!" Winthrop exclaimed in some heat. "I should regard myself as gravely deficient if the marriage legalities were not entirely in order."

"Oh, I don't mean that dear fellow. I mean: was Annie's true and free consent given at the altar? I am speaking, mind you, of a woman's psyche. The greatest lawyer in the world need not be ashamed to have failed to plumb *those* murky depths."

Winthrop was shocked that so respected a member of the community should not devote even a passing glance to the moral aspects of what confronted them. "Even assuming that there was a chance for some respectable separation," he countered, "surely it is jeopardized by the presence of such a cad as Bleecher."

"Oh, come now, Bleecher's not as bad as all that. He's not the first man in our society to make up to a flirtatious wife. Carrie and I have found him an agreeable extra man for dinner parties, and even you will admit that he has an eye for a picture. Did you see his 'Toilette of the Odalisque' at the *Beaux Arts* show last winter? Many people preferred it to 'The Abbess Detected,' which took first prize."

Winthrop stifled the impulse to parade his opinion of the immorality of last winter's *Beaux Arts* show. He recollected that Andros' own 'Halt of Cavaliers' had been the runner-up. "Bleecher's taste in art is not going to help matters if he runs off with Annie. He has already implicated Jane King in their friendship. If you and Mrs. Andros receive him in Yonkers, he will not hesitate to tell the world you have taken his side."

"His side? How can a man in his position have a side?"

"You will forgive me, sir, if I am totally frank. To me the facts are too grave for parlor manners. It is my conviction that Bleecher is not even the decent simulacrum of a gentleman. He hopes to become your nephew-in-law and to force you to champion him in society."

Andros was suddenly very still. "Force me, you say? How?"

"By implicating you and Mrs. Andros as accomplices in his adultery."

How was it that Andros managed to quicken the air about him? He did not so much as twitch an eyeball or stir a muscle, yet Winthrop felt a throb in the atmosphere, as if, deep within the older man, some heavy cylinder had started to revolve.

"Mr. Bleecher will find that he has mistaken his party," Andros said dryly. "What steps do you propose?"

"I propose that you keep Annie at Yonkers this week and see that Bleecher is not allowed on the grounds."

Andros' shaggy head went up and down several times. "The latter is simple enough. But my niece is a grown woman and married. I can't force her, Winthrop."

"We all know how Annie looks up to you. You've been a father and mother to her, as well as an uncle. She'll do as you say."

"You have more confidence in my power over young ladies than I do."

"I have utter confidence in your powers!" Winthrop exclaimed, feeling that it was the opportune time for a show of emotion that was only half feigned. "And the day we New Yorkers lose faith in Lewis Andros, we'll have faith in nobody!"

This was a bit strong, and Winthrop feared that he might have gone too far. But no. Andros rose, and Winthrop rose with him. Once again the big hand gripped his shoulder.

"Winthrop, my friend, you may count on me. I shall lie before Annie's door like an Indian servant and guard her with my life. As for Mr. Bleecher, I shall not soil my hands with the likes of him. But I have some strong young men on the place—not to speak of two Russian wolfhounds—who may be less fastidious. You had better warn him to stay in the city!"

"I knew I could count on you. With your permission I shall drive out to see Annie in the morning. And in the meantime I guarantee Charley's good conduct. The matter may yet be contained."

2

At breakfast the next day in Union Square, Rosalie lingered at the table after the boys had gone off to school.

"Don't you think it might be better if I went to see Annie with you? Or even if I went in your place?"

"I'd rather not have you mixed up in this, my dear."

"Oh, Winthrop, I know all your theories about sparing the gentler sex. But you and I must occasionally deal with particulars and not always with generalities. I know as much about this situation as you do. That is, if you've told me the whole story."

"I've told you all I know. A man, of course, may have his own insights."

"And a woman hers. In such a case a couple would be better than one."

"Listen to me, Rosalie. I am not claiming any masculine superiority. I recognize that you might handle Annie quite as competently as I. It is not you, Rosalie Ward, whom I wish to keep clear of this sordid affair. It is you, Mrs. Winthrop Ward, the mother of my sons."

Rosalie raised her hands in mock surprise. "Men make such interesting distinctions. A woman would never have thought of that!"

Winthrop looked down at his newspaper and tried to read about President Buchanan's diplomatic reception. It proved impossible. Would Rosalie never give up? His tense fingers crumpled the journal.

"If you only didn't enjoy it so much," Rosalie continued. "I think I might mind the whole thing less."

"Enjoy it! Charley's humiliation?" As Winthrop stared across the table at his impassive tormentor, he felt his eyelids suddenly smart with angry tears.

"I didn't mean to imply that you enjoy Charley's humiliation. I meant that you enjoy the prospect of correcting Annie."

"I have always been devoted to Annie!"

"Oh, I know *that.*" Rosalie's face hardened as she moved to a more direct offensive. "Where do you think I've been for the last seven years not to know that? You're obviously jealous of Jules Bleecher."

Winthrop felt the sudden drop of anger in his heart. So that was it. So like a woman. So rather touching, really. He should have anticipated that Rosalie, like any good, loving wife—and who was a better, a more loving one?—was quite incapable of the smallest objectivity with respect to any member of his family. She was jealous, quite naturally, of anything that presented a potential wedge between her and him. She had always resented his love of Charley, always despised Annie . . . wasn't it really better that way? How else could he be sure that she loved him?

"I am certainly not going to try to rebut your last statement," he said with what he intended to be an air of amiable dignity. "At the risk of appearing stuffy and self-complacent—if that be not giving myself the benefit of *your* doubt—I should say it would be beneath my dignity. I confine my defense to this: if I get any pleasure, as you aver, out of this whole sorry affair, it is the pleasure—and a very mild one, I assure you—that every man is entitled to derive from the sense that he is doing his duty."

"Oh, go to see Annie, for heaven's sakes," his wife retorted brusquely. "I don't even want to come with you after *that.*"

Winthrop had been looking forward to the drive up to Yonkers,

well muffled, on that cold but pleasant December day in his new
runabout with two fast trotters. There might have been in it some of
the excitement of an unexpected holiday. But now all was made as
bleak as the winter sky by Rosalie's relentless denigrations. Why was
it so necessary to her content—or to at least the lessening of her per-
ennial discontent—to pull him down so? She was always quick to
flare the egotistical motive under the seemingly generous actions in
him. But when it came to some ranting, bushy-bearded abolitionist
who wanted to blow up the world to cover his own failures—did she
flare any ego? Oh, no! Then Mr. Bushy-beard was a saint, a prophet!

The sight of "Oaklawn," one of the last summer residences in
Yonkers, always made him sit up. To Winthrop it was a thing of
peerless beauty, Richard Upjohn's masterpiece, and he would have
liked nothing better than to recreate it in Newport. The approach
was down a long straight avenue, soft even in winter, under two
brown Gothic archways, at the end of which was the glazed brown
multi-turreted, castellated structure with tiny windows in the turrets
and painted tin awnings over the larger windows of the main floor. A
groom waiting at the front door took his carriage, and Winthrop was
ushered at once into a small study with wicker furniture, lamps with
beaded shades and several small dark examples of the seventeenth-
century Italian school.

"Mrs. Ward will be with you in a moment, sir."

And indeed Winthrop already heard the rustle of her skirts. Annie
came hurrying in and threw her arms around his neck.

"Oh, Winthrop, sweety, at last! I've been dying to see you!"

She was dressed in black, as if in mourning. It perfectly suited the
pallor of her complexion and served as a sepulchral setting for her
long raven hair and thick eyebrows, her thin long figure, her flat
chest. Yet for all of this Annie was the antithesis—and herein, as
Winthrop well knew, lay the secret of her immense charm—of the
death look in her garb and complexion. For she was all movement,
all life, all gaiety. Even now, as she took in his effort to assemble his
features into a becoming sternness, she burst into a peal of high
laughter, too infectious to be as mocking as she may have meant it to
be.

"Oh, Winthrop, that *look*. Please, not that look. You're going to
make me die of giggles when I want to be so serious. When, really,
I've got to be serious. This is no time to play the Puritan ancestor.
We have things to discuss. Things to decide."

"I don't know what we can have to discuss but your promise never again to see or communicate with Mr. Bleecher."

"Not to see Jules!" Annie stepped back and stared at him as if he had said something ridiculous. "But, of course, I can't give up Jules. He's the only man who's made life tolerable for me in the past year. Jules *amuses* me, Winthrop!"

"Will he amuse you enough to make it up to you if Charley repudiates you?"

Annie uttered another high peal of laughter. "Oh, quite enough! Would Charley really do that? Repudiate me. What a beautiful word!"

"I doubt that you'd find it so beautiful if it happened. What would become of you, Annie?"

"I suppose I'd have to go to Paris. Isn't that what fallen women do?"

"And what would you live on?"

"What would I live on? Why, what do I live on now? My own income, thank you very much. Or would the law—*your* law—give that to Charley?"

"No, that would not go to Charley. But may I remind you that your money's all in trust, and that your trustees have a certain discretion about the payment of income. If you were living in Paris with a man not your husband . . ."

"With a paramour!"

"With a paramour, then. Your trustees might see fit to accumulate the income until you came to your senses."

Again that laugh! Winthrop reflected that his ancestor, Wait Winthrop, would probably have hanged this girl in Salem.

"Confess you're bluffing!" Annie challenged him. "Trustees may be afraid of sin, but they're much more afraid of law suits. And I'd sue them. Believe me, I'd sue!"

"Well, even *with* your income," Winthrop retorted, with a touch of impatience, "what sort of future would you have in Paris? No respectable people would receive you."

"How terrible!"

"And Bleecher, cad that he is, would desert you the moment he felt like it."

"Ah, that he wouldn't." Annie did not laugh now, and her eyes had a sudden gleam. "I might leave Jules, for *I* am a bit of a cad, but he would not leave me. You underestimate my charms."

"I have never underestimated your charms. But what I think you have underestimated is the difference it would make to Bleecher if he found you a social liability instead of a social asset."

Annie paced the length of the little room. She stood for a moment, her back to him, before turning. "You're playing a role, the family friend, the family lawyer, the guardian of morals. I wish you'd stop. I want to talk to you seriously."

"What about?"

"Well, in the first place, Jules is not what you think him at all. He loves me dearly, faithfully. I should trust him implicitly, even in Paris. I know when a man is not to be trusted. Charley is not to be trusted. Besides, he hates me."

"He's your husband. He's the father of your child."

"Oh, Winthrop, be reasonable. Are you trying to tell me that Charley loves me?"

"Deep down, yes."

Annie laughed again. "Angels save us from that 'deep down'!"

"But you can't give up your marriage just because you and Charley have a misunderstanding!"

"A misunderstanding or an understanding?"

"Either." Winthrop tried to look his most earnest. "A marriage must be worked on. Even if you don't believe it's a sacrament, you should recognize that our society is based on it. And your child—how can you abandon her? A court, you know, would give her to Charley."

"Then I'd hardly be abandoning her."

"Tell her that when she's grown up!"

Annie at this looked grave. "Ah, yes, I can imagine what you Wards would have done to her. Even you, Winthrop." She sat down on a plush stool and folded her hands soberly in her lap. Winthrop remained standing. "Yet you were my best friend after my marriage," she continued wistfully. "You were all kindness and sympathy and understanding. At first I thought you were too stiff, too moral, too much older, and, of course, I knew that Rosalie disliked me. She hates feminine women. But then, gradually, I came to recognize that you loved Charley and, through him, me. I loved Charley, too, in those days, but as I began to understand his weaker side, I became frightened. And then I saw that you understood it, too, and were trying to help me. I accepted your help, perhaps too greedily. It was naughty of me, but Rosalie's anger made it such fun."

Winthrop had turned away, pained by what she had said about

Rosalie hating feminine women. It was true, of course. "Go on," he muttered. "But leave Rosalie out of it, please."

"She was never really in it. What kind of idiot says there can't be a friendship between a man and woman? *We* had such a friendship. Now don't say I'm being cruel!" Again her laugh pealed out. "You know it was true—on both sides. And you helped me, that's the point. But all those books we discussed together, all those poems and plays—what were they really about? *Jane Eyre* and *The Scarlet Letter* and *Madame Bovary?* They were about passion! Do you remember when we went to see Rachel in *Phèdre?*"

"What are you getting at?" Winthrop asked abruptly.

"Simply that those books taught me that passion is the whole thing in this world. That if you miss it, you miss everything!"

Winthrop was able to turn back to her now, sobered by the enormity of her misconstruction. "But those books and plays all point out the pitfalls of illicit love. Look what happens to Madame Bovary and to Phèdre and to Hester Prynne. *Jane Eyre* ends happily, it is true, but only because she keeps away from Mr. Rochester until his wife dies."

"And until he goes blind," Annie added with a giggle. "But it doesn't matter what happens to the heroine *afterwards*. The point is that the great experience is passion. Maybe it's punished—*tant pis*. But it's still worth it. For without it, what are you? Phèdre doesn't give a hoot about going to hell. The only thing that keeps her from Hippolyte is that he won't have her! But Jules, dear Winthrop, is no Hippolyte."

"Do you love him?"

"How you bite the word!" Annie shrugged. "Perhaps I do. More than I do Charley, anyway."

"Annie!"

"Oh, go home, Winthrop, if you can't talk. What did you come out here for? Jules is willing to give up everything—his job, his career, his position in New York—to go off with me. How many men would do that?"

"Many. Who had as little to give up as he."

"You're not fair. Uncle Lewis tells me his prospects are excellent. He's the rising journalist on the *Daily Post*. Everyone's talking about him."

"If they're not, they will be. When *this* thing breaks."

"Well, what do you offer me instead? A dull, loveless brownstone life, paying and receiving calls and learning to look the other way when Charley exercises the right of his sex to seek his pleasures elsewhere. Oh, Winthrop! A woman needs a faith greater than mine to make her stick to such a course. What do you offer for my pleasure? Or don't women count at all?"

"There's your child."

"Nothing else?"

"Well, isn't there art? As you've just said?"

"So life is made up of bad people who live and good people who read about them?" Annie gave herself over to the longest and most exuberant of her laughs. "And Uncle Lewis who does both!"

For the first time Winthrop joined in her laughter. She came over and fixed her dark eyes with a smiling intensity on his. "Let me ask you something," she said. "If you will promise me an honest answer, an absolutely honest answer, I will promise to consider taking your advice."

"Only to consider it?"

"Oh, that's a great concession for a naughty lady who's contemplating an illicit trip to Paris."

"If she really *is* contemplating it."

"Well, if she isn't, what do you have to worry about?"

"All right. I promise to give you an honest answer."

Annie nodded and removed her hands from his shoulders. "I want to know if art, if the life of the imagination, makes up to *you* for the dullness of your life with Rosalie."

Winthrop stepped back. For a moment he considered leaving the house without a word. Then he remembered his mission.

"Suppose I reply that my life with Rosalie is not dull?"

"Then I shan't believe you. I know there has to be something outside of your marriage that keeps you going. And I doubt that it's the law. I do you the honor of supposing that when you recommend to me the consolation of the life of the imagination, you are recommending a consolation in which you have a strong personal belief."

Was it his growing belief that she was *not*, after all, in love with Bleecher that brought the sudden exhilaration to his heart? Not that she was in love with Winthrop Ward, or ever had been—that was manifest. He was too middle-aged, too spare and lean, too ascetic, too darkly garbed, for such as she. She liked him, played with him, understood him—in part. Was he really and truly in love with her? Did it matter if he never voiced it? He would have to remember to

pray all the way home and to give thanks to the Almighty that
Annie had never guessed!

"I am waiting for your answer, Winthrop. Does the life of the
imagination make up?"

"Make up?"

"You know for what!"

"Yes," he said at last. "It does."

The wonderful girl knew when not to laugh. She became even
paler. "Thank you," she half whispered. "I know what that cost you.
Go to Jules. Talk to him. I'm in your hands. Good-bye."

When Winthrop went to the door to the hall, she had already
disappeared up the staircase. Her young aunt, Carrie Andros, was on
the landing. She came hurriedly down to speak to Winthrop. Her
big soft worried eyes seemed to pop out of her heart-shaped face. She
was a child, a child who had already borne four children to the old
bull.

"Is it all right, Winthrop?" she asked tensely. "Can things be arranged?"

"I trust so."

"It'll be all right between her and Charley?"

"Let us pray."

"Ah, yes. Let us pray, by all means." But Carrie Andros' anxiety
seemed now to give way to a sterner mood. "And let us pray, while
we are at it, that Charley will appreciate the sacrifice that she is
making."

Winthrop stared. "The sacrifice, Ma'am?"

"The sacrifice of passion, Winthrop! The sacrifice of everything
her heart has dreamed of."

Winthrop was too stupefied to reply. Was it possible that adultery
could be thus publicly denominated in the front hall of a mansion
built for Lewis Andros by the architect of Trinity Church? Was *this*
what the world had come to? Had Annie and her aunt been
confiding in each other, whispering of plans for escape and love? Of
course they had! Had Carrie not used that same vulgar word?

Winthrop disposed of his embarrassment as best he could, aided
by a quick bow, and took his immediate leave. But on the way back
to town, amid a lightly falling snow, he allowed himself to speculate
if there was any essential difference between the ladies of the highest
Manhattan society and the commercial dames of Mercer Street! He
did not remember the prayers he was to make until he was on the

barge over the Harlem River, and he then recited them with chattering teeth. Happily, it was never too late.

Back in town he drove directly to the Patroons' Club where he wrote a note to Bleecher, requesting him to call that night at Union Square on a matter of the utmost importance. He sent the note to the *Daily Post* by messenger, together with one for Rosalie, instructing her to leave word with the servants that Bleecher should be ushered into the library if he called but not received upstairs. Then he went to the bar where he was sure of finding Charley.

"Bleecher will come to my house tonight," he told his now rather shaky cousin. "I plan to give him this one chance. If he will agree never to address your wife again, in conversation or by letter, I shall advise him that the Wards will take no further action against him. It will simply be understood that he will abstain from all further social relations with our family."

Charley seemed to have some difficulty taking this in. "And if he refuses?"

"Then we destroy him."

"In a duel? Thanks for the 'we.' Do you know that Bleecher's a first-class shot? He fires one bullet between the wife's legs and the next between the husband's eyes. Don't you give a damn about me, Winthrop?"

Winthrop contemplated Charley's sagging pale cheeks and moist, rolling eyes. Why, he wondered, was panic so contemptible? It was sickening to consider what the wretched Bleecher was costing them, but the worst casualty of all might be his own love for Charley. Could nothing in their family survive the raid of this big buzzing, gilded bee, this coprophagous poetaster?

"No, of course there will be no duel. Why should you submit your life to Bleecher? Gentlemen don't duel in New York, and if they did, they wouldn't duel with the likes of him. No, I mean destroy him financially and socially. I'll close every pocketbook and front door in New York to him!"

"How?"

"You'll see, my boy. Just leave it to me. And in the meanwhile I want you to purge your mind of all those filthy thoughts about your wife. I know you've been under a great strain. Otherwise I should not tolerate your language. But you must get this through your head. Annie has *not* been unfaithful to you. I'll go to the stake for that. She has been indiscreet, yes; she has been foolish, yes; she has been naughty, yes. But she has not been wicked. She has not submitted to the lewd embracements of that fiend."

"What makes you so sure?"

"Because I know Annie. And because I know she loves you." Winthrop stared Charley coolly in the eye until the latter had to look away. "You and she have had your difficulties, I know. Annie is a very emotional creature and inclined to hysterics. She leaps to conclusions. She probably decided that you didn't love her any more and that her marriage was over. So she turned in desperation to flirt with the first man available, who happened to be Bleecher. She needs help, Charley, not abuse. You and she are going to be all right, I promise you!"

Charley was again the surly schoolboy, but this time the schoolboy who has misread the calendar and finds that his vacation is almost over. Winthrop decided that he had better stay and dine with him. In the course of their meal and a bottle of wine Charley was finally induced to give his sullen word that he would welcome Annie back from Yonkers if she would promise never to see Bleecher again.

This accomplished, Winthrop returned to Union Square, where he found Molly waiting in the front hall to tell him that a Mr. Bleecher was in the library. He could see through the half-open door the stocky back and curly black hair of his detested visitor. Bleecher was studying his little Kensett, a Newport seascape.

"Ah, there you are, Ward," he exclaimed, turning to flash his dark, impudently friendly eyes on Winthrop. "I'm admiring your Kensett. Such a subtlety of coloring. It's hard to tell where the sea stops and the horizon begins. I can see why people speak of your taste as advanced. While the rest of us are buying Italian peasant scenes and Turkish market places, you're putting up your money for something as good as this. Congratulations!"

This appeal was to Winthrop's most vulnerable side, for he fancied his own eye as a collector. But that night he was unassailable.

"Never mind the compliments, Bleecher. May we get right down to business?"

Bleecher stared at him for a moment, then smiled and nodded briskly, as if he, for one, could never have been responsible for such a breach of good fellowship. "I'm at your service, Ward. I assume from your tone that you prefer to remain standing?"

"Much."

"Very well. Excuse me." Bleecher went over to a table and

crushed out his cigar in a bowl. "Let us eliminate the last traces of conviviality."

Winthrop declined to notice the sarcasm. "Your correspondence with Mrs. Charles Ward has been discovered."

Bleecher's bushy eyebrows rose. "Do you imply that it was concealed?"

"I most certainly do. It was delivered clandestinely, through Miss Jane King."

"It was delivered through Miss King. Let me ask you something, Ward. Whom do you represent in this matter?"

"The family, of course. The outraged family."

"I see. But do you represent Annie?"

"Do you refer to Mrs. Charles Ward? I do indeed. *And* her husband."

"You mean you are speaking to me tonight with Mrs. Ward's authority?"

Winthrop could not resist a little snarl of satisfaction at the note of surprise in his antagonist's tone. "That's a bit of a shock to you, isn't it, Bleecher? Yes, I am speaking to you tonight with her authority. I received it today at Yonkers."

"Where she is residing, I gather, as the virtual prisoner of her uncle. Mr. Andros had better remember that there is such a thing as habeas corpus in this country."

"Can it be invoked by the would-be seducers of married women?"

Bleecher advanced a threatening step towards his host and stopped. He took a heavy breath. "It should be invocable by any man who champions the cause of a poor woman shackled to a swine like your cousin."

Winthrop's heart was beating so hard now that it hurt. He closed his eyes and counted to ten. Then he cleared his throat. "I suppose we had better avoid epithets. Are you prepared to give me some assurance that you will have no further communication with Mrs. Ward?"

"Does *she* ask that?"

"She has placed her case in my hands."

"Then what assurance can you give me that she will be allowed to live a life free from the constant apprehension of violent abuse and drunken threats?"

Winthrop trembled on the verge of incoherence. "Do you presume to treat with me, sir?"

"And why not? Have I not enjoyed Mrs. Ward's confidence? And that of Miss King? Do I not have letters from each? Do you think, Ward, that you are living in Turkey, where women are kept in harems and put in sacks and thrown in the river if they are disobedient? Let me disillusion you. The days are past when a married woman can be incarcerated by an old bulldog of an uncle while the family lawyer lays down ridiculous terms to her friends!"

"There is no more to be said, Mr. Bleecher. Kindly leave my house."

When Winthrop heard the reverberation of the slammed front door, he stirred himself from his reverie and strode to the table where Bleecher had deposited his ashes. Picking up the small crystal bowl which contained them, he dashed it to pieces in the grate. He heard a short laugh from the hall.

"How you must have enjoyed that!" Of course, it was Rosalie.

3

On New Year's Day the principal families of Manhattan maintained open house, but it was the custom of the hosts to desert their wives and to join the call-paying throng. Winthrop, when weather permitted, would start in his carriage as low as Canal Street, where a few old relatives still held out, and, proceeding north up Broadway, would make as many as a dozen calls—including one to his own house— ending at his Aunt Joanna Lispenard's on Forty-fifth Street. But on January 1, 1860, he set about these calls with anything but a New Year's spirit. Though careful to keep a holiday look in his eye, he was concentrating on grimmer matters, and his sips of eggnog were mere tokens. Still, there had to be an element of excitement in the execution of a clever plan, and Winthrop was not despondent as he made his way quickly through the crowded drawing rooms and clicked his glass against those of friends.

By the time he had arrived at Lewis Andros' square brownstone house on the corner of Great Jones Street and Broadway, he had accomplished the minor part of his mission. He had placed suggestions in half a dozen important ears. But the big job was still before him. When he spied old George King, the white-haired, tight-lipped, soft-voiced "landlord of the Bowery," at the end of Andros' crowded picture gallery, where Christian slaves and lions, Western sunsets and hunting Indians looked like canceled postage stamps amid the waving arms and nodding heads, he put down his glass, made his way towards him and led him apart from the others. Mr. King listened, nodding sagely, as Winthrop rapidly and succinctly delivered his message.

"Bleecher's name will come up at the next meeting of the Admissions Committee," King responded.

"Then I am just in time. I am sure you agree, sir, that we do not wish such a scoundrel in the Patroons'."

The King eyebrows formed a brief, black triangle, an odd patch under a cloud of white. "If we were to lose every member who had ever lusted after his neighbor's wife, you might be surprised at the gaps in our midst. To tell you the truth, Winthrop, there is a certain solidarity among men in these matters. I am not even sure that the scoundrel, as you call him, would be blackballed on your facts."

"A neighbor's wife! How about a fellow member's wife?"

Again the triangle appeared, higher, isosceles. "You didn't mention that to be the case."

"I had hoped it would not be necessary."

"Ah, but I'm afraid it is. And what is worse, I shall need to know which member."

Winthrop hesitated. "It's a very delicate matter."

"But you are asking me to perform a very delicate task."

"That is true, sir. It is my cousin Charley."

"Charley Ward! Dear me." King shook his head to indicate that Winthrop had not improved his case. "Charley Ward is not in very good odor at the club. He imbibes too much, and two years ago there was some trouble about a bill . . ."

"I paid that, Mr. King."

"Yes, no doubt, my dear fellow, and everyone at the Patroons' admires and respects you—I shouldn't be at all surprised to see you in my chair there one day—but don't you think that these things are better patched up or hushed up? Surely, Charley has nothing to gain by letting this sorry tale get about. Mightn't it make matters even worse for him?"

"Do you imply, sir, that the board might *still* elect Bleecher?"

"Well, it's hard to predict these things." King's shrug was a bit impatient now. "Mightn't it be better not to risk it? You would lose so much more in defeat than you would ever gain in victory."

"I am sorry, then, Mr. King, that I cannot spare you my further information. Bleecher used your daughter Jane as his intermediary. She carried his letters to Annie so that Charley would not know." Winthrop did not quail before the old man's acidulous stare. "You cannot think that I would say such a thing if I were not sure of my facts."

Both men now looked across the gallery to where Annie Ward, precariously reunited with her husband, and Jane King were giggling together. Jane was small and dark and sounded very silly. Charley Ward, standing beside them, seemed absorbed in his dark glass.

"I shall take care of the matter you speak of, Ward," the old man said gratingly. "But God help you if your facts aren't right!"

"Happy New Year, Mr. King," Winthrop rejoined coolly, with a departing bow. "I hope it will be happier for all of us—but one."

As Winthrop walked up to Annie, she threw back her head to emit the famous laugh.

"Hello, King Arthur," she greeted him in her deep voice. "Here are all your court! There may be a few dents in the Round Table, but nothing that can't be hammered out. If one has a good hammer. And you always *do* have one, don't you, dear?"

"I try to please." Nothing could dampen Winthrop's sudden exhilaration. Here were Annie and Charley together, and his plans for Bleecher were working!

"What have you been saying to my father, Winthrop?" Jane King asked with a little grimace. "I never saw such a scowl."

"Oh, I'm sure he'll tell you about it," Winthrop responded cheerfully. "Don't you and he have little father-daughter chats from time to time?"

"Angels protect me!" Jane turned to Annie. "What do you suppose Winthrop's been telling him?"

"I hope he's told him what you've been up to," Charley said to Jane with a sneer. "I daresay the old man won't fancy the kind of service you supply to Annie's journalist friends . . . oh, dear!" Seeing Winthrop's frown, Charley clapped his hand over his mouth with mock dismay. "I promised not to mention a certain name, didn't I? I promised to leave *him* to Cousin Winthrop!"

"And you had better keep that promise, too," Annie retorted with heat. "Or our so-called reconciliation will be of brief duration."

Winthrop, seeing Lewis Andros in the doorway, escaped to his side. "Have you a word for me, sir?"

"Yes. Are you calling on the Cranberry Hardys today?"

A wrinkle of scorn slid over Winthrop's face. "I wouldn't normally."

"Well, I suggest you do. His store takes a full page advertisement in the *Daily Post* twice a week. A word from him to the editor, and

Bleecher's out of a job. I've sent my son-in-law to broach the matter with Hardy. It's up to you to close it."

Winthrop's nod was military in its abruptness. "I'm on my way, sir."

Cranberry Hardy had built the largest mansion in Manhattan, larger even than Mr. Astor's. Its four tall stories were encased in white marble, covered by a high mansard roof and studded with clusters of Corinthian columns. Hardy was the greatest merchant of New York and the proprietor of the largest department store, but the money was new and the family plain, and the Ward ladies had never called. Winthrop, however, had met Hardy in Trinity Church business matters and had received his New Year's bid. It was the perfect chance; he was not expected to bring Rosalie.

He donned his friendliest smile as he passed through the crowded reception rooms of the marble mansion. He was careful to betray none of the condescension that he felt for the overopulent interior, filled with marble statues from American studios in Rome: a Cleopatra, an Augustus, a Miles Standish, two fighting gladiators. Winthrop recognized none of the guests; he wondered if Hardy recruited them from the store's personnel.

He found his host puffing at a large cigar and talking to a small, respectfully listening group of younger men. Hardy was a bald, heavy-jawed man with tiny, glistening eyes. He broke away without a word of apology to his audience when he saw Winthrop. Taking him firmly by the elbow, he propelled him to a corner.

"So you'll call, Winthrop Ward, when you want a favor from the merchant. Is that about the size of it?"

"So it might appear. But it also so happens that I was planning to give myself the pleasure of calling today in any event."

"Without the Mrs.?"

"My wife is receiving today."

"How would I know? She didn't ask me."

"She will next year."

Hardy snorted. "Well, enough of that. I shouldn't be too rough with a man who comes to bid me a happy New Year. But this business of Jules Bleecher sticks in my craw. What's it to me that the man's a bounder? Why should I care if he hankers after one of your society matrons? Can't you take care of your own? Must I get the poor lecher fired for you?"

"We hoped that you might regard our cause as yours," Winthrop answered smoothly. "And that you might agree that such a wrong inflicted on a gentleman like my cousin affected all the leaders of the city."

"I ain't in your crowd, Ward."

"Isn't that your choice, sir?"

Hardy stared. "Are you telling me that I could get into the Patroons'?"

Never had Winthrop's mind worked so fast. "I am not telling you that you could get in. That would be a question for the Admissions Committee. But I can certainly tell you that I should be glad to write you a letter of endorsement."

Hardy snickered. "I know that dodge. 'Dear Board of Admissions: I promised Mr. Cranberry Hardy that I would write a letter for him. This is the letter. Very truly yours, Winthrop Ward.'"

Winthrop breathed in relief. Now he had him. "Mr. Hardy," he said in a higher tone, "I cannot conceive what there may be in our past relations to justify your impugning my honor. If I were to write for you, it would be to heartily endorse your candidacy. And I should stand by my letter. After what you've just said, of course, there can be no further question of that."

He turned to go, just slowly enough to give Hardy the time to catch him by the arm. "Don't take offense, Ward. I was too hasty."

"I'm afraid you were."

"Maybe one day I'll ask you for that letter. But not yet a bit. In the meantime, thank you. Tell me, what's old Andros going to do if I don't bring him Bleecher's head on a platter? Have the Bank of Commerce call all the store's demand loans?"

"Not at all. Mr. Andros is simply asking a favor from one business leader to another. He may be in a position to return it one day."

Hardy put his thumbs in the pockets of his red waistcoat and balanced to and fro, his lips pursed as if to whistle but emitting no sound. "Well, I confess that I wouldn't mind having a few more friends in your crowd. God knows, Jules Bleecher doesn't mean a damn thing to me, and he's probably a horse's ass anyhow. But I don't much care for the idea of old Lewis Andros sending first his son-in-law and then you. Damn it all, Ward, if Andros wants Bleecher's head, let him come here and ask for it!"

"Today?"

"Well, there's no time like the present, is there?"

"I can't guarantee it, but I'm on my way back to Great Jones Street!"

4

Ten days later, at nine o'clock in the evening, Winthrop again received Jules Bleecher in the library at Union Square. This time Winthrop sat at his desk, touching his fingertips together, his face impassive, grave. Once again his heart was beating uncomfortably, but this time the discomfort was punctuated with the tickling of a fierce jubilation. Bleecher, with darkened countenance, was walking up and down the Persian carpet.

"My first impulse was to call you out," he was saying, "but I knew that would do no good. You burghers don't fight. Then I thought of going to your office with a horsewhip. But that would have been playing into your hands. Your friends on the bench would have put me in jail for a year or more. And then, thinking it over, I began to cool off. I began to be even interested in what had happened to me. What sort of a man are you, Winthrop Ward? Or are you a man at all?"

"What I am need not concern us, Bleecher."

"Oh, but it concerns *me*. I find myself without a job and without a friend in a city of brownstone fronts with locked front doors. How the hell did you do it? And why? You're not her husband. You're not even a very close relation." Bleecher paused to stare at his silent host. "It couldn't be that you're in love with Annie yourself?" He shook his head slowly as Winthrop failed to move a muscle. "No, that would be impossible for a snowman like you. But I still must ask of someone, as Othello asked of Lodovico:

'Will you, I pray, demand that demi-devil
Why he has thus ensnared my soul and body?'"

Winthrop's lips tightened in contempt. How typical of the poetaster to turn to Shakespeare in his ranting! "You and I, Bleecher, will be bound to disagree on which is the demi-devil. You have lived much abroad and cannot be expected to understand the customs of simple American gentlemen who still believe that a marriage vow is sacred and that homes should be protected."

"But from whom, in the name of God? Your cousin is the one who has threatened his own home from the beginning. Have you any idea, Ward, what his wife has had to put up with?"

"I think I have an idea."

Something in Winthrop's tone made Bleecher stare at him again.

"Maybe you're not a snowman, after all. Be frank, Ward. If you did what you did out of jealousy, I'll forgive you all. I'll even shake your hand!"

Winthrop rose. The exhilaration had departed from his chest. "We could talk all night and never understand each other. Let me put my last proposition before you. You have in your possession certain letters from Mrs. Ward and Miss King. Is that not so?"

"Why should I tell you?"

"Because I want them and because I'm in a position to barter for them. If you will deliver them to me, I will ask the *Daily Post* to re-employ you as a foreign correspondent. You will be able to live in London or Paris. I have no doubt that you will find life in one of those cities, particularly the second, preferable to our quiet existence on this side of the Atlantic."

Bleecher looked at him now with something like fascination. "And will the *Daily Post* do as you tell them?"

"I think so. If my proposition be endorsed—as I trust it will be—by certain gentlemen of prominence in this town."

"Like Messrs. Hardy and Andros. I see. And now the bounder is supposed to crumble. Or, like Shylock before Portia, be sent to renounce his faith. Only you have the wrong script, Ward. In *my* script, the villain turns upon you with a splendid defiance. You may take your proposition and cram it up the aperture—if indeed there be one in a snowman—in the nether part of your frozen body."

Ward averted his eyes from his foul-mouthed visitor. "I suppose I should expect such talk from you."

"You will be relieved to hear that I am removing myself from your 'quiet existence.' I have a standing invitation to come to Richmond and write a column for the *Enquirer*. It will be pleasant to be among gentlemen again. Perhaps I can help to warn them in the South what they are up against. They think, because they know how to fight bravely, that they are bound to prevail in a struggle with men of straw and men of ice, such as I have met up here. But they may well be wrong. If your millions of labor-slaves are ever harnessed into an army and sent into bloody battle by such remorseless bigots as you and Andros and Hardy, who can tell the outcome?"

"Then you keep the letters?"

"What I may do with the letters must remain the one little cloud of uncertainty on your cerulean sky of fatuity. Keep your eye ever peeled on it, Ward! Keep your umbrella in constant readiness!"

"Even if you want revenge on me," Winthrop protested earnestly, "must you take it out on Annie, too? Must she live in the daily fear of seeing her letters printed somewhere?"

Bleecher's gasp was incredulous. Then he burst suddenly into a harsh, raucous laugh. "Annie! That teasing, tantalizing, little bitch? Do you honestly think she'd give one holy goddamn if I told the world she copulated with sailors every Saturday night on a public pier?"

"Get out of my house!"

"You don't know her, Ward."

"Get out of my house!"

"I can't go fast enough."

Winthrop drank two whiskies before he went upstairs. Rosalie was at her dressing table, already in her nightgown. As she removed her earrings, she studied his face in her mirror.

"You didn't get the letters."

"No," he replied with a sigh, sitting down on the bedside.

"I didn't think you would. But it doesn't matter. He'll never do anything with them."

"Now what makes you say that?"

"Because he's a gentleman."

"Oh, Rosalie! Are you trying to annoy me?"

"No, dear. But I think you should face a fact every now and then. Even a disagreeable one."

"He's going to Richmond. He loves the Southern aristocracy. Slaveholders! How does *that* go down with your abolitionist principles?"

"Very badly." Rosalie's smile was obscure. "I never said I liked him, Winthrop. Or that I approved of him. I merely said he was a gentleman. To me that is a technical term. But one can deduce certain things from it. And one is that he'll never use those letters."

"And what about me? Am I a gentleman?"

"No, I don't really think you are."

"Rosalie!"

"I don't really think any man in New York society is. It's not what we go in for here."

"I'm tired. I'm going to bed."

"Good, dear. Do."

But later, in the dark, she put another question to him. "Tell me something, Winthrop. Do you really think you have done a good turn for Annie and Charles in salvaging their marriage?"

"I did what I had to do."

"What *you* had to do? Why you? Nobody else felt that way. Certainly none of our friends or family. You were the designer of the whole plot. Has it ever occurred to you that you've been playing God, Winthrop?"

"Maybe that's what I meant by doing what I had to do. Maybe there are times when one has to play God—when everyone else seems to forget He exists."

But Rosalie seemed unimpressed by his religious turn. "Do you suppose that's how history's written?" she mused. "Like a play being put together for the dress rehearsal? With one little man rushing about, shouting directions and trying to get people into the right costumes? Not necessarily a powerful man—simply a man with an *idée fixe*. A man with a sense of how things should at least *look*. Even a fussy man, a . . ."

"Rosalie, I want to go to sleep."

When a silence of several minutes followed by gentle snoring indicated that he had no further interruption to fear, Winthrop moved his lips in silent prayer:

"Dear God, if I have ever thought of Annie carnally, please forgive me. Remember that I have never given her or anyone else the right to say so. My conduct has been correct, even if my heart has been sinful. And let me face the facts of my motive in doing what I have done to Bleecher. Did I destroy him because I was jealous? Perhaps. But would I not have done so even if I had not been wickedly attracted to Annie? *Yes!* Yes, I would have! So is it a sin to enjoy performing a task essentially done for thee, O God? Is it wrong if jealousy give a fillip to doing one's duty? Make me humble, dear God. Crush me, overwhelm me. I am nothing, nothing, nothing . . ."

Winthrop felt calmer now and hoped that he would doze off before his excitement returned. Two drinks! He should never have had two drinks. Oh, why had he remembered them? He was wide awake again, watching the curtains gently blowing in the moonlight. The *Enquirer?* The Richmond *Enquirer?* Bleecher would be writing for *that?* Was that not the rag which had urged secession that very morning, suggesting that the Southern States place themselves under the protection of Louis Napoleon? What traitors! How could one govern a nation with such firebrands trying to pull it apart?

"Dear God, of course I know that we must allow our Southern States to live in peace. But if in thy great wisdom thou seest fit to permit them to strike the first blow, if thou turnest thine eyes away and allowest them to secede, *then* will it be wrong if we leap to arms with joy and jubilation in our hearts and if we bring the devastation of thine anger to their fair land, burning their plantations with a cleansing fire and chastising their rebel people with the sword? Or even with worse? Wilt thou blame us if their women are raped by the very slaves whom we have freed, if . . ."

He started as he heard Rosalie's voice. "What's wrong, Winthrop? Are you having a nightmare? You're rocking the bed!"

(VI)

The Arbiter

PORTRAITS OF GENTLEMEN, especially those commissioned by institutions—hospitals, colleges, clubs—of their directors or trustees, are usually so flat and pompous that the rare exceptions to this rule tend to become prized as considerable works of art. The likeness of Adam Winthrop, executed for the Patroons' Club in New York by the British-American painter, James Shannon, and hung in the principal salon to celebrate the opening of its new home in 1902 was hailed by conservatives and radicals alike as the portrait of an era. The enthusiasm which its exhibition engendered matched that aroused by the new edifice itself, a square Georgian temple of red brick and white marble, whose fine proportions and simple majesty made its neighboring châteaux and palazzos on Fifth Avenue seem as fake and fussy as time has proved them.

The portrait was large, even by Shannon's standards. Against a background of gleaming crimson folds, seated in a high black Italian chair, the subject exploded at the viewer out of the dazzling whiteness of his dress shirt and vest. A silk opera hat rested at his feet; one hand grasped the ivory top of a cane; the eyes, gray-white as pearl, looked out with a reflective serenity and a guarded welcome. Everything about the figure, its pose of easy erectness, of studied relaxation, of being happy to "sit" but only if the artist will get on with the job, was benign, aristocratic, even authoritative, yet in the fine, spare lines of the face, in the carefully trimmed, pointed beard, in the almost audibly sniffing aquiline nose, there lurked a sense of reserved decisions, of unexpected tolerances, even of possible gentlenesses. The model might have been a sexagenarian Marcus

Aurelius, heir and administrator of a golden empire beset with problems that distressed him.

That was the way Adam Winthrop himself liked to view it. Every afternoon at half-past two when he entered the clubhouse for the hour of whist that followed his session in the treasurer's office, he would pause to take himself in. Club attendants and members who saw him thus engaged had learned to look discreetly away. It was not tactful to intrude upon the president communing with himself. Adam noted this with a silent chuckle. "What a pompous ass they must take me for!" he reflected. "Little do they know that I, too, am wondering what lies beneath that high Winthrop brow. Shannon is a greater artist than Sargent. Sargent insinuates. Shannon admits that he hasn't a clue!"

On a windy March afternoon of 1903 Adam found Charles Buell hovering in the doorway waiting for him to finish his daily session with his likeness. Charles, whom nobody ever called Charley, a small, fussy, balding, sulky man, who had no occupation except as the efficient but officious treasurer of the Patroons' and who bristled with resentment at the attitude of fellow members who, while accepting the fruits of his industry, still sneered at him for it, was always on tip-toe at the president's arrival, as if his daily conference were in danger of being skipped, which it never was. Adam followed him now to the office. It no longer irked him that Buell stood aside to let him walk in first. He had learned to accept the other's aggressive toadying.

"I really don't know what we're coming to," Buell began mournfully, "what with waiters asking ten dollars a week, and the House Committee seriously considering a ladies' day on New Year's. However, I suppose we can survive *those* things. But what we surely cannot survive is any further depreciation in the quality of our membership. Look at this letter that came in today. George Schuyler is actually proposing Mr. Arnold Gordon!"

"I presume from your tone of shock that Mr. Gordon is a Jewish gentleman?"

"If that's not a contradiction in terms! He *was* a Jew, as Schuyler puts it. As if there could be a 'was' in such a case—just because the man now calls himself an Episcopalian and owns half of Long Island City! He certainly owns Schuyler. If that's going to be our standard, let us fling open the doors and ask the whole world in."

The president contemplated his indignant treasurer with tempered amusement. As a young man Adam had briefly contemplated a

church career, but he had been put off by his studies of the New
Testament. The first century A.D. had not attracted him, and ever
afterwards he had tended to associate Jews with early Christians in a
composite image of violence and bad breath, of fiery comminations,
of long, wagged fingers and shaking beards. He preferred to think of
himself as some togaed pro-consul, exquisite, cultivated, broad of
view, a Gallion, or, again, a Marcus Aurelius, turning with a faint
shudder of distaste from that shrill, semitic sect which saw only sacrilege in beautiful statues and a second coming in every thunderstorm.
But as an art collector Adam had developed something like reverence
for Jewish taste.

"I don't see what you have against Jews, Charles," he reproved
him. "They're the only people who in these money-grubbing times
have the sense to admit they love money. As a result they can afford
to care for other things as well, like art. But your New York Christians—they're the worst. Because they won't ever admit their passion
for money, it gobbles them up!"

"Really, Mr. President, I sometimes find it hard to tell when
you're joking. Do you mean to imply that you're in favor of admit-
ting Hebrews?"

Adam smiled at the angry little man, half ashamed of giving in to
the temptation to bait him. If Adam Winthrop were to espouse the
cause of Jews, let him take it up with his peers. "Well, if I am in
favor of it, Charles," he replied affably, "it is not for the benefit of
those who change their names and put financial heat on George
Schuyler to get admitted. What else is on the agenda?"

"Harold Bell would like to buy our little Ferrers painting of Trinity Church. He wants to give it to the Historical Society. He's willing
to pay anything you ask. We could fix the furnace and the acoustics
in the hall."

"A thousand times no!" Adam was immediately aroused. "Will
this cramming of beautiful things into museums never stop? Is there
to be nothing left in a gentleman's club?"

"I told him you'd say that."

"Good. Tell him so again."

When Adam left the office, he paused at the top of the marble cir-
cular stairway to delight in the little 1810 view of Trinity Church
that hung at the landing. One could imagine some American Jane
Austen coming out after a Sunday service and strolling down Broadway to the Battery.

"Could I talk with you a moment, Adam? I know you're going to the Whist Room. It will only be a minute."

There was certainly nothing of Jane Austen about Bob Guest. In only the middle of that cold, clear afternoon there was already a hint of liquor on his breath. Bob was big and strong and ruddy and had been considered—until almost yesterday—a fine enough fellow. But the last pretense of youth was gone at forty, and there did not seem much place in a middle-aged world for an idleness that was no longer picturesque or amusing. Adam's curt nod conveyed his disinclination for a lengthy interview.

"You couldn't let me have another thousand, could you," continued Guest, "until the first of the month?"

"I could, of course. *Should* I, is the proper question. You have never repaid me, Bob."

"But I will. You know I will."

"It's the last thing I know. Unless you're counting on Ada to finish her new novel and have it a great seller."

Guest flushed. "I didn't think that *you*, of all people, would fling Ada in my face."

Adam eyed him coldly. "Oh? Why did you not?"

"You should know what the answer to that is."

"Should I? But I don't."

"Oh, come now, Winthrop, you don't have to take that tone to me. Haven't I left you and Ada alone?"

"If you mean that my inclusion in your wife's social circle is one of the great pleasures of my life, I do not deny it."

Guest smirked. "All right. That's what I mean. Now do I get my grand?"

"Let me understand you, Bob, first. Do you imply that there is a connection between this accommodation and my being received in your wife's drawing room?"

"No, no. Of course not."

"You're quite sure?"

Guest gave up, defeated. "Quite sure. Look, Winthrop, I apologize."

"But for what do you apologize?" Adam continued inexorably. "For *thinking* that there might be such a connection?"

"No, not even for that. I apologize for troubling you with my troubles."

"Ah, then, that's quite all right, my dear fellow. You shall have your check in the morning. And now then, if you will forgive me, I think my whist table awaits me."

Adam played cards until a quarter to four and then took a hansom home. It was nearing the time for his call on Ada Guest, but he had observed a stain on his white waistcoat which would have to be changed. This was the more a nuisance in that Adam hated to go home in the afternoon. In the morning sunlight or by candles at night, the house gave him a constant joy. He had labored over it, room by room, with his friend, Ogden Codman; together they had created a perfect eighteenth-century Paris *hôtel* in a wilderness of what Codman called "New York Renaissance." As Adam now let himself in with his key to the dark front hall, goddesses in *biscuit de Sèvres* gleamed at him from their marble niches, and through the double doorway to the dining room tapestries flung spangled yards of emerald and sapphire over gray panels. There hung his great collection of *fêtes-champêtres*: Watteau, Boucher, Lancret, Chardin, Vanloo.

But the afternoon light, the dim, bleak, winter afternoon light, chilled the warmth of the colors, made all a ghastly gray-blue. It darkened even the picnics till they seemed like prints in a doctor's office; it filled the stately silent house with a sense of death. In the afternoon Adam seemed to hear in his corridors envious vulgar voices whispering: "He's dead, Adam Winthrop, as dead as his perfect mansion." As the glass, grilled front door closed slowly behind him, he shrugged, with quick, impatient defiance. Was ugliness life? Was banality vigor? Why should they all hate his house so, hate *him* so, but that his concept of beauty showed up their grime?

Gates, the old butler, stood watching him in unsurprised silence from the dining room. "Seeing you're home early, sir, would you care to do the place cards now?"

Adam always seated Violet's dinners. If he had chosen the house, she chose the guests. And what guests! In thirty years he had not made the smallest nick in her preconceived idea of "society." Moving now past the shining damask, the clustered wine glasses, the porcelain centerpiece of Neptune's chariot rising from the sea, Adam scanned the beautiful calligraphy of the cards that Gates handed him. But no, no, what could one do? "Mr. James Steele." "Mr. Paul Steele."

"Can my wife never give a party without all her siblings?"

Gates remained impassive.

Adam, putting a card down in its place, smiled suddenly at the memory of his old grandmother Cabot's comment when he had begun courting Violet Steele. "The trouble with marrying nouveaux riches is that you sink to their level. They never rise to yours. Their level becomes the new high, and that is how society is continually debased." But a real voice broke in on his reflections.

"What are you doing home at this hour?"

Violet, in the doorway, in a pink dressing gown, supported herself with one hand to the edge. Her face, marble colored, was rigid; her eyes haggard. She tippled in the afternoon, but had usually recovered by eight. The dinner party was her discipline.

"I had to change my waistcoat. It has a spot."

"Oh, I see. A spot. Out, out, damned spot." Violet came in wearily and sank into her chair at the head of the table. "It would be terrible, wouldn't it, if Mrs. Guest were to spy a spot? Almost as bad as a run in her blue stocking."

Adam turned at once to dismiss Gates, but he had underestimated the butler's tact. He and Violet were already alone.

"Don't be so concerned about Gates," Violet continued pettishly. "There's precious little he doesn't know. When I heard your voice down here, I wondered for one ridiculous moment if you might have come home to see *me*."

"You mean for a particular reason?"

"There would have to be one, I suppose?"

"What are you getting at, Violet?"

"What, indeed? We're beyond the foolishness of wanting to see each other without a reason, aren't we?"

Adam felt the old ache in his heart at the hopelessness of their situation. "What is the use, Violet, of our quarreling after thirty years? We are what we are."

"If we even quarreled, it might be something."

"I suggest that we're doing well enough. I . . ."

"Don't say it!" she cried. "Don't say we're civilized. Can't you see what being civilized has done to me? Everyone else does. My brothers and sisters all do. Our daughters do. You've built your beautiful temple, but what am I but a prisoner in it? You've walled out life, Adam. That's what you've done."

Adam sighed. First the afternoon light and now this hackneyed complaint. "I haven't walled out your dinner parties, if you call them life."

"Go ahead. Sneer at my friends. They're all I have left."

"What about everything here? This house, the pictures, the furniture? They're all yours."

"Things." She looked scornfully about. "What do I care about things? You're the one who gets a kick out of things. Because you have no heart, Adam."

He decided to try once again, for the thousandth time. "What you resent is not my heartlessness but my happiness. You think it's heartless of me to be happy when you're not. But your misery is a quicksand, my dear. If I fell into it, you'd be no better off. With old age in sight, it's a case of *sauve qui peut*. It is true that I derive joy from the paintings in this room. But that joy is open to you, too."

"I suppose Mrs. Guest is open to me?"

"If you mean by that, is it open to you to form a friendship with a brilliant intellectual woman, yes, it is!"

"A *friendship?*"

"Yes, a friendship, Violet."

He left her now and went upstairs to change his vest. When he came down, Violet had retreated to her room. Adam stood before the Lancret, his eyes moving carefully from figure to figure, left to right, across the canvas. But instead of the consolation that he expected, an ugly thought came to mind. Was it possible that all those charming forms, all those gallants and ladies, some sitting, some standing, some lying, half-embracing, listening to a lutist, two dancing, one playing with a monkey, one glancing up at two doves in a cage, that all that delicate cream and green and yellow, all the tender pink of the marble columns of the little temple of love in the background, all the deep lush emerald of the surrounding forest, were only disguises for a party as vapid and turgid as the one Violet would be giving that night? Well, thank God, then, for Lancret! If *that* was what he could make out of it, did he not justify the existence of his tawdry model?

2

Ada Guest's house was in West Twelfth Street. It was a converted coach house, so that one entered the huge front parlor, painted white and hung with Japanese screens, directly from the sidewalk. Like Ada's mind the room was a jumble of the good and less good, of the very fine and the occasionally sentimental. If her intellect took everything in, it threw very little away. There were three splendid Louis XV *bergères*, given her on three Christmases by Adam; there were paintings, on easels, of illustrations for Ada's fiction: the Christian girl in the arena seeking her lover in the crowd, representing an earlier phase, and a portrait of the heroine of *Perdita*, closely modeled on Ada herself, as an example of the more realistic later novels. There were bright chintzes everywhere, for Ada had been an early client of Elsie de Wolfe.

As he had come that day by specific invitation and was expecting at least a small tea party, Adam was agreeably surprised to find Ada alone. But she rose, as she always did, even with company, to cross the room and greet him by taking both his hands in hers. He never failed to be pleased by this candid way in which she acknowledged his principal place in her salon. Ada's looks had been the kind of pale, soft, blond prettiness that everybody had agreed would fade with the first crinkles of middle-age, but at forty-five she was as handsome as ever. Her hair, reddish-blond, was pulled loosely back to a knot behind; her eyes, large and green-gray, shone with intelligence and humor.

"I saw Bob at the club today," he told her when they were seated by the small fire.

"Did he hit you for another loan?"

"He said something that disturbed me. He implied that our relationship was meretricious."

Ada watched him with amused eyes. "And I trust that you assured him to the contrary."

"How could I?"

"How could you? But think of my reputation, Adam!"

"Well, of course, I had that to think of. But how could I be so ungallant as to assert that ours was a case of simple friendship?"

"Oh, Adam, you're divine!" she cried, clapping her hands. "You are the most perfect gentleman in the world."

"I trust Bob is not going to get nasty at this late date."

"Oh, you know Bob."

Adam did not quite like the candid contempt of her shrug. He had distinct ideas of how even indifferent wives should speak of their mates.

"Let Bob look after himself," Ada continued. "One of these days I shall be rich enough to repay all your loans."

"You must be rich, by all means, but not to repay my loans. Allow me the luxury of thinking that I had a tiny stake in the career of a great American novelist."

"Ah, but that stake isn't the money!" she remonstrated with indignation. "That stake is the loving interest that you have taken from the beginning. It's all your editing and correcting and *believing* in me. The believing's been the great thing."

Adam noted with a benign amusement that she omitted any reference to his ideas for stories, several of which she had used. This was quite right. An artist had to have ego.

"I've been having a terrible tussle with Estelle." She shifted now to the work in progress, whose plot she and Adam regularly discussed. "I can't seem to make the social whirl attractive enough to be fatal to a creature of her keenness. If society is only dangerous to butterflies, why is it worth writing about?"

"Society is dangerous to people who need an excuse for not making something of themselves," Adam responded in a very definite tone. "I have been giving some thought to Estelle, and I think I begin to see the way. Let her be disappointed in love. Let her be so hurt as to need the anodyne which society offers. There she will meet Nicholas, your sterile dilettante, who is trying to hide his business failure in a drawing room success. By the time she has discovered her mistake in marriage—for he will marry her, if only for the money—it is too late. She is hooked."

Ada's silence was a clear tribute.

"You *do* see it," she mused. "It's phenomenal how you see it."

"Thus she will balance your heroine, who finds her salvation in a flight from society with a true artist. I think you have the germ of Nicholas now. But there's something that is holding you back from developing him fully. I think I see what that is."

She stared with a shade of apprehension. "What?"

"You're afraid that he will come out too much like me."

"But you're no dilettante, Adam!" Ada burst out, too strongly. "You have the finest eye for prose I know. And for painting! Why, my dear, people like you are the reason people like me write at all!"

"I like to hear you say that. If I have contributed anything, in the smallest way, to the development of your genius . . ."

"Oh, Adam, stop!" She rose and came over to put her arms around him. "Don't you think I know, you old darling, what you've done for me?" Here she slipped a thick wad of paper into his breast pocket. "These are the last two chapters. Introducing Enid. I think it's a breakthrough. A new level. Read them when you have a chance."

"If Bob should come in now, he'd think the worst."

"Let him!" she snorted. Then, as if the very reminder of her husband iced her warmth, she returned to her seat at the tea table.

Adam, as the maid came in, resisted the impulse to straighten the hair which Ada had ruffled. The front door was opened to admit two men. They were Hubert Hinds, the architect, long-nosed, bushy-bearded, large of frame and burly of muscle, who might have seemed dirty had he not been so obviously clean, and John Clark, the art collector, tall, alabaster, spindly, with long light hair. When the two were seated on either side of Ada, they might have been contrasting Toby jars on opposite ends of a Victorian mantel.

Ada looked from one to another of her visitors, smiling mysteriously, and suddenly clapped her hands. "I asked just the three of you here today because I wanted to be alone with my three most valued friends. I have some great news. And you will be the first to hear. Bob and I are moving to Paris. We have taken a flat in the Rue Monsieur. Now just a minute!" She held up her hands as all three started to exclaim. "Let me anticipate some of your questions. I feel that the time has come in my life for a change of mental air, for a new inspiration. I want to spread my wings!"

Hinds stood up to emphasize his instant, hearty accord. "My dear Ada, you are doing the real right thing. If it had not been for my years in Paris at the Beaux-Arts, I should not be the man I am today. Europe is a must for every serious artist. I don't say that the time is not coming when we'll take the lead over here, but that time is still a long way off."

"The same is true of our museums," Clark added. "At the rate we're buying, New York will ultimately be on every European's grand tour. But, as Hubert says, not yet. You're taking the right step, Ada. Don't let anyone persuade you otherwise!"

Ada's gaze of half-concealed anxiety was now directed at her principal friend. "Don't look as if it were the end of the world, Adam," she pleaded. "You know you come over every year. I expect to show you off to all my new friends in Paris. You'll still be my biggest lion."

"Shucks, my roar will sound like a squeak there with everyone crowding around the American George Sand. I can just hear them: 'Who's that old Yank in the corner? Some relative of Ada's? Why are Americans so infernally loyal?'"

Ada laughed, relieved by the seeming lightness of his tone. "On the contrary, they'll be saying: 'Did you meet that delightful Mr. Winthrop? Who would have thought that brassy, pushing bluestocking would have such a charming friend?'"

"Well, we shall see. Of course, I'll come over, if only to view you in your glory. How will Bob like Paris?"

"Oh, he's going to work on his water colors. Paris will be just the place for that. I've always thought Bob had a real talent."

Adam reflected with a wry amusement that there was nothing quite so obtuse as a clever woman faced with a hopeless obstacle. "So Freia is deserting the gods," he observed with a sad shake of his head. "Valhalla will become old indeed."

"But surely you sympathize, Adam? I'm starved, literally starved for good minds. Oh, of course, I've had the benefit of yours and Hubert's and John's, and I'm forever grateful, but it's only made me greedy for more. You should know—you, Adam, of all people—what New York is. Violet's dinner parties, my dear! Think of your own incomparable descriptions of them."

"But that's just society, Ada. You haven't explored the universities or the literary life of the Village."

"Have *you*?"

"I'm not a writer."

"Well, if you were, you'd know how hopelessly departmentalized New York is. The academicians are all uptown, writing theses, and the intellectuals are all downtown, drinking beer. There's no real mingling, as in Paris."

"Paris will be fun, I admit," Adam responded with a shrug, "but what has it to do with your writing? Everything you need for your art, Ada, is right inside of you. You might even lose a few drops of it by traveling too far from your source. You're not like Hubert here, who has covered the east side of Manhattan with Renaissance palaces, or John, who has covered his walls with Renaissance paintings. They are basically Europeans in America. But you're a Yank, first and foremost . . ."

"Now just a minute, Adam," Hubert broke in indignantly. "I insist that my style represents a combination of the Romanesque with certain Pueblo Indian aspects . . ."

"And you totally ignore my Copley collection!" exclaimed John.

"Gentlemen, gentlemen!" Ada cried out in a voice of sudden, sharp distress. They were all silent with astonishment as she rose now, pale and agitated. "Please, will you go now! I'm sorry. I am too upset by what Adam has said. I am going to my room."

She hurried from the chamber in an evident crisis of nerves. Adam turned to the others, seemingly unperturbed, and offered them a lift in his Daimler. All the way uptown Hubert and John repeated their arguments in favor of Europe, urging him not to distress Ada unduly with a stubborn and obviously hopeless opposition to her plans. How could he stand in the way of an artist and the selection of her environment? Who knew better what Ada needed? He or Ada? Adam simply shrugged.

"It seems to me, gentlemen, that you fail to recognize the simple signs of a bad conscience. Ada knows what this move will do to Bob. She wants to be rid of him, and she can't face her own motives."

Home, in his dressing room, Adam dismissed his valet and sat down in his big leather armchair to read the two chapters which Ada had given him. For thirty minutes he read, very slowly, with total concentration. Then he arose with a sigh and strode up and down the room.

Ada had been quite right. She *was* approaching a new level in her writing. She was doing at last to the fullest what he had from the beginning coached her to do: she was reaching into her own heart and mind and biography to pull out the very essence of Ada Guest and use it as her raw material. Raw? The new character in her novel, Enid Avery, was herself, undisguised! Enid's story was Ada's own, that of a bitter little Boston girl, fired with a fury of shame for her shabby, sentimental, evasive, slippery father, and her futilely snobbish, penny-pinching mother. Ada's style was at once blunter and straighter and stronger. It seemed to have arisen, with a gaunt integrity, from the ashes of her old imitations of Robert Louis Stevenson and Anatole France. Adam knew now that she would become the kind of writer who tells, over and over, the saga of her own passions and frustrations, like those actresses (including some of the very greatest) who always play themselves.

There was a knock. "I expected you down, sir. Shall I decant the wine?"

"Yes, Gates. I'll be right there."

He continued to walk up and down his dressing room. Torn in different ways, he could hardly endure the idea of greeting Violet's guests. He wanted to go to Ada and tell her that she was writing a great book. But was there any limit to the human price she was willing to pay? She was already using him, as Nicholas. She was preparing to drag Bob to Paris where he would drink himself to death. And now she flung herself, a final log, on the bonfire of her insatiable fiction.

"She's a monster!" he cried aloud, and stopped to view his own astonishment in the mirror. "It's not art at all. It's nothing but a kind of screaming diary."

Where was the discipline of the age of reason? What was writing

like Ada's but a chalking on walls? Strong, perhaps, but wherein did
the strength lie? Ada wanted to stand out from the masses by shouting her name in a louder voice than anyone else. And *that* was art?
And *he* had encouraged it? Adam turned to contemplate a small
Hubert Robert, a favorite, that showed the courtyard of an old con-
vent with a fountain in the noonday, Provençal sun. Could Ada do
anything like that? Perhaps it would be just as well if Paris, like a
fine fountain spray, should douse some of the fires of her Yankee
genius.

Again a knock. This time it was his valet. "Please, sir, the mistress
says you're to come down."

"I'm coming, damn it!"

He slammed the door, quite uncharacteristically, in the poor
man's face and returned to his Hubert Robert. His forehead was
damp with sweat. Had someone pulled a dirty wash rag over his beloved canvas? Why did it seem faded? Why did it seem so dull?

3

Adam as a young man in the years immediately following the Civil
War had felt like the Biblical character in the parable of the talents
who could think of nothing better to do with his money than bury it
in the sand. Too young, before Appomattox, to have fought, he
suffered from the guilt of being the sole male survivor of his family.
His father, the general, had died before Vicksburg and his two older
brothers in the Wilderness campaign. What could he do to justify
such sacrifices?

Not that the world cared. All that it seemed to want to do in 1870
was to forget the glorious past. In Washington, the President whom
Adam's brothers had followed to their deaths had ears only for cor-
rupt underlings. In New York a ring of shady manipulators controlled the courts and the legislature. Even in Boston materialism
pervaded the dark streets and wintry air. Adam, trained at Harvard
and Oxford, a student of ancient law and modern painting, the best-
dressed man on Beacon Street and the undisputed billiards champion
of the Pilgrims Club, looked about him with gravely searching eyes
to select the most vulnerable spot on the public dragon in which to
implant his javelin. He decided at last to join the young Henry
Adams and his group of eager reformists who were articulating their
rather scholarly protests in the pages of the *North American Review.*

After some months as a researcher for others, Adam decided to strike out on his own with a major piece on Ambrose Steele, the Wall Street speculator who was generally considered to represent the nadir of financial irresponsibility. To his astonishment his subject showed the greatest cordiality about being interviewed.

"Of course, I know what you're up to," Steele told Adam cheerfully. "You want me because you think I'm the worst. I'm not, but history will deem me so, and you'll get the credit of discovering it."

"Why aren't you the worst, sir?" Adam asked, taken aback by the old rascal's friendliness.

"Because I face what I am and make no bones about it. But that's precisely why I'll be damned. I'm not a psalm-singer like the other pirates. There'll always be an historian to find some virtue in a hypocrite."

Adam, looking down at this funny, almost unkempt little gnome of a man, with watery smiling eyes, scraggly beard and bald head, saw that his problem would be that he was going to like him. He declined Mr. Steele's invitation to stay in the Fifth Avenue mansion while doing his research, but he found himself a constant guest for meals. In the course of that extraordinary winter he not only became irreparably fond of the undeniably crooked Mr. Steele; he fell in love with his daughter.

Adam knew none of the people who came to Mrs. Steele's afternoon receptions at three o'clock, when the thick red velvet curtains had been pulled so that the malachite and dark Egyptian things could glint in candlelight. They were probably recruited from a list of her husband's debtors. But the six Steele children, three boys and three girls, were charming. They were cheerful, frank, handsome, fresh. The wispy old man seemed to have had nothing to do with their procreation—their genes must have come from the stupid, tongue-tied, handsome mother. And Violet, gray-eyed, blond, teasing, was the pearl of the clan. To Adam's dazzled eye and ear her high laugh seemed to rip out a corner of the huge dead parlor through which came pouring in all the dancing glories of spring, as in the first act of the *Walküre* when Siegmund throws open the door of the darkened hut.

"Why do you write about Papa?" she asked him. "Who wants to read about stocks and bonds and reorganizations and such dull things? Why don't you write a beautiful romance? About a proper young man who comes down from dark old Boston and meets an outrageous girl?"

Even Adam's assurance about his article began to weaken. When he tried to discuss this seriously with Violet, she simply laughed at him.

"What's it to me what you write about Papa? So long as *he* doesn't mind? And what makes you think that any but a few cranks and bluestockings will ever read it?"

This argument was taken up on a more serious level by Mr. Steele himself. One evening after dinner he took Adam into his study which, filled with black mahogany and ebony statuettes, was even murkier than the rest of the house. There he delivered a lecture.

"I know that people never take advice, but you strike me as unusually intelligent, and I'm going to give you some. I understand your wish to reform the world. The trouble is that you can't. What will be will be—and when it will be. One day the people of this country are going to decide that businessmen have too much power, and then they're going to take that power away. Just the way they decided to get rid of the English and to free the slaves. Now when that time comes, the people who had the idea earlier, the reformers, will lay claim to the victory, and they'll get it, too. But they won't deserve it. Martyrs always die in vain. Those old Romans would have finally become Christians had every lion in the arena gone hungry. So don't waste your life, Adam. Marry Violet. She's a lovely girl, with a good temper, and no brighter than her mother which, in my opinion, is an asset. She will have a considerable fortune, and I will see that you have a say in its expenditure. In fact, I'll make you trustee for the whole family. Now, I know what you're going to tell me: that you don't want to be the appendage of a rich wife. You won't be. Never mind that fools will say you are. Just look around you and see what's happening in this New York of ours. We're beginning at last to grow up into a city. A great city. We've started an art museum. We've started a natural history museum. The people have decided that they want culture, and they're going to get it. I may not believe in pioneers or in martyrs, but I do believe in captains of ships. Get on board, Winthrop! There's a great future for you here."

Adam felt that it was rather small of him to make the point that he nonetheless now made. "Is it a condition, sir, that I should give up my piece about you?"

"Don't be an ass. Write anything you like. Get it through your head, my boy, once and for all, that I mean what I say. Whether you write your article or not will make no difference to anybody in the world, including yourself. Or perhaps only to yourself. Satisfy that Boston conscience of yours. Give it anything it wants."

Adam married Violet and did not write the article. Or at least he did not publish it. He decided that to do so would be an act of pettiness, an unbecoming effort to have his cake of good conscience and eat it, too. For he had been finally convinced by Ambrose Steele. He believed now that the only way to clean dirty money was to spend it well. And once he had made up his mind that he was on the right track, as a Winthrop and a gentleman, he was not going to be so weak as to stumble off into the bushes because the path of duty happened to head toward marriage with a beautiful woman whom he loved. It even comforted him a little to know that fools would always regard him as a fortune hunter and a dilettante. This would compensate in part for what might otherwise seem too heaping a slice of luck.

Adam's mother had been reconciled to the match, not only by the prospect of her daughter-in-law's dowry, but by her concept of the latter's personality as a "razed tablet" on which her clever son would be able to write whatever he wished. In this latter idea she proved wrong. Violet's father had been right about her: she was good, but she was stupid. Adam discovered early that his wife was utterly incapable of any development in taste. She had been passionately anxious to add Adam to her life, but purely as the gem of her small collection of sentimentalities, never as a guide or mentor. Oddly enough, although she perfectly comprehended the social value of the Winthrops, it did not occur to her that Adam himself might know about such things. "Society" to Violet would always be the people who had been snooty to her before she became Mrs. Winthrop.

Her siblings were like her. When Ambrose died, he left them even richer than expected. They were enchanted by their sudden fortunes —the mocking old man had always kept them close—and they proceeded, except for Adam, to spend their money exactly as their neighbors did. Never were uglier houses built or uglier works of art purchased; never were more beautiful horses raced or more trim yachts sailed. The Steeles retained their youthful spirits and enthusiasm into prosperity. They danced till late on Saturday nights and sang hymns lustily in church on Sunday mornings. They dressed in bright colors and gave liberally to charitable causes. But when middle age began to play with lines around the corners of their eyes and the edges of their lips, they became dull. And when they became dull, they became unhappy—in a fitful, bewildered, childish way.

Only Adam prospered with the years. *His* house was a museum; his paintings admired even by the great European collectors. He was a trustee of the Metropolitan Museum, the Metropolitan Opera, the Museum of Natural History, the Brooklyn Museum, the New York Philharmonic. With the exception of Mr. Morgan's, there was no more respected voice in the cultural life of the city. Adam used to say to himself that he lacked only two things to make his life perfect: God and an intimate friend. He eventually reconciled himself to the absence of the former by his emulation of the agnostic Roman spirit, but of the latter he continued to dream. And then one night, at a dinner party, in his fiftieth year, he met his candidate. Somewhat to his surprise, it was a woman, a pretty woman in her early thirties, with gray-green eyes and a liveliness that set off charmingly her immediate and obvious interest in himself.

He had known and disapproved of Bob Guest at the Patroons'. He knew that he spent more money than he had and drank more liquor than he should and was presumably a trial to the poor childless wife at home who "scribbled" to help with the unpaid bills. But now he discovered that Mrs. Guest was far from pitiable. She talked with competence of the Egyptian additions to the Metropolitan collection, of Melba's Marguerite, of Howells' last novel. And she could listen, too. Adam's only reservation lay in his suspicion that, like many intellectual women, she might lack degrees in her mental laboratory, that everything might be jumbled in together, the windows of John LaFarge with the windows of Chartres. He asked her about her own work, which he confessed to having not read.

"Why should you read silly novels?" she responded quickly. "Why should you read even serious novels? You have a real life."

"Can one life be more real than another?"

"Oh, yes. Mine isn't real at all. That's one of the reasons I cover paper with words. But you run great institutions. You buy beautiful things. You are Adam Winthrop, the *arbiter elegantiarum* of New York."

"Mrs. Guest, your flattery is outrageous!"

"But I mean every word of it." Here she paused to look at him steadily and altogether convincingly with those wide-open gray-green eyes. "I have always wanted to meet you."

"Dear lady, where have you heard about me?"

"From my husband, among others. He sees you at the Patroons'."

"I shouldn't have thought that Bob, excellent fellow as he is, was one to care much for beautiful things."

"He isn't. But I have my own way of interpreting what he says."

By the end of the following week Adam had obtained and read all of Ada Guest's published works. Her novels were uneven. She had a fondness for historical fiction and a tendency to overwrite, but there was a hard underlying strand of intelligence, like an underground railway which keeps surfacing among the backyards and gardens of a suburb. Adam made out at once that the rails were worth more than the suburban gardens. When he called on Mrs. Guest in her tiny brownstone where she then lived, he found her enraptured that he should have discovered any merit in her work. She begged him to take away and criticize the manuscript of a novella about Saint Luke in Rome, composing his gospel. For all her seeming submissiveness he already had a sense of being taken over.

"It's a clever theme," he told her on his next call. "But we mustn't let people say you're copying *Le Procurateur de Judée*."

"Will you help me?" she asked simply.

Soon they were meeting regularly. Adam was careful to confine his role to a criticism of plots and a pruning of language. He never actually wrote a single sentence of one of her stories. Where he was sure that he was of most value to her was in demonstrating that her bluebird, like Maeterlinck's, was at home. When she wrote of historical characters, for example, Mary Stuart or Dolly Madison, she tended to be too high and noble, but when she wrote of her late grandmother, an alcoholic abolitionist, or of an uncle who was a fashionable quack, she was clear, crisp, vivid, sarcastic—in a word, devastating. Ada Guest ethereal was inclined to pomposity; Ada Guest realistic was shrewd and pungent.

As their friendship deepened, the world began to discuss whether or not they were lovers. It became a popular topic; people took sides. In fact, neither of them ever wanted to be. They discussed the question only once, at Ada's suggestion.

"I am so afraid," she told him one day at tea, "that you will think, because you're a gentleman, that you ought to make love to me. Please don't. It would spoil everything. To convince you of this I must say something rather crude. It will probably hurt your feelings, but after it's been said, it will never have to be repeated, and that issue will be closed. I am not attracted to you. There! It's done. And now let me add something to soothe your wounded male ego. It is not because you are not attractive. Far from it. It is because of your age and your intellect. Like many bluestockings, I am attracted to younger, rather brutish men. That is a very low taste and one that I trust I shall have the character not to indulge—a second time."

Adam would have vastly preferred that she should not have

brought the subject up. He regretted that she lacked the sensitivity to understand that his tact would have perfectly coped with the situation, that he would never have offered himself where he was not wanted. And, of course, his male ego *was* wounded. Her statement about younger men only made this worse. But he was able to derive considerable solace by a private laugh at Ada's expense. He reflected with an inner chuckle that no female of fine feeling, no expert in the art of pleasing men, would ever have been guilty of such crudeness. "For the prize in flat feet," he snorted to himself, "give me a woman writer any day!"

"You may depend upon me, my dear," he responded aloud with a benign smile. "I shall keep the beast within me at bay."

4

The Patroons' had an office reserved for the president to which Adam sometimes repaired when he wanted to be quite alone. The window overlooked the park, and on the afternoon of the day following his receipt of Ada's news of her proposed removal to France, he stood by it for ten minutes, watching the ambulation of children and nurses and the flights of dirty pigeons over the bare trees. He could see an outdoors cage of the zoo and one old tattered buffalo, which never seemed to move.

"Pardon me, sir. Mr. Guest has just come in. He says he'll see you in two minutes."

"Thank you."

Adam turned to contemplate two paintings which rested on easels facing his desk. They were examples of what was beginning to be called the post-impressionist school. The signature on the first canvas was "Bernard"; on the second, "Gauguin."

"I mustn't keep thinking of Ada," Adam said aloud to himself. "I mustn't think of her except when I *mean* to think of her."

The door opened to admit Bob Guest.

"Ah, there you are, my dear fellow," Adam greeted him. "I want to have a word with you about this great change in your life."

"Isn't it really more of a change in yours?"

Adam looked up in surprise. But no, Bob had not been drinking. He looked cooler than usual, more composed. The slight, faintly mocking air of deference that he usually adopted towards Adam was in abeyance.

"Quite so. New York will be the loser. We shall all feel grossly abandoned."

Bob was inspecting the paintings. "Are these yours?"

"No. They're here on approval. The gallery that owns them has suggested that I might wish to buy them for the Metropolitan. What do you think?"

"I don't know. The colors seem wrong."

"The colors *are* wrong. Do colors have to be right? One should try to keep an open mind. Otherwise one ends up thinking that Italian painting ended with Guido Reni and French with Corot."

Bob shrugged and turned away. "Of course, I know nothing about it."

"Well, you'd better get used to it. You'll be seeing a lot of art in Paris."

"Is there any kind of club life there?"

"There's the Jockey, of course. But they're not renowned for their cordiality to American gentlemen who don't speak their tongue."

Bob flushed slightly. "I can learn French, Adam."

"My dear boy, I know you can. But the French are the most terrible linguistic snobs. We like to hear our language spoken with a slight accent. But they regard it as a kind of affront."

"I suppose there are plenty of Americans in Paris."

"Oh, yes, a whole colony."

"What do they do?"

"Criticize French servants and damn their native land."

Bob transferred his gaze back to the Bernard. "Is there much sport?"

"There's some very good hunting, but it's tightly controlled, usually by the old families. They won't be Ada's cup of tea, or she theirs."

Bob turned angrily now to his tormentor. "What you're saying is that I won't have any life abroad. Is that the gist of it, Adam? Except as a kind of appendage of Ada's in expatriate literary circles? Do you think I don't know you'd say anything to keep Ada in New York?"

"Of course, I want to keep Ada in New York. But, believe it or not, I am thinking of you."

"I do *not* believe it. When you think of me, it is with contempt. You regard me as a complacent husband who borrows money from his wife's lover."

"I am not your wife's lover!"

"No, but half the town thinks you are. Anyway, why should I care? She hasn't had anything to do with me that way for years." Bob came over now to the desk and sat down opposite its occupant, leaning forward to fix his eye on Adam's. "There are things you don't know about me, Adam. One is that I am very grateful to Ada. If she wants to go to Paris, to Paris we go. She has put up with my drinking and my uselessness. She has made a home for me. She has never thrown in my face the disappointment of her marriage, or the inequality of it."

"But surely, at the time Ada married you, it was considered a step up for her!"

"Perhaps. By the ignorant. She was a Miss Nobody from Boston, and I was the 'dashing club man,' 'old New York,' and so forth. But the real truth was that she was a genius, and I was already a drunk. And when she found that she had the worst of the bargain, when I was disinherited by Uncle Joe whose favorite I'd always been, what did she do? Leave me? No such thing. She turned to and scribbled her head off and brought in most of the money on which we've lived. Even counting the loans I got from you!"

Adam looked away from that shameless stare with a cough of distaste and gazed for some moments out the window. "I never denied that she was an admirable woman," he said at last. But when he turned back to his visitor, it was to find himself alone. He stared from the Gauguin to the Bernard to the Gauguin again. Then he rose with a sigh of impatience and rang for the page to order his car.

He found Ada alone in her living room, putting tags on the furniture that was to be placed in storage. They had not met since her summary dismissal of him and Hinds and Clark. She was obviously still tense, for she continued her nervous activity, leaving him to sit with the cup of tea that she had rather grudgingly poured for him.

"Do you think I should leave my books?" she asked. "I wonder if it isn't better to read *only* French for the first year. I want really to immerse myself in this experience."

Adam ignored the question. "I've just been with Bob."

"Oh, Adam, you're not going to bring that up again!"

"I simply thought . . ."

"What can I *do?* The plans are all made."

"I thought that instead of living in Paris, you might get a house in the country. Bob likes dogs; he likes to ride. He might even do a bit of farming."

"But I've already taken the flat in the Rue Monsieur!"

"I know. But you could take another. I could loan Bob the money . . ."

"No, no, *no!*" Ada cried in exasperation. "I refuse to be saddled with any more debts. And I refuse to spend my life running two households! I have waited for years for this opportunity, and I'm not going to give it up now. What has Bob ever done for me, I'd like to know? Honest to God, Adam, it is really too much to be told, after ten years of struggling to preserve an incompatible marriage, that I must now give up my one chance for happiness so that Bob may be slightly less bored than he already is!"

"But Bob cares so for you. I think you may be the only person in the world he really cares for."

"Oh, cares," Ada wailed. "He has a fine way of showing it! Has he ever tried to care about anything that interests me?"

"He can't, Ada. It's beyond him."

"If you want to help Bob, here's something you can do," she suggested suddenly in a changed, eager tone. "Urge him to stay here. Urge him to take a room in the Patroons' for the winter. He'll be perfectly all right here. And I'll promise to come back in the summer and take a cottage in Newport or Southampton or wherever he wants and spend three whole months with him. There! Isn't that fair? You can't say that's not fair, Adam. Do it for me. Please!"

"Fair?" He shook his head. "I don't say it's fair or unfair. I say it won't work. For Bob."

Ada looked at him hopelessly. "You really think it's my duty to give up Paris, don't you? Perhaps even to give up New York and live in the country, on a farm?" She paused, as if to give him a last chance to redeem himself. "You *do* think that, don't you?"

"Yes, I'm afraid I do."

At this she jumped up, making no further effort to conceal the violence of her vexation. As she strode up and down the small, empty room he could see that her arms and shoulders were trembling.

"There is a great difference between you and me, Adam. And I think it may clear the air to say what it is. You have been able to adapt yourself to the hothouse air of a New York social life. You breathe it in easily. I believe it even nourishes you. You can go to any number of stifling dinner parties and see any number of stifling bores. You have built a refuge within yourself from which you peer out and derive amusement from the sight of the other animals. You are kind to your wife and good to your servants. You execute all your obligations and perform all your duties. You are an inestimable friend. But it is not difficult for you to be these things. As a canary is yellow or a jay blue, so is Adam Winthrop a good citizen. But I am made of different clay. I cannot really breathe any more in New York. You have been very flattering about what you choose to call my genius. Well, if I have a bit of a spark, even just a touch of talent, don't you think I owe it something? Shouldn't I move my literary seed—such as it is—to a soil and a climate where it can grow? Or is the only obligation in life to devote myself to the hopeless task of trying to make a man happy who can't be made happy? And whom I never should have married in the first place? My God, Adam, is *that* what you really think life is all about?"

"I did not mean to suggest any such sacrifice. I see your genius—and I am happy to reaffirm my belief in it—quite differently. I think the best soil and the climate for it are right here in New York."

Ada stopped now to stare at him. Suddenly she threw back her head and uttered a mocking laugh. "That, Adam, is the first insular statement I have ever heard from your lips. Do you really owe poor little old New York that much loyalty? You, the arbiter of elegance, the cosmopolite! But you couldn't possibly have said anything that would more fix me in my resolution that I must go abroad. That you, my principal refuge, my oasis in the Manhattan desert, should prove a mirage is the final warning. I must go and go now!"

Adam rose, with a dry smile. "And I, too."

Ada's air of hesitation now suggested that she was debating an irrevocable step. "Shall I tell you something else, Adam? *You* have been the real reason from the beginning that I'm leaving New York. Does that seem strange to you?"

"Very. I had no idea that I could matter so much."

"Well, you do. When you first started coming here, I regarded you as the principal ornament of what I was presumptuous enough to consider my salon. I was very proud indeed of my little collection of enlightened gentlemen. I had, after all, in addition to yourself, a leading architect, a well-known judge, a university president, a museum director. But I discovered in time that there was a strange common denominator to my small group. It was a concern with form over substance, with technique over action. You are dry, Adam, all of you! Dry with the dust of New York, derivative rather than inspired, clever rather than forceful. Hubert Hinds, as you say, builds Renaissance villas, and John Clark buys Renaissance paintings. The old Puritan fire has gone out. What you really hate is not my going to Europe, or anything that will happen to Bob. No, what you really hate is my new book. You hate its force and life! You hate it because you're dead, and it's alive!"

"It is your child, my dear, all yours, but maybe I can give it a kind of godfather's blessing." Adam turned now to the doorway.

Ada took a quick, remorseful step to his side. "Oh, Adam, forgive me. I'm wrought up. I don't know what I'm saying."

"You've never been more articulate, my dear. I see now that you are simply fulfilling your destiny. One of these days you'll write a wonderful novel about a woman who rid herself of the man she married before she knew what she was worth."

Ada stepped back. "I had no idea you could be so cruel."

"Learn, then. For you will make use of me, too. Oh, I can see it, again and again! The future will be full of university theses written about the question of who was the model of the arid dilettante, the cold epicure, the bloodless formalist, who appears so frequently in the novels of Ada Guest. He won't be hard to find. I shall have my little black spot in your shining sun."

"Adam!" She suddenly threw her arms about his neck in a violent reversal of mood and pressed her head to his shoulder. "Whatever we say to each other, I'll never forget my debt to you."

"Thank you, Ada," he said serenely. "That is more than generous. Now I must go."

5

Three years later, on a cold March evening, Adam sat at his corner table in the vast square bar of the Patroons'. The ceiling, sixty feet high, was decorated with a fresco that showed Peter Stuyvesant, standing by a fort with the harbor behind him, receiving a wreath from a tall Indian goddess representing the spirit of Manhattan. Immense canvases, gilt framed, covered the walls with dusty revolutionary ardor. The massive bar, on which sixty men could lean, ran down one whole side of the chamber. Adam sat alone at a corner table, as was his wont when expecting a friend for a private talk.

He looked at his watch. Bob Guest was now a minute late. He had ordered the soufflé for eight. Well, he would eat it at that time, Bob or no Bob. He lifted his gin to his lips and experienced its cold consolation. He enjoyed the sudden rattle in the steam pipe under the window. Outside was freezing weather. It was agreeable to feel safe, safe from the cold, the poor, the women. There had to be moments, even in the best organized lives, when a man gave in to the urge to

shiver, to bundle up, to stamp his feet in an ecstasy of imagined security.

He supposed that he was preparing himself for the intrusion of
Bob. The latter was not apt to enhance illusions of safety. Word had
come from Paris about his increased drinking, his womanizing. Ada's
greater fame and income had simply expanded the audience of his
follies. But now that Adam caught sight of the red face above the
light tweeds approaching him through the tables, he was agreeably
surprised. Bob's stride was firm, his aspect resolute. Adam was again
surprised to hear his now seated guest order a lemonade.

"Is that a taste you picked up in Paris?"

"That is just one of the things I picked up in Paris. My education,
Adam, was considerable."

"How did you leave Ada?"

"As well as a woman can be who has got precisely what she
wanted."

"Surely you don't refer to your absence?"

"No. As to that she was quite indifferent. I gave Ada something of
much greater value. I asked my lawyer to instruct hers that I should
not oppose her suit for divorce."

Adam nodded slowly several times. "So it's come to that. At last."

"Why should I stand in Ada's way? The proceedings should be
simple enough. There's no question of settlements or of custody of
children."

"Does she wish to remarry?"

"I doubt it. But she certainly wishes to be free. Let me tell you
about it now, and then we can have a pleasant dinner over other subjects. When I went to Paris, as you may remember, I was determined
to be good. I was going to learn French. I was going to moderate my
drinking. I was going to see if I couldn't be a proper husband to a
great writer. Well, things started well enough. The apartment was
beautiful. Ada wrote in the mornings, and in the afternoons we went
sightseeing—always, of course, to places she picked. The evenings
were more social. Ada managed to put together a kind of salon, if a
rather frowzy one: expatriates with artistic leanings who were 'misunderstood' at home, sexual deviates who thought they were geniuses
because they were persecuted, retired pedants, rich old maids. But I
was always polite. I mixed their drinks and listened to their stories.
And do you think Ada appreciated it?"

"Not a bit."

"How do you know that?"

"I know Ada. It's a dangerous thing to get between a woman and her favorite grudge. She was determined that you were a trial to her."

Bob looked at Adam admiringly. "You *do* know her. Ada became more and more irritable. And even bossier. She found what she called my Philistinism unbearable. But I could have put up with that. After all, I had heard that song often enough at home. What broke me in the end was the condescending kindness of her new friends. There was one of them who particularly rubbed me the wrong way, an old bachelor, Percy Hunt, the major-domo of Ada's little court. He was always 'including' me, the desiccated bastard. 'And now let us hear from dear Robert,' he would keep yapping. 'What do *you* think, Robert? Oh, indeed? Now *that* is interesting. Did you all hear what Robert said?' It drove me wild, Adam! Hunt was always delegating one of the little group to take care of me. It wasn't Ada's idea. I might have been touched if it had been. But she couldn't have cared less. The sorriest old Sapphist in her salon cared more about me than she did."

"You're very free with Ada's friends."

"Well, I can always tell if a group is out of the top drawer or not. I was born with that smell. Ada had it, too, but she's lost it. She wants to be a frog so big you can't even see the puddle. The great American lady of letters surrounded by her adoring court! Obedience and homage—that's what she's after now."

Adam wrinkled his nose. "She was more selective here."

"Ah, but she was just a little frog here. She's grown up now. But let me finish my sad tale. I began to be maddened by my gentle treatment as Ada's illiterate husband. I started drinking again. There were scenes—I won't go into them. But Ada complained to her group about her maltreatment, and, Christ, you should have heard the wails and ululations of the old eunuchs and dried up cows! 'Poor Ada, what her husband puts her through!' I was made to feel a brute, a cad. When I came into the parlor they all stared at me as if I were a mad dog. I took up with other women, whores mostly. The wails became deafening. 'Ah, dear, *dear* Ada!' And do you know what I began to understand, Adam? Ada was putting it all on! She was deliberately acting the martyred wife to her gallery of wizened dilettantes. She was determined to be rid of me, to drive me out and to be the wronged spouse to boot. Oh, yes, however wronged, she had to be right!"

Adam, sipping his gin, felt uneasy and depressed. He did not doubt Bob's story; he could put it together only too sharply himself.

But it was sickening to him to have to accept such meanness in a woman whom he had helped to shape. "She's an artist," a voice within him murmured. "She's the finest writer you've ever known. You had a role in the creation of her works. What more do you want in a lifetime? Was Wagner kind? Didn't Shakespeare leave his wife to go to London? Don't you remember the Dickens' scandal?"

Bob's tale rose now to its climax:

"Finally I asked myself: 'Who do you think you are, Robert Guest, that you should win a game with the smartest woman in America? Do you think she's ever going to come to you and beg for a divorce? And what good would such a petty triumph do you? Let her be right! Ask *her* for it. And maybe when she's rid of you and happy in her own self-indulgence, she'll write her greatest novel. You can do *that* for letters, Robert Guest, you worthless drunk!"

"You mean you can do it for yourself," Adam corrected him sternly. "You can do it for sobriety and manhood."

But Bob seemed hardly to take this in. "What about you?" he asked. "Will you be going over to Paris to see Ada?"

"Oh, no. I doubt that Ada will want to see me again. Ada has all the material on Adam Winthrop she can possibly use."

"She's got enough of me, too." Bob's tone for the first time that evening was bitter. "You've been a true friend to both of us, Adam. It mortifies me to think I used to accuse you of being too close to Ada. As if anyone could be!"

"Oh, Ada has her passions. Your revenge will be that you may come to represent something to her that she has too lightly put aside."

"You mean if Europe doesn't work out?"

"Yes. And it may not. Take Ada's last book. I thought I could detect already a note of dryness. Of Gallic polish. The beginnings of intellectualization. It's not the right air for her. In France she has nothing but her past. That in time will dim. She ought to come back, but she won't."

"What a tragedy."

"A tragedy, Bob? Isn't that a strong word for it?"

"If Ada doesn't achieve the first rank in literature, where are you and I?" Bob asked, shaking his head. "What have we been but early chapters—or maybe footnotes—in the great biography?"

"I think we make too much of geniuses." Adam peered down into his gin as if to make out the future in it. Decidedly, he rejected Bob's version of his role. "Genius is a combination of so many things. The luck to be born at the right time. The luck to spot the things in which people of the future will be interested. The luck to have the right subject and the right audience cohere. The luck to run into the people who inspire one. The luck to have any readers at all. There is something petty and peevish about this modern yearning for literary fame. Look at Shakespeare who did not even bother to print his plays! And think of the author of the greatest two-volume novel ever written: the Gospel according to St. Luke and the Acts of the Apostles. We hardly know anything about him. Was it Luke or somebody writing under the name of Luke? And who was Luke, anyway?"

Bob smiled. "Are you trying to tell me that Ada is vulgar?"

"Oh, my poor friend. I'm sorry. Yes, she's very vulgar. The way she has treated you is in the worst possible taste."

"And you wouldn't change places with her?"

"Never!"

"I don't believe you."

"Don't, my dear fellow, if you don't want to, don't. Have it your own way. Good heavens!" Adam checked the clock on the mantel with a glance at the heavy gold watch that he removed with difficulty from his waistcoat pocket. "It is after eight. We have dallied tonight. I tremble for the soufflé."

(VII)

The Mystic Journal

THERE HAD HARDLY BEEN a time in Danny Buck's fifty-six years when he had not been spoken of as living in the shadow of Titus Larsen. But in the earlier time this condition had been less umbrageous. Through a Worcester childhood of the eighteen-seventies, in public and high school, through Boston University and Harvard Divinity, through their joint proprietorship of a private day school in Boston, right up to the climactic moment when Larsen had received his call to become headmaster of the great boys' academy at Farmingdale, the two had considered themselves as a kind of pedagogical and ecclesiastical partnership. It was true that Titus had always been the senior partner and Danny the junior, but after Titus had accepted the Farmingdale offer, upon the condition, soon accepted by its board of trustees, that Danny Buck go with him as chaplain, the distance had widened to a point where they could hardly be called partners at all. In the next quarter of a century Titus had become the great New England headmaster, revered, quoted, admired, feared, loved, hated, while Danny had been simply "Mr. B," his confidant, his executive assistant, his man Friday, never his gray eminence.

The difference was further accentuated by their physical sizes. Danny Buck was "little Mr. B," an amiable, joking, kindly fellow, with bushy gray hair, a bristling gray mustache, deep brown eyes and a rolling gait. Even though capable of quelling an army of boys by raising his voice to a thunder peal in a rare burst of temper, he was still known as a basic "softy" because of his tender heart. The headmaster, on the contrary, was a kind of Jove. The boys never knew what to expect of *him*. He was a huge, gaunt, craggy man with an ugly, pale, big-featured face under straight, slick brown hair parted in the center. He could be as still as a rocky mountain peak and move as rapidly as a startled lizard. His eyes were small and piercing, but of a radiant blue that might have been a benign sky or an avenging heaven. Ambling ceaselessly about his campus, "prowling" as some said, "overlording it" in the term of others, an ominous or beloved but to all tireless overseer, he was as central a feature as the Gothic dormitories, the red brick gymnasium, the startling great ark of the Frank Lloyd Wright Library, as indigenous as the sky-reaching elms and the emerald grass on a June day. Titus Larsen had become a synonym for Farmingdale.

He had even reversed by his marriage the social head start which Danny Buck had originally had on him. In Worcester, Dr. Buck, Danny's father, a beloved pediatrician, had perched on a higher peg than that occupied by Larsen, Senior, a foreman at the pencil factory. And Danny's mother had boasted descent from colonial governors, including Winthrop and Dudley, while Mrs. Larsen had been a mere hospital nurse. But when Titus and Danny, as the two young clerical proprietors of a fashionable Boston day school, had found themselves invited, on rare occasions, to the houses of their pupils, it was Titus who had plucked the fruit of such opportunities. He had planted himself in the affections of none less than a Miss Lowell. This young lady, a determined soul, had not only overcome the natural objections of her family, but had actually put her father to work to make her suitor more eligible by Lowell standards by obtaining for him the Farmingdale position. As first lady of that school, through the ensuing decades of their happy marriage, she had continued to enlist parental and financial support from the great families of Beacon Street and Commonwealth Avenue.

Danny had never consciously resented his friend's success. Indeed, until his own marriage in 1912, twenty years after Larsen's, he had been hardly aware that it was something a subordinate might be expected to resent. He had been perfectly content with his own place on the steps to the throne and with his role of spiritual advisor to four hundred boys, brands to be plucked from the crackling bonfire of a New England materialism. Little "Mr. B" was loved on the campus in a way that the headmaster never sought or even desired to be. If the latter was a high, judging deity, was not the role of the pleader, the interceder, the Virgin, an equally attractive one? Danny was simpler but more human than his superior. He could swap funny stories with the smallest boy and join in a rousing chorus with the glee club. And he had an esthetic side, too, far more sensitive than

Larsen's, manifested in his love of Milton and Shakespeare and the language of the King James Bible. Oh, yes, he had his own domain at Farmingdale.

It may seem odd to have compared the diminutive but virile Danny Buck with the Virgin, but until the age of forty-seven, when he married Abby Frost, ten years his junior, he had been sexually pure. She was the spinster daughter and housekeeper of a retired Latin teacher, Lyman Frost, who lived just off the campus. Plain and prematurely gray, she was widely respected for her cheerfulness in what struck most observers as a rather bleak existence. Danny had long admired the high spirit with which she assisted Mrs. Larsen on "parlor nights," when the boys played games at the headmaster's, and the unfailing patience which she showed with her long-winded, senile progenitor. It seemed to him that if there were one perfect Christian soul in that academic community, it might be hers. Suppose he were to offer to share her burden? Suppose he were to bring love to that benighted heart? Would their union not be something beautiful, something that showed God's glory in what seemed a rather gray patch of the Farmingdale quilt?

It had come as a distinct surprise to Danny that his proposal did not surprise Abby more. She seemed to have a clearer idea of her worth than he had imagined. But what came as an even greater surprise was the abrupt transfer of her allegiance to him. Her father was placed in a nursing home—a very pleasant one, it was true, and near enough so that Abby could visit him daily—and the brightened-up, renovated Frost shingle cottage became a school social center second only to the headmaster's house. Abby loved the husband who had liberated her quite as strongly as he had hoped she might, but at the same time she placed herself firmly in charge of a career that she considered to have been grossly neglected.

"Titus Larsen has taken advantage of you ever since you were born," she used to tell Danny. "It's high time that you were appreciated for yourself."

There were days when Abby's love and warm heart made their home the patch of glory that Danny had originally envisioned. But there were others when her bustling presence about the campus and his vision of her flying gray hair and eager eyes, his vivid sense of her intentionally offered contrast to the sleek, chic smoothness of the headmaster's wife, caused Danny pain and even mortification. It was as if he were some humble knight, seeking to slip unobtrusively from the tourney to the refuge of a nearby cloister, only to hear his shrill recall by trumpet and the proclamation of his martial prowess against all challengers. Abby was bound to see to it that her Danny had his due. Perhaps, misguided female, she even wanted him to be a bishop!

"You don't have to worry about these things," she would insist. "You just go ahead and be yourself. Leave the public relations to me. I think I see where I'm coming out!"

And indeed she might have come out almost anywhere had she not been struck down by cancer. Her courage to the end was almost unbearable. It would have been a kindness to her loved ones had she once broken down. And when it was all over, and Danny was almost suffocated by the hot pillow of genuine sympathy that was pressed down upon him by a thousand hands, he wondered with near indignation why God had not taken *him*. Why could the dread disease not have torn at his innards? How welcome it would have been!

In time Danny learned to live with the spectral companion of his relief at being alone again. After all, God had made man subject to temptation, and this was manifestly one of them. The Devil hoped to snare him with despair: despair that he could be a Christian and at the same time feel anything but desolation at the loss of such a light as Abby. No, a man had to face everything, including the smallness of his own nature, the meanness of his soul.

He was happiest now in chapel. It was an oblong edifice of rusty-red stone with two rows of vast stained-glass windows which blinded the eye on a sunny day. The pews, on either side of the aisle, faced each other under a top row of Gothic choir seats. Memorial slabs for the young dead were everywhere to be seen, and by the font at the end of the nave an immense marble angel brooded over a marble lieutenant who had died in Cuba. When Danny preached on Sundays, the school, the parents, the visiting trustees, the parish, the neighboring village itself were all his. Then the quiet little man seemed to be sublimated into the rich, resonant voice, so slow, so articulate, at times so almost awesome, seemingly controlled by that steadily rising and falling white-robed arm.

"The parlance of the modern world, my boys, is full of new terms which aim to make weak men feel at ease with themselves. Why do I drink? I have an anxiety problem. Why do I steal? I have a compulsion. Why do I murder? I am obsessed. Why do I covet my neighbor's wife? My flesh controls me. True, perhaps. But boys, there still exists a simple adjective that we should never forget. Why do I do these things? Because I am wicked! And, boys, I bless that word, wicked! It gives me back my will. It gives me back my choice. It gives me back my soul!"

He knew that he was a great preacher. He could sense it in the hush of the packed chapel, in the silent, pressed handshakes after the service. Larsen's sermons were full of hackneyed terms and repetitions. Larsen had the school, but Danny had the chapel. They might have been some old emperor and pope of the Middle Ages, a Henry IV, a Gregory VII, dividing the rule of man's body and man's spirit. Oh yes, they were a team, or at least they had been. Abby had never comprehended that.

But Abby had died in 1915. Two years later Danny went to the trenches in France as an army chaplain, though he was over fifty. On a leave in October of 1918, he made a pilgrimage to the ruins of the great medieval abbey at Cluny, once the religious center of France. During his week there he would sit for an hour at a time in the shell of the remaining tower, trying to visualize the immensity and grandeur of the ancient church. And then, of a sudden, it came to him one morning, a vivid, living sense of a reconstructed interior, with a high vaulted ceiling, impossibly high, and windows that seemed to thrust their Roman arches heavenward like fireworks, and cold, aching cold, with mist permeating the interior and a distant choir chanting a blood-curdling Dies Irae. He was no longer Danny Buck, or perhaps he was a forebear, a monk in medieval times who was indifferent to all hardships and dangers so long as he could spend his waking hours in the great church, which was a kind of heaven, or anticipation of heaven, or perhaps heaven itself, at least that part of it caught by the intersection of the earthly and the heavenly arcs. Danny seemed to be passing into a kind of trance; he felt that he might even be losing consciousness.

But he did not lose consciousness. On the contrary, he found himself sitting up all at once very straight on his seat in the empty chapel with a distinct image in his now alert mind. The image was of Titus Larsen. He, too, was apparently in Cluny, but he was a gargoyle, way high up in the tower, on the outside, far above Danny's head. And he was not a grinning gargoyle, either. The square head with the small staring eyes was solemn—solemn and hostile. He was staring out over the Burgundian countryside of whose beauties he was totally unaware, looking north towards the war front where the Germans were in retreat. But Larsen was unconscious of the Germans, too. He might have been thinking of nothing but himself. Of himself and his own bad temper.

Danny was considerably upset by this image. He supposed that it must represent a latent hostility to the headmaster. Had he always, deep down, hated Larsen? This was an idea that would not have been shocking to some of his younger friends who kept up to date with the latest medical opinions from Vienna, but it was very shocking to Danny, who believed that a true Christian was judged just as much by what he thought as by what he did—perhaps more so.

He returned to the front just in time for the armistice, and in the celebrations that followed, and even on the troop ship going home, he found himself much preoccupied with the question of his new attitude towards his old friend. When he returned to Farmingdale, however, he discovered, almost to his relief, the possibility of a different, though sadder, solution to his Burgundian revelation. For Larsen, in the year and a half of Danny's absence, had drastically changed. He had become like the gargoyle Buddha! Had it been intuition on Danny's part? Had he divined from the long years of his intimacy with the headmaster just how the latter would change at just this critical time of his life?

Danny was not the only member of the faculty to note the change. Far from it. The other teachers, always conscious of his intimacy with the headmaster, were cautious about criticizing the latter, but in the short time that it takes in any academic community, the truth came out. Danny even learned the opinion of the younger masters that the headmaster was undergoing a kind of male menopause. He was sharper, louder, intolerant of criticism. He ruled by fiat rather than consultation. And he was particularly violent in his religious opinions. He refused even to speak to his daughter Hilda, who had married a divorced man. He walked out of a public dinner in Boston because the speaker of the evening had simply predicted the ultimate reuniting of the Catholic and Protestant churches. His sermons were full of wrath.

Larsen's attitude towards Danny had also changed, but there seemed to be nothing personal about this. It was part of the general pattern. He avoided his old friend and shunned intimate talks. Under ordinary circumstances Danny might have considered taking himself and his sermons to another school, but these were not ordinary circumstances. If Titus Larsen was going to pieces, it was Danny's duty to remain at his post. Perhaps that had been the meaning of the image at Cluny.

2

In early October of 1919, shortly after the opening of the school term, Danny had a conversation which seemed to justify his gloomiest apprehensions. It was with Ethelred Eames, chairman of the Farmingdale Board of Trustees. Eames, a muscular bachelor of fifty, was considered the most brilliant investment banker on Federal Street. His passionate devotion to the school, combined with his large donations, enabled him to dominate his board. He was one of those shrewd, practical men of affairs whose emotional life is concentrated on a totally retained but highly idealized image of happy school days. The boyish Ethelred Eames survived in the man of middle years like an artificial organ.

"I know your loyalty and devotion to Titus, Danny," Eames told him as they walked on a Sunday afternoon through the golden woods by the slowly eddying river, "but it is your bounden duty to set the school first. I may have to consider putting to the board the advisability of Titus' forced retirement. But before I take any such drastic step, I must be absolutely sure of my facts. That is where you must help me. I want you to promise to keep an eye on Titus throughout this school year."

"Keep an eye on him?" Danny interrupted indignantly, stopping to face his interlocutor. "How can you say such a thing, Eth? What else do you suppose my life has been but watching Titus Larsen?"

"I am aware of that. But there are eyes and eyes. What I want you to do is to cast a cold, clinical eye on our friend. For the good of the school, Danny. For *his* good." Eames let himself go now by throwing up his arms. "For the glory of God, if you will."

"I do not will," Danny retorted severely. "And what do you suggest I do after I have completed this cold analysis? Go to Titus Larsen in the Garden of Gethsemane and kiss him on the cheek? And then collect my thirty pieces of silver from you?"

"You're not going to succeed in provoking me, Danny. Do you think that I have not rehearsed this scene a dozen times? It is too serious for melodrama."

Danny walked on again, staring into the muddy water of the sluggish stream. What was Eames doing but reciting his own fears?

"When you have completed your cold analysis," Eames continued inexorably, "you will necessarily know what you consider to be in the school's best interests. I suggest that it may help you to keep a journal, with carefully recorded facts and dates. If you decide that Titus should retire, you will surely, as his oldest friend, deem it your duty to tell him so. And if he rejects the suggestion, I do not see what you can do but resign. Your continued association after any such discussion would be unthinkable."

Danny paused to think this out. "And my resignation, I suppose, would be your signal."

"It would be *a* signal."

"I see. So I should never have to speak to you."

"Or to any of the board," Eames responded eagerly. "You won't even have to tell me now if you have shared my suspicions. I ask nothing of you, Danny, don't you see? Nothing dishonorable, that is."

"Nothing and everything. Suppose I go now to Titus and report our conversation?"

"Go ahead. What can he say? There is nothing you can possibly do that will not assist me."

"Assist you in what?"

"In finding out what I have to find out. What it's my obvious duty to find out!"

"Eth Eames, I believe you're some kind of fiend!"

"Even a fiend can love his school."

At this point Eames saw that he had gone as far as he needed. He was a man who knew when to let well enough alone. Abruptly now he turned his talk to what was wrong with the Farmingdale football team. He discussed this for the rest of their walk while Danny, not attending to him, pondered his earlier words.

Danny was deeply troubled in the next days. It appeared to him that he was already entangled in Eames's net. For the eye that he now fixed upon the headmaster, in chapel, in assembly, in dining hall, at evening prayers, was the eye of the diagnostician. Nothing of Larsen's exterior would henceforth escape Danny Buck, not the least flicker of those leather-like eyelids, not the smallest twist of that thick, rugged neck. In the brief time that it takes a suspicion to evolve into a policing force, the master of Farmingdale had become a fat beetle wriggling under the pin which his junior had inserted in the middle of his shiny black back.

"I think, if you don't mind, Danny, I'll take the sermon for Thanksgiving. I know it has been traditionally yours, but this year I feel I have a particular message . . ."

What did *that* mean? Or again:

"I have been wondering, Danny, about the effect on the boys of card games on parlor night. I realize that for the most part they play harmless things like hearts or old maid, but some of the older ones have recently been playing bridge. Does that not tempt them to gamble? Katherine, I admit, thinks I make too much of this . . ."

Danny had always been interested in writing, and as a young man he had even contemplated a career as a novelist. But he had always had a lurking sense that it might be wrong to fabricate human souls and play with them like dolls. Had God not given us real humans to care about? After he received his call to the ministry, he limited his literary talent to the composition of sermons. Compiled in a volume entitled *Talks to Boys* and published by Little Brown these had enjoyed a considerable success. Now he began to wonder if Eth Eames's idea of a journal might not result in a book at least as morally useful as the Little Brown volume—even if it had only one reader, himself. Why should he not seek the objectivity that he so desperately needed by sketching Titus Larsen in the pages of a notebook? He would be careful to use the same thick, expensive paper on which he wrote his sermons.

One Saturday night, sitting up late, he began the experiment.

Entry 1

Titus Larsen has always professed to care a great deal for his parish. Of course, this is limited to the school grounds, for the Bishop understands that the headmaster of a church school cannot be expected to undertake ordinary parish duties. But the boundaries nonetheless include the cottages of the masters and, here and there, a household not directly connected with the academic community. To watch Larsen shining his ecclesiastical benignity on an individual of the latter category is always diverting. He makes a great show of sweeping the litter of his headmaster's life to the floor in order to devote his total attention even to the poorest and humblest of his flock. "Busy, Mrs. Naitches, certainly not!" he exclaims to the old crone in his doorway. "Come in, come in, by all means, and let us discuss the adventures of human souls!"

Today he kept his board of trustees waiting twenty minutes while he was closeted with Mrs. Naitches. When he emerged at last, it was to lead her slowly past the open doors of the board room so that all might observe his intent air of listening to the widow's high, deaf chatter. Richard III, in the great scene where he demonstrates his piety to the Mayor of London, was not a more consummate hypocrite!

*

Danny now contemplated the above, written out in his round, clear hand, without a single erasure or correction, with awe. Already it seemed a thing with an existence independent of himself. Would the paper even tear if he tried to tear it? But he did not try to tear it. He put it away carefully in a leather folder in a locked drawer.

A week later he took it out and reread it. It struck him that the two paragraphs were prosy, even prim. Why did he take such satisfaction in his analogy to the scene in *Richard III*? Would a man who was deeply and morally committed to the examination of the fitness for office of his closest friend and immediate superior indulge in such literary flourishes? Was there a place for art in the truly serious task? Had that not been the reason for his early distrust of fiction and his confinement of his literary talent to sermons where God might be expected to keep it in rein?

For the next few weeks Danny made no further entries in the journal. When he caught himself reflecting, after some peculiarly turbulent remark of Titus Larsen's, that it would make a fine passage for his notes, he reproved himself. What he was committed to do was to form an impression, to make an assessment, and for this no jotting down of clever comments and no composition of beautiful paragraphs was required. He did not, after all, have to justify himself. He had only to be just.

The episode of Dillon Low, however, seemed to require a further entry in the journal. Danny found that he could not handle it alone. Dillon Low was a teacher of English, a bachelor, and the master in charge of a fourth form dormitory in Satterlee House. He was thirty-five, although he appeared younger, and had a delicate, blond charm, despite his air of intensity. He was, if anything, too conscientious about his pedagogical duties and seemed to have no life outside the school. Danny, on more than one occasion, had had to counsel him to moderate his enthusiasms.

"It is not complimentary to God, Dillon," he had warned him, "to assume that He expects the impossible."

"I drive myself no harder than you do, dear Mr. B."

"But you, my boy, are not an old widower. You must try to relax and enjoy life."

Danny had become very fond of Dillon, and the latter had

confided to him his secret yearning to become a minister. Only he was not sure that his call was a true one. On Sunday afternoons the two would walk by the river to discuss God and man at Farmingdale. Danny had been almost ready to recommend that the great step be taken when the crisis broke.

After it was over, Danny reached for his journal almost as he might have reached for a pain killer. He had to put down his impressions somewhere. The blank white page to which he turned seemed to wrinkle and throb before his intently staring eyes. It might have been a thirsty mouth, or two great sucking lips which would attach themselves to his very heart and drain out the painful picture there. He blinked and looked away. He sighed and coughed. At last he took firm hold of his pen.

Entry 2

This is how it started. Last summer Dillon Low went on a walking tour of the English lake country. Carried away by thoughts of Keats on a similar expedition, he wrote some overflowing epistles to Timmy Stearns, a thick-set, muscular fellow who had been assigned to Low for extra tutoring in English. Stearns, when school reopened, happened to show these to a malevolent friend of his, Alan Webb. Webb interpreted the letters in the vilest possible way and, snickering, passed them about the form. Stearns, a well-liked boy, did not choose to risk his popularity by siding with a teacher. He joined the snickerers.

When poor Dillon at last grasped what was going on, he came to me in the greatest distress.

"I was trying to describe what it felt like to be smitten with a sudden overwhelming sense of the English poets. The English in Keats's day were much less inhibited about emotion. I don't know how they came to be as stiff as they are now. Consider Shakespeare's sonnets, Mr. B!"

I looked into his dazzled, boyish, absurd blue eyes and sighed. If he dwelt with the English poets, where did the snickering boys of the corridors and dormitories of Farmingdale dwell?

"We must live in this world, Dillon," I cautioned him. "Half the troubles of mankind arise from misconstruction. A bachelor master who writes affectionate letters to a handsome boy is always going to have to face raised eyelids."

"Mr. B!" he cried, jumping up. "Surely, you don't think . . . you, of all people . . ."

"No, my dear fellow, I think nothing. I should vouch for your morals anywhere. But we have to concern ourselves with the appearance of evil. To so many of our benighted brethren it is the same as evil itself."

"You mean I shouldn't express myself candidly to a friend?"

"Not when that friend is a boy at school. Look where your candor has got you. But I shall speak to Webb. I shall see that he delivers those letters to me. Let us hope that will be the end of it."

I made my talk with Webb as brief as possible. It is always very painful to me to dislike a boy at Farmingdale; it seems the repudiation of a teacher's most basic duty. But there are cases where it is impossible to avoid this, and Webb's is certainly one. He is the son of very social and worldly parents, so spoiled and arrogant that he cannot manage to hide his contempt for so poor a creature as a schoolmaster. I marvel at the resources of a deity who could create him and Dillon Low out of the same human material. The boy actually had the effrontery to ask me what I wanted the letters for.

"Never mind that," I told him gruffly. "All that need concern you is that you have been passing around letters that were written neither by you nor to you."

"Excuse me, Mr. Buck. I had the permission of the recipient."

"But not of the sender! You will deliver these wrongfully published letters to me. All of them and at once. Unless, of course, you wish to appeal to the headmaster, in which case you run the risk that he may take an even graver view of your offense."

No boy ever dared to take a chance on what Titus Larsen would think or do, and the letters were delivered to me within the hour.

Webb, Dillon informed me, had been scrutinizing my position as senior master. With the sharp nostrils of an old time European palace courtier he must have flared the declining intimacy between myself and the headmaster. Or is it all simpler than I have supposed? Have things reached the point where Larsen is making critical remarks about his faculty—and me—to the boys themselves?

What, at any rate, I next discovered was that Webb was circulating copies of Dillon's letters which he had made before surrendering the originals to me. As this was direct disobedience —at least as I interpreted it—I took the matter up directly with Larsen. Naturally the headmaster asked to see the letters, and I gave them to him. When he had had a chance to read them, he sent for me again. I did not like the suggestion of a smile that played around the corners of that big crooked mouth over that granite jaw.

"This is a bad business, Danny," he began. "A very bad one."

"I quite agree, sir." It was always my custom to address him as "sir" when we discussed school business. "Webb has not only behaved with shocking malice. He has challenged my authority, and through mine, yours. It seems to me that he should be at least suspended."

"Have you stopped to consider how that would look, Danny? Have you tried to picture the reaction of Mr. and Mrs. Webb when they learn their son has been suspended from Farmingdale for warning his form mates that intimacy with Mr. Low may be expected to result in overtures of an indelicate sentimentality?"

"Indelicate?" I stared at Larsen's small, intent eyes. "Do you mean that you think Low has been capable of sodomy? Surely you wouldn't keep him in the school a minute after such an idea became a conviction!"

"May I remind you, Danny," the headmaster retorted testily, "that before this morning, when you brought me these repellent epistles, I had no conception that Mr. Low was capable of writing such filth. All I knew was that I disliked him."

"You disliked him!"

"That surprises you? I found him soft. I had been wondering if Farmingdale was the place for him. Knowing what I now know, I am decidedly of the opinion that if a disciplinary question has been raised, it concerns Low far more than it concerns Webb!"

"Then you must believe that he has been guilty of some kind of immorality," I said, shaking my head sadly. "For the life of me, I cannot see that the letters prove that."

"I do not say that the letters prove that. I simply state that a headmaster must recognize where such things may lead. Soft sentiments followed by soft letters may be followed by soft embracements."

I turned away impatiently from what seemed to be almost his leer. "I have considered him a candidate for the ministry," I said gravely. "I am convinced that he is as pure in body as in soul."

Larsen now adopted the faintly weary look of the man of the world, of the great archbishop who envies the simple parish priest his isolation from secular cares. "My dear Danny, there are moments when I wish I had a faith in human nature like yours. But it behooves a headmaster to keep abreast of the times. The writings and discoveries of Doctor Freud have become a part of the world in which we must live."

"I am quite aware of Doctor Freud, Titus."

"Then you should be aware of the role played by the subconscious. There is little doubt in my mind that Dillon Low is at least subconsciously homosexual. These letters are love letters. Read them, Danny!"

"I have read them. They are affectionate letters, it is true. They may even be called sentimental. But I am convinced that they were never intended to arouse improper sentiments. The mere suggestion of that has been enough to reduce poor Dillon Low to a near breakdown . . ."

"But the very violence of such a reaction," Larsen broke in triumphantly, "must in itself point to a kind of guiltiness!"

"Because an innocent man would not be shocked?" I cried, staring at Larsen until he turned impatiently away. "How am I to value such innocence? I tell you, Titus, that when you judge a man by the evil which you read into his subconscious, you are usurping God's role. What is this subconscious of yours but original sin? Surely we do not condemn a man who lusts but triumphs over his lust? And you would condemn one who does not even *know* that he lusts?"

"I am not really concerned with your friend Low," Larsen replied, thoroughly irritated now. "I am concerned with protecting my school from the most repulsive of vices to which boys' schools are subject. I had rather rid myself of ten innocent masters than have one child corrupted!"

"I suggest then that you employ only women teachers."

"Danny, you're being ridiculous. But I tell you what I'll do. I'll meet you halfway. I'll give Mr. Low a fair chance. I shall ask for his pledge that he will never write another letter to a boy or see any boy alone except in his study in the School House during class hours. I shall also suggest that his continued tenure may depend upon his early marriage."

"My God, Titus!"

Larsen arose. "Will you tell him that I wish to see him now? Or shall I send for him?"

"Send for him, by all means. I want no part in your matchmaking."

I returned to my own study, into which, a half-hour later, Dillon burst with stricken countenance.

"Do you know what he told me, Mr. B?"

"Come with me to the chapel, my friend. I prefer to discuss it with you there."

In chapel we sat together in two of the choir seats. It was late in the afternoon, and the organist was practicing a piece by Purcell.

"You must learn, Dillon," I told him gently, "that what has happened may be a message from God. He has put men like Titus Larsen on earth for a purpose. That purpose, in your case, may be to try your faith. You must learn to put him aside. You must learn to stand on your own feet—to be a man."

"Aren't you begging the question, Mr. B?" Low asked in a horrid, sneering tone, and I realized now that I could only pray. Larsen had reached him.

*

Danny, rereading this entry, was shocked by the final sentence. What had he meant by saying that Larsen had "reached" Dillon? Was that not a dramatic, even a melodramatic, conclusion? Did it sound like Daniel Buck or did it sound like a modern novel? Was he trying to assess his thoughts about Titus Larsen, or was he engaged in the composition of a twentieth century *Pilgrim's Progress*? What gave him even more concern was that he could not recollect consciously thinking that Larsen had ever "reached" Dillon before he had actually penned that word in the journal. When had this conception of the headmaster as a satanic agent struck him? Did the evidence not point to the fact that his theorizing and his journalizing were not necessarily one and the same thing? And if this was the case, was it not possible that the journal had some kind of an independent existence of its own, an existence which might well be evil?

Danny closed the notebook now and looked at its black leather cover with something like repulsion. It had a smooth, smug, gleaming, fatuous look. It seemed to be saying: "Insult me if you wish. Rant and rave at me. Slam me shut. Lock me in drawers. But you will come back to me. You will open me up. You will write your horrid thoughts in me. You have no alternative. And you know it!" He picked up the notebook and threw it in the top drawer of his desk and turned the lock. He resolved once more that he would not write in it again.

But the fatal temptation came back the very next week. On the following Monday every boy and master at Farmingdale was discussing the profanity of Jim Rogers and what Larsen was going to do about it.

Danny had always had ambivalent feelings about how to punish swearing. Traditionally, this had been regarded as a serious offense by the church; its prohibition was the sole function of the Third Commandment. Torture and even death had been known as punishments in ancient days. But Danny felt that he should not altogether ignore the fact that many of the boys at Farmingdale came from homes where fathers, older brothers and even mothers, took the Lord's name in vain as a matter of routine conversational emphasis. The boys so exposed grew up to believe that such language was evidence of strength and virility and that the abstinence from all expletives denoted a speaker as effeminate or "namby-pamby." He had finally made it his own practice to give a boy who cursed six black marks, for each of which the boy had to put in an hour of physical labor on Saturday afternoon. But Danny made it a condition that he had actually to hear the boy cursing. A report would not do.

The headmaster took a very different view. To him profanity was an intolerable offense. "If you lived in the White House, you wouldn't cry, 'President damn it!'" Larsen used to point out. "And if you lived in Buckingham Palace, you wouldn't exclaim 'King damn it!' Why should we allow boys on God's campus to cry: 'God damn it!'? No, Danny, I won't have it. The swearing boy must be sent away!"

Fortunately, Larsen's attitude was so well known at Farmingdale that no master or prefect would ever report a case of profanity to him, and if he asked for what unspecified offenses certain black marks had been handed out, he was told: "Smutty talk." And so great was the awe inspired by the headmaster's presence that there seemed little danger of any oath resounding in his immediate ambience. But the Devil was never at a loss to find an occasion, and Danny now found himself once more seeking the key to open the desk drawer for the hateful journal.

Entry 3

Last Sunday, when Larsen and I retired to the robing room after communion service, we found that the boy whose duty it was to fill the chalice had overestimated the number of communicants. There was a considerable quantity of the consecrated wine left over. It is theoretically the duty of the participating priests to consume this.

"I don't suppose the good Lord expects us to edify our Sunday lunch guests by appearing tipsy, do you, Danny?" Larsen asked me with his stony wink.

"It isn't as if it were a Haut-Brion."

Larsen chuckled in his gravelly way. "Well, here goes." He opened the narrow Gothic window of the little room and flung the contents out. He did not look before he acted, and the wine found an unexpected target, for our ears were assailed with a screeching volley of billingsgate. I do not recall the exact terms, but it is certain that our Lord was described not only as misbegotten but concupiscent, and the Virgin . . . well, as not that. I had assumed that it must be some village tramp awakened from a drunken doze under a bush in the garth when I saw Larsen, who was looking out the window, change expression.

"Rogers!" I heard his startled shout. "Rogers, you will go at once to my study and wait until I arrive."

"Not Jim Rogers?" I gasped in dismay.

"Unhappily, the same."

Jim Rogers was a sixth former, a prefect, expected to graduate in the spring with high honors. Furthermore, his father had donated the great west window of the chapel in memory of the World War dead.

"You must remember, Titus, that it was your fault. You should have looked first."

"It was my fault that I splattered the boy, of course. But was it my fault that those drops of consecrated wine elicited such . . . such horrors?"

"It was the shock. You surprised him."

"It was the shock which revealed all too clearly the phrases uppermost in his mind. Oh, Danny, who is to say that the blessed wine has not accomplished more after the communion service than during it? Laugh at me if you choose, my friend, but there may have been something in the slap of those drops on that boy's head that made the Devil jump out and snarl!"

"Well, if the Devil's out, what more do you ask?"

"I'm afraid he popped right back in again. Rogers, I must surmise, is a vicious youth."

"Oh, Titus, vicious? He's had some bad example, that's all."

"You know as well as I that such an outburst of scurrility could have come only from a hardened user of profanity. Think of the example he must have been setting to younger boys!"

The story flew about the school, and by lunch time four hundred boys and forty masters knew it. The general speculation was that Rogers would get off with a mere six black marks because of his family's wealth and position, factors widely known to weigh heavily with the headmaster. But I reasoned differently. Titus Larsen is a strange composite. If he likes to cultivate the wealthy, he likes also to impress them. When he reaches into his war chest for one of Jehovah's thunderbolts, he can be decidedly democratic, if not downright radical, in his selection of targets. For one must never forget that he tends to identify himself with the deity, which makes him greater than even the wealthiest parents.

I was not surprised, therefore, when he summoned me on Monday morning to his schoolhouse study to tell me that he had decided to expel Rogers.

"I know there'll be a great outcry, but we shall have to face it. I spent two hours in prayer early this morning. At the end of it I felt refreshed and convinced that I had come to the right conclusion. God does not wish to have his name taken in vain at Farmingdale. Let us establish that principle, once and for all, and let the chips fall as they may. What can happen, after all? Parents may remove their boys, and the trustees may close the school. Or get rid of your humble servant. Do you think I care? Will I not have forced them to declare before the world that they have created a school, theoretically devoted to God, but actually abandoned to his vilification?"

There was something splendid about Larsen as he declaimed this. After all, as none knew better than I, there *was* a definite risk of his deposition. His apprehension of this may not have been entirely oratorical. And although I understood that a sense of the drama of one's martyrdom may reduce its agony, there must still have been a residuum of pain to Titus at the idea of stepping down from his great post in a conflict that was bound to appear ridiculous to at least as many persons as those who found it noble. I viewed the craggy features of my old friend's set expression, took in the dull gleam of those small blue eyes and had to conclude that, whatever his faults, however vast his ego, here was a man.

"You're a hard one to disagree with," I told him. "And wherever you go, I'll go with you—even in dissent."

But where I next went was to his house to call on Katherine Larsen. I knew that she would never intervene with Titus unless she were convinced that such intervention was not only essential but sure of success. In such a case, however, she could be depended on to act with tact and speed. She received me in her front parlor while she worked on her needlepoint. She was the neatest, darkest, trimmest little lady in the world. All her movements seemed to be concentrated in her darting hands. Her lips were a thin line, her nose a little beak, her eyes large and blackly intelligent. She heard me to the end without a word of interruption.

"I am afraid the graduate reaction will be unfavorable," I concluded. "Particularly in Boston."

"Why particularly there?"

"Because that is where we find the concentration of the school's principal families."

"Do you intimate that such families approve of profanity?"

"Far from it. But they will find a reaction as violent as Titus' . . ." I paused. "Unseemly."

"Is that the term you're really looking for, Danny? You're not usually at a loss for words."

"I am embarrassed, Katherine. Shall I say vulgar?"

"I see." She nodded, her dark eyes smiling at me. But not her lips. No, not her lips. "The *gratin* in Boston and along the North Shore will find it vulgar—or shall I say, hick—to make such a to-do over a few cuss words in frequent use in the best circles. Is that it?"

"Precisely."

"And where is God, Danny, in all of this?"

"The law has a maxim: *De minimis non curat lex.*"

"The law cares not for trifles. For *lex* you would substitute *Deus?*"

"I should, Katherine."

She seemed impressed by the gravity of my tone. "Then why bring in me? And my family—at least by implication?"

"Because Titus cares so much for your opinion. And for theirs."

"He does not seem to."

"Ah, but that is because it has not been expressed. You see, Katherine, when the rest of us approach him, it is from without. He is standing up there above the portcullis ready to pitch boiling lead down on our heads. You come from within the citadel."

"Judith in the tent of Holofernes." Now at last she laughed. It was a rather dry cackle. "Well, I can try, anyway."

*

Danny did not bother to note in the journal the results of this conversation. Rogers was suspended from school for only a month, which he spent with his family in Palm Beach, sending irritating post cards to his snowed-in classmates at Farmingdale. But this minor victory for the forces of reason and moderation was followed by yet more crises. The furies seemed to be hounding Titus Larsen that winter, and Danny found himself making so many entries that his journal threatened to become a diary. He had a giddy sense of riding some plunging, driven craft on a turbulent sea, headed towards a whirlpool, or, worse, a gigantic sea monster, a mammoth white whale. Surely, Ahab had been no grimmer than the headmaster, posted up there on the quarterdeck, at all times and in all weathers, staring grimly ahead at the misty moral horizon. Danny's doubts deepened about his own role in all of this. Was he, of the simpler faith, of the lesser worldliness, to end up as a temporizer, a conciliator, a trimmer?

Conference followed conference about morals on the campus; faculty meetings proliferated. The masters who served liquor in their houses—were they breaking the law? Were they not at least breaking the moral law by encouraging bootlegging? Could it be tolerated? And what about boys reported to be drinking on the vacations? Drinking, in some cases, to excess? Did the headmaster's jurisdiction extend to this? If not, should it be pushed to it? A bachelor master had announced his engagement to a divorcée whose marital troubles had created great scandal in the Boston evening papers—should his future wife be made welcome at Farmingdale?

It sometimes seemed to Danny that Larsen grew worse as the journal lengthened. It was as if the headmaster, a character in search of an author, had somehow become aware of his junior's jottings and was determined to take them over and blow them up into the great moral novel of the post-war period.

And then, finally, came the episode of the cheating in Sixth-B Science. This cheating had existed for years and was well known to all but Titus Larsen. There were no more than fifteen boys in the class, all drop-outs from the classics. Mr. Hoadley, the teacher, was amiable, but old and dull and rambling. It was his practice to start each period with a ten minute test, and while the class was engaged in writing out the answers, he would slowly chalk a précis of the day's lecture on the blackboard, his back turned to the boys. It soon became the accepted practice of the class to have a single member, chosen by turn, prepare the day's lesson, write out the answers and pass them about for the others to copy. So established had this habit become that it was not regarded as "real" cheating. Indeed, there were boys who took willing part in it who would have been shocked by the suggestion that they had so much as glanced at a neighbor's paper in a "real" examination. But unhappily that winter Mr. Hoadley's Sixth-B had gone too far. He was more senile, they more impudent, and the day had come at last when all fifteen papers had been couched in precisely the same language. The scales had fallen from the old man's weary eyes, and he had taken the offending papers to the headmaster.

Danny observed the next day that there was a good deal of going in and out of the headmaster's study in the schoolhouse. No less than half a dozen masters must have been closeted with Larsen, each for fifteen minutes at a time. The chatter in the corridors was even louder than usual. An air of tenseness pervaded the classrooms. It was evident that Danny was not going to be consulted, which could only mean that Larsen had determined on some grave step which was bound to meet with his junior's disapprobation. And what could that be but the expulsion of fifteen sixth formers one month before their graduation?

Danny returned from his Latin class to his own study at noon, close to tears. It would be the ruin of Farmingdale—at least of the school as he had known it. The expelled boys would never get into college, at least the college of their choice; the parents would be wild, the trustees and graduates outraged. Even if Larsen survived the tumult, what kind of school would be left with half the boys and all the faculty hating him?

Danny stood by the window and looked out at the glorious elms waving gently in the mild early spring breeze. He glanced up at the cerulean sky. He closed his eyes, and his lips moved in prayer. Then his lips ceased to move, and he reopened his eyes. He looked up again at that sky, up and up. He felt himself translated into that blue. His heart began to beat more rapidly as he recognized once again the mystic experience, and he feared that its very beating would interrupt the trance. And then, suddenly, it was over, but it was all right. His prayer was answered. All that he had to do now was to seat himself at his desk, open his journal and turn to a fresh page.

Entry 22

Larsen sent for me immediately after assembly this morning. He was at his most grave, but it struck me that he seemed more subdued than in other critical moments, as if he had received some shocking personal news. His voice quavered slightly.

"You have heard, of course, about Sixth B Science? What are we coming to, Danny? Widespread, unabashed cheating going

on under the very eyes of the instructor! The boys have behaved like the children of poor immigrants in a public school.
Worse! And one of them is a prefect. A prefect, Danny!"

I explained as best I could the sorry tradition of cheating in
Hoadley's class. Larsen surveyed me with eyes of incredulity.

"You are telling me that there are two standards here at
Farmingdale? That a boy may cheat in Class A but not in
Class B?"

"Not really. The vice is confined to a single course. A single
poor exception."

"Which you *knew* about, Danny?"

I shrugged. "Let us put it that I had heard some rumors."

"About which you did nothing?"

"Exactly!" I saw my way out. "About which I did nothing.
So it is really my fault. Not the boys' at all."

"I cannot go that far." Larsen blew out his breath in a deep
windy sigh. "Cheating is still cheating, even if the police force
is lax. It can only be eradicated by a drastic operation."

"Let me resign, then."

"You, Danny, resign? You want me to cut off my right hand?"

We stared at each other in the happy surprise of our suddenly
renewed intimacy. "If thy right hand offend thee . . ." I began.

"No, Danny!" he interrupted, jumping up to come over to
me that he might seize and shake that offending member. "You
and I started together, and we'll end it together! The saddest
part of the past year has been my growing sense of your aliena-
tion from me. Let us heal that rift, my friend."

"You have felt it, then?" I asked in surprise.

"How could I not?"

"I have wondered if you did not simply regard me as an im-
portunate ass. An old friend, to be sure, but one who was getting a bit dotty, possibly a nervous wreck, a war casualty . . ."

"Oh, Danny." Larsen seized me by the shoulders and shook
me violently. "Don't talk that way. You remember what Oc-
tavius said of Antony:

> 'Yet if I knew
> What hoop should hold us staunch, from edge to edge
> of the world, I would pursue it.'

That is how I feel."

"Perhaps there is a way," I suggested now. "Suppose at chapel
next Sunday I tell the school the story of the cheating in Sixth
B Science?"

"Surely they all know it by now."

"Yes, but I mean the *whole* story. How I and other teachers share the guilt by having looked the other way. Suppose I tell them that we all, teachers and boys, bear a joint responsibility for this misfortune—everyone but the headmaster—and that I then ask God for our forgiveness as we rise to our feet."

Larsen had taken his great hands from my shoulders. His blue gaze was serene. "I accept your solution, Danny. With only one amendment. Do *not* except the name of the headmaster. He bears the greatest responsibility of all. For it was he who made the gap between himself and his faculty so wide that none dared tell him what was going on."

I was too moved to answer, but I gripped Titus' hand.

*

Danny looked up from his journal at the boy who had entered after knocking.

"Please, sir, the headmaster wishes to see you."

"The headmaster's wish is my command, Tanner," Danny replied cheerfully as he rose to stride down the corridor to Larsen's study.

"Oh, Danny, come in," the latter called out. "Close the door, will you?" When Danny had complied, the headmaster continued in a tone that was almost matter-of-fact: "You have heard, of course, about this cheating mess. It's all most distressing, and I can only blame myself for putting off so long the nasty duty of telling poor old Hoadley that he's got to go. Retirement for any devoted teacher is hard enough, but when, like Hoadley, it's been his whole life, and he has neither wife nor child . . ."

"I understand his situation. After all, it's my own."

"Ah, but you, my dear fellow, have a hundred interests, besides being a priest. You will never want for occupation. But Hoadley, without his classes and his laboratory, without his papers to correct and his boys to take on bird walks . . . well, I don't like to think of it. But go he must. I gather that Sixth B Science has become a kind of circus, severed from the rest of Farmingdale and subject to its own laws or fantasies."

"Then you're not going to penalize the boys?"

"For what?"

"For cheating."

"Can you really call it that? Apparently it was the custom of the class. There is evidence that some of the boys sincerely believed that Hoadley himself had sanctioned it. How is one possibly to clean up a mess like that?"

"It's difficult to say. Yet I am sure there were boys who took deliberate advantage of Hoadley's age and condition."

"You are severe, my dear Danny. You are severe. If I allow the near-senile to continue to teach, I must expect the boys to behave badly."

"I suppose that is so."

"It has to be so, I'm afraid. Now will you, Danny, do me a favor? Will you go to poor Hoadley, my sacrificial heifer, and tell him to wait upon me in this chamber? And please give him some hint of the dreadful ceremony in store for him, so the agony may be broken in two and the initial shock not fatal."

3

Some weeks later Danny Buck and Ethelred Eames again walked on the bank of the sluggish river. The air was velvet and full of the season's potentialities. Danny was happy, and Eames was aware of his happiness, if puzzled by it.

"So you actually burned the journal?"

"All but the last entry—the false one. I kept that because it was true."

"Do you mean to tell me that you think that the journal had an actual effect on Titus? That it caused him to say things and do things that he might not otherwise have done?"

"Possibly."

"But, Danny, that's crazy! You're saying you believe in devils."

"In a way. For that is what the journal represented. Its creation was an act of deep personal disloyalty. I was motivated by jealousy and resentment. The presence of these ugly things may have been somehow communicated to Titus. How I do not profess to know. But I believe that they aggravated the same ugly things in him."

Eames stopped to stare open-mouthed at the container and utterer of so much naiveté. "And so, when you resumed your old loyalty, you may have helped to drive some of the ugly things out of Titus?"

"I think so. Yes. Laugh at me if you will."

"I am not going to laugh at you, Danny. Far from it. I am not going to laugh at you at all. It is not a funny matter. But forgive me if I say this: that I deem it fortunate that there exist a few benighted creatures like myself to carry on the daily work of the world. For I happen to consider it my duty, as chairman of the board, to determine whether or not the headmaster is doing his job. For you, of course, nothing can be that simple. What concerns you is not the capacity or incapacity of Titus Larsen to be headmaster, but the moral capacity or incapacity of Daniel Buck to judge him. The drama for you is all in *you*. You are happy now, obviously. Why? Because it has been decided that Titus Larsen is qualified to continue in Farmingdale? No. Because it has been decided that Danny Buck was almost a sinner and has now ceased to be! What does it matter, I ask you, what happens to a million schools and headmasters so long as Danny Buck saves his own soul?"

Danny smiled tolerantly. "You are like the knights of the Middle Ages who wondered what help all those monks were, shut up in a monastery, praying."

"Damn right I am!"

"But, Eth, how can a priest purport to save the souls of others until he has saved his own?"

Eames's expression was that of a man who was used to disappointment and knew how to handle reverses. "All I can say to *that*, Danny Buck, is to propose, as once before beside this river, that we change the subject. I want you to tell me about next year's football team . . ."

(VIII)

The Triplets

NATICA SELIGMANN HAD BEAUTIFUL black hair parted neatly down the center, green-yellow eyes and alabaster skin drawn tightly over facial bones of an exquisite regularity. She was small, agile and strong. In her daily morning exercises, clad in black leotards, she could cross her legs behind her neck. But in the evening, receiving her friends in the Sutton Place apartment that overlooked the East River, backed up by the strong, vivid fabrics of her annually redecorated living room and the large samples of her collection of abstract impressionists, arrayed in floating golden gossamer by Alfredo, no one could have seemed more feminine, more *petite*, more fragile. Her husband was also small, but just as finely made. Ernest Seligmann had a bright, clear boyish face with bronze curly hair. His eyes were blue and smiling, though they seemed to penetrate to your very heart. He wore blue evening shirts, with a hundred delicate ruffles, ruby cuff links, and sparkling pumps. How could they be so successful, so popular, so rich, and not yet thirty-five?

Natica had been born a Burrill, which was stuffy old New York, but her mother had been one of the Winthrop triplets, beautiful daughters of the beloved Harvard philosophy professor, who had made such great marriages—on the second round. Lila, Natica's mother, was now married to Eric Skent, who owned World Prints, largest of paperback houses, and her sisters, Elise and Jane, were the consorts of Ashley Ford, the electronics magnate, and Mike Spartos, the Greek shipper. Natica's own husband, Ernest, had the blood of half the great German Jewish families of New York in his veins and a handsome handful of their money in his pockets. He was now in the state attorney general's office and headed for the very tip-top.

But it was not in worldly goods only, or in grace and beauty, that Natica and Ernest dazzled the urban scene. What was even more remarkable was that they were so advanced. They were liberal democrats who had not been shaken by the nomination of McGovern. Their most elegant parties were never without a portion of black guests. Their two little girls went to the Dalton School, and Natica had removed her name from the Social Register. They raised large sums for civil liberties, were active on the junior committee of the Museum of Modern Art, and helped to support the *New York Review of Books*. The only hint of a conservatism not wholly outgrown was that their nude portraits by Alice Neal were hung in their bedroom.

Nobody was more aware, however, than Natica that even where the mise en scène is totally decorous, there may still exist backstage gray and dusty things. One evening, when she and Ernest were neither dining out nor entertaining, he brought in a bottle of champagne to the living room as the herald of important news. Natica at once made her mask more masklike. What was she ever waiting for but disaster? Oh, yes, she saw the dark deity, up there behind his thunder clouds, Zeus, Jehovah, hirsute, inexorable, peering at her. Let Natica make just one mistake, just *one* . . .

What was this?

Ernest was charming. He never raised his voice. His smile and his chuckle concealed his deep seriousness from nobody. Everyone admired Ernest.

"As you've probably suspected, it's the kind of thing I've always secretly wanted. It should give me the chance to write that book on constitutional law, *The Court to the Rescue*. You know, the one I'm always yacking about? How the right wing has got so damn clever at blocking civil rights legislation we have to depend on the courts?" As Natica did not even blink, he proceeded, with a self-conscious cough, to explain. "I've told you, darling. Busing, redistricting, abolishing the death penalty—all those things we owe to the courts."

Why was he telling her this? She knew all this. Why was he, always so cool, suddenly so nervous? Was he afraid that she was going to tell him that she loved him? But he knew that she knew how he disliked any intimacy, except in copulation, brief but regular. Why had she fallen in love with a man so guarded? Did he even perceive that she loved him? Did he care? Of course, he never wanted to hurt anybody.

"It's a small law school in a small town upstate, Durham. We'd have to drive to Buffalo for our flings. But I'd be teaching at last. Not only constitutional law but contracts."

Natica was surprised at how clear she was, even how calm she was. It was as if she had always expected it. "I take it that you have accepted this job."

"I have."

"Without even a hint to me? Without so much as a by-your-leave? Why, Ernest?"

"Because I have observed that the women of your family are always at their best with a fait accompli."

"My family? You mean the triplets? On the contrary, they are at their best in undoing the fait accompli."

Ernest managed a dry chuckle. "Like their first marriages?"

"Precisely. Does it never occur to you that I might seek to undo mine?"

"Oh, Natica." He turned away, as if now she were being childish.

"It ought to. Where do I fit into this scheme of yours? Since when have I been the type for a small college town?"

"You'd be the hit of hits, darling."

"Do you really believe that?" Natica sat up cross-legged on the sofa, holding her glass in both hands. She took a long sip of the champagne. "Of course you don't. In a political career we're a team. In the life you project, I'm at most an adjunct, at worst a liability. How can you switch the rules of the game on me like that?"

"I never committed myself to a political career."

"You mean in writing? I suppose not. But the man I married exuded from every pore that he was made for the big league."

"You didn't marry Ernest Seligmann!" he exclaimed with sudden heat. "You married the future attorney general. The future senator!"

Natica had been waiting for this. She had even had to give him the opening. "So that's where you come out!" she cried bitterly. "You want to say it's all *my* fault. You've never been loved or understood, have you? You married a hard, dashing woman of the world who saw you as a kind of ski lift to success. And all the time you were made for books and pipes and ivy-covered walls and some nestling little sparrow who would chirp in your fatuous ear how wise you are. Has she been selected already, this sparrow?"

"Must you be so dramatic?"

"Has she been selected already, this sparrow?"

"Of course she hasn't. I want you to come with me. I didn't realize that had to be said."

"Oh, but it does, Ernest."

"Very well then." He faced her with an expression of assumed gravity. "Please come with me, Natica."

What did he mean? There was always that little spark of sarcasm glowing in the back of his eyes like a pink bulb to simulate a fire in the grate of an apartment house lobby. Ah, but he was so sure it was a real fire! She felt choked by the ancient frustration, the ancient suspicion. No matter how cleverly she dressed or acted or loved, the others, the loved ones, were bound to catch her in flagrant default. Because they were always looking, damn them!

"Why should I? What is there for *me* in your small town? Now you're going to tell me I shouldn't look at it that way. I should ask: what is there for the small town in *me?* But, you see, I know they won't like me. People don't like me. *You* don't like me. Oh, perhaps you love me. Anyone can be loved." Natica rose now and looked down into her champagne glass. It was one of the good ones, of carved crystal. She hurled it suddenly into the fireplace where it shivered into a hundred fragments.

"That must have been fun," he observed.

"Leave me alone. Go away."

"Where shall I go?"

"Anywhere you want. Go teach a course. I'm going to cry, and nobody ever sees me cry."

2

Natica had been ten, an only child, when her mother had left Ted Burrill. The court which had awarded Lila the divorce had given her custody of her daughter, and Ted had not even objected. But Natica had. She had seen the not-to-be-missed opportunity of putting her beautiful mother in the wrong, and her cries of "Daddy, Daddy," which had not been heard while he was under the conjugal roof, rang out now in his absence. But the reaction of the triplets was disappointing. Listening outside her mother's door, as Lila, according to her invariable custom, consulted both sisters, she heard the following:

"Of course, the poor darling is utterly right!" Lila wailed. "She *should* visit her father. If that's going to be a rough experience, it's still part of her education. I'd like to protect her, but how? How can I let her grow up believing that I'm a selfish bitch who's torn her from the arms of a loving dad?"

"It might be kinder in the long run." This was Aunt Elise. "Kinder than letting her find out that Ted doesn't give a damn."

"No, no," retorted Aunt Jane. "I agree with Lila. After all, it isn't as if Ted were a fiend. He's not going to beat the child."

"Exactly, Jane. So I've arranged to have her spend the summer with Ted's mother in Southampton. Ted should be there at least on the weekends. He can't miss his golf, after all."

That summer had been one long humiliation. Old Mrs. Burrill, a rough, hearty woman, whose vigor and plainness were the outer cover, not of that heart of gold which they were meant to suggest, but of something bleaker, lived in a big ramshackle summer cottage with her two married daughters and their children. The Burrills joined households in July and August for economy's sake. Natica felt a hopeless outsider in the noisy, homogeneous throng and suffered from the aspersions constantly cast at the higher living style and greater splendor of her mother's family. "Of course, you can't expect steam yachts here," she was daily warned. "If it's Greek billionaires you're looking for, you'll find we go in for a different commodity: good, plain, decent, old New York."

Her father might have made up for everything—oh, yes, easily—but he was obsessed with a desire to make money on the stock market. He wanted to be rich because he wanted the things that money could buy, and he never learned that only those become rich who love money for itself. All weekend long he played golf or drank with fellow brokers and talked about the perils of communism. When Natica returned to her mother after Labor Day, she knew that she did not want to go back to the Burrills. She would have gladly forgiven the atmosphere of failure that pervaded the house, but not their revelry in its stink.

The life to which she now resigned herself was one with three mothers. If Lila and Eric Skent went on a winter safari to Africa, Natica and her baby half-brother were placed under the care of Aunt Elise Ford, and if Aunt Elise was away, Aunt Jane Spartos would fly in from Paris. There was no end of villas and ranches and clubs and shooting lodges, but it seemed to the children of the trio as if they were all owned by a benevolent syndicate which prescribed uniform rules throughout its little empire. The sisters took the same interest in their nieces and nephews as they did in their own offspring. It was a well-known story around town that when Lila and Jane, boarding a plane from Washington to New York, had unexpectedly run into Elise in the first-class section, they had drawn lots as to which should get off. It was out of the question that all three should risk themselves on one flight.

Rebellion, even dissent, was very difficult, for the triplets always backed each other up, and the self-asserting child found that he or she had to argue with not one but with three intelligent and reasonable women. And their approval was seducing. When Natica began to realize that she was going to be pretty, she could not help but be thrilled at the confirmation in the eyes of three such experts. Yet she still struggled to maintain some of her native distrust. There was a sour little Burrill core deep within her that seemed to have something to do with her very soul. For did one want to be smothered, even in niceness?

Take, for example, what happened to any project of a triplet's child. It was immediately seized upon by the mother and aunts and improved beyond all recognition. Did Natica want to spend the summer as a counselor in a camp for poor children? How splendid! But wouldn't it be better to go to Uncle Ashley's great rest home for the disabled in New Hampshire where that amazing Doctor Campion had achieved such miracles? It would be an education just to *watch* him. Or was Natica looking for a job in a reformatory? How relevant! But, if one might make a suggestion, would it not be more instructive for her to work in Uncle Mike's model prison on that island off Mycenae where the most astonishing experiments were being tried? Natica wondered if she were to become an anarchist and seek to blow up City Hall, whether the triplets would not provide her with a bomb kit, made at Tiffany's.

Of course, what she was watching for was some *proof*—not just abundant, overpowering evidence—that her mother and her companions of the womb were engaged in ceaselessly gobbling up the very cake which nonetheless continued to remain stalwartly in their possession. How else did they manage, with their looks and their clothes and their warmth and their charm, *always* to be on the side of the angels? Natica remembered what Granny Burrill had told her, with obvious invidious reference to the Winthrop trio: "Whenever, my child, you go to a really good dinner party—where all the guests are congenial, articulate, charming—take another look at your hostess. You'll find she's not a nice woman. For what has she done with her lame ducks? And her bores?" Well, Granny Burrill was certainly nice by those standards. There was never any question of what *she* had done with her bores. But Mummie? Could it be a coincidence that everyone under her roof had at least one trump to play: a trump of wealth, a trump of beauty, a trump of genius, a trump of power, a trump of influence? The jongleur of Notre Dame would have been as welcome to Lila Skent as to the Virgin, but only on condition that he danced.

On the very afternoon before her own coming-out party Natica had dared to suggest to her mother that their life was vanity. Lila had simply folded her in her arms.

"Oh, my precious pet, don't look at me with those burrowing Burrill eyes and say such dreadful things. Can't you love and let love? All I want is for you to be useful in this world and have fun. Those are two very difficult goals. Put together they represent almost an impossibility. But we can try, can't we?"

Natica later fixed that moment as the date of her final surrender to the triplets. The party, which followed it, was a beautiful party, one of the last of its kind, with two great marquees on the Skent place in Roslyn and dancing until dawn followed by swimming, with champagne served on the rafts. Everyone said it was Scott Fitzgerald moved up to 1956, but everyone still enjoyed it. A week later Ted Burrill committed suicide, solving his ever-worsening financial problems messily by firing a shotgun into his mouth in the messy living room of the Southampton house. Natica sat in the front pew with her broken old grandmother. Afterwards she had to tell Mrs. Burrill that the Skents would guarantee her support, and she would always remember how quickly that venerable lady made her compromise.

Lila, who seemed to know everything, knew that her daughter, as a post-debutante and Barnard student, would need a fresh stimulus in life, and for this role she chose Harold Ainsworth. He was the only man with whom all three of the triplets had been supposed, at one time or another, to have been in love. At fifty, he was short and plump, with thick white hair, a bland, unwrinkled countenance and sharp, restless, laughing eyes that seemed to be trying to reach one from behind the wall of his habitual reserve. He was a famous trial lawyer, the author of two brilliant books on government, and had been a democratic senator from Connecticut. Married, but living considerably apart from his wife, he attended all the parties of the triplets, who spoke of him as a leading contender for the national ticket. Following Lila's suggestion, he took a benign, avuncular interest in Natica, who was greatly flattered.

"My friends at Barnard don't think much of this kind of life," she confessed to him one night at dinner. "They think I ought to live up at the college and be very serious about everything."

"They think you're redeemable, then?"

"Oh, yes, they're perfectly willing to give me the benefit of a doubt. But they think I ought to be on my own, whatever that means. What good would it do me to give up what I have only to spend the rest of my life getting it back?"

"None, provided you like what you have now."

"I think I do." Natica gazed about her. It was a dinner at Aunt Elise's. "I like the paintings on the wall. I like Rothko and Kline and de Kooning. I like the people in this room. Or at least I like their looks and their talk. And I like you, Harold. I like your kindness to me. I boast about it to everyone. I drop your name outrageously."

"If you like what you've got, you're a rare nineteen. And a lucky one."

"Well, I *think* I like it," Natica said with a little frown. "But it bothers me that every time I peek out of my world I seem to see people looking up at me with sourness and anger. They hate the triplets!"

"They envy them."

"Well, of course, that's it. The triplets own the world. The rich Jews like my stepfather, the rich Greeks like Uncle Mike, the rich Wasps like Uncle Ashley—they all bow down to the triumphant sisters. And the triplets don't mind people hating them. Unimportant people, that is. But *I* do. I'm like my father. I'm afraid!"

"You don't look afraid."

"That's because I'm so well made up."

"Well, then, always be well made up, my dear," Ainsworth advised her with a smile. "A good mask is as good as a fortress."

"A mask, yes. That's what I'm putting on. A mask to make me look like my mother."

"Why should you want to look like her?"

"Because she's successful. If you're successful you're strong, and if you're strong, you needn't be afraid."

"Afraid of what?"

"Of being found out, of course." Natica was beginning to be impatient with what she took to be his disingenuousness. "Of being caught in the act of having nothing whatever inside of you."

Ainsworth seemed struck at last. "I see. But what makes you suppose that your ma and her sisters have that much inside of *them*?"

"Do I dare assume that they don't?"

"Ah, that's it!" he exclaimed. "That's it. The triplets are so manifestly the fine flower of a great tradition. Who dares to challenge them? They have combined their great ancestor's passionate mission to save the world with all that is beautiful and luxurious in the world to be saved. We may suspect, at least down here in benighted New York, that the mission is defunct and that its lovely ministers are frauds—or let us say illusions—but what have we that is better?"

"I have nothing that is better. But I have my mask."

Ainsworth nodded almost grimly now. "Let us keep our masks on, by all means."

"Do you wear one, too?" she asked in surprise.

"Haven't you found that out yet? Of course I do. I wear the mask of the cynical, liberal, oh-so-charming politician, too intellectual not to despise the obvious goal of power. Just the way other people in this room wear masks of sincerity, or passion, or rugged individualism, or just plain niceness."

"Everybody but the triplets?"

"Yes! Everybody but the triplets. For they *are* masks! The masks our civilization wears."

Natica liked to think, in the next two years, that she was under the spiritual guidance of Harold Ainsworth. His advice on any step in life was sure to be wise and humane and practical, and it had the added advantage of being a total justification of the step taken, at least in the eyes of the triplets. Natica began to feel surer of herself as she took in the effectiveness of the portrait that she was painting of the image in her mirror. When she read in the evening papers that "Natica Burrill gave to the little gathering that particular blend of chic and cultivation that is the patent of her mother's family," or that "Natica seems the embodiment of all the virtues of the triplets and will carry their flag to yet higher peaks," she smiled, but it was the smile of an artist checking on a work in progress.

There was one subject, however, that Natica had not yet discussed with her mentor, and that was marriage. It was obvious that her particular career required a great marriage. A girl did not spend hours at the hairdresser and a fortune at Bendel's; she did not slave at her French and German; she did not perfect her bridge and her riding in order to become a doctor or judge. But, unfortunately, it was no longer fashionable to plan a great marriage. The schemers of Natica's day had to operate underground. Sex had become such a sacred cow that even the boldest felt obliged to fall in love with their victim. It was characteristic of Ainsworth's genius that he should have understood this. It was he who, unsolicited, produced Ernest Seligmann from his own office.

"It would be fatal to say this to most bright girls," he told her, "because they'd immediately react the other way. But Ernest is your perfect mate."

Natica watched him closely without saying a word.

"To begin with, he's a near genius," he continued. "He was not only editor-in-chief of the *Harvard Law Review*—he's a fine mathematician. He has charm and drive and kindness. And he's an expert fisherman. He even plays the violin!"

It was not necessary for Ainsworth to mention that there was also a great fortune, now almost a requirement for a liberal aspirant to high office. Nor did he have to speak of Ernest's being Jewish, which could give to his courtship the romantic touch of family conflict, real or imagined—it didn't matter which—that would lift it out of mercenary considerations in the eyes of all the world, including those of the principal participants. Natica could fancy what he was saying to Ernest:

"The one thing, mind you, I don't expect from you is the obvious. So *don't* say she's a spoiled society brat. It happens to be precisely what she's not. She stands aside, in the wings, and takes in the whole show."

Natica liked Ernest from the beginning. She liked the way he always seemed to be smiling at people without an actual grin; she liked his wit and his even temper. She found him at once critical and pleasantly amicable; concerned yet almost languid, curious but unimpressible. He had the same good manners with all men, great and small, yet he left the distinct impression that this smartly tailored, diminutive, neat and boyishly handsome observer was not fooled by any false front and that whoever you might be, your rank was not beyond the reach of Ernest Seligmann. He took Natica out for two weeks before he kissed her, but when he did so it was as if he had known all along that he might.

"You and I have got to go slow," he warned her. "We're just too good to be true together."

Natica worried over the fact that the course of true love, like everything else in her young life, was too smooth. She and Ernest never seemed to quarrel. The triplets were delighted with the match, as were the senior Seligmanns. The only hint of awkwardness was that Ernest's father looked askance at Natica's stepfather, whom he described scornfully as a "concealed Jew." But religion and race otherwise were not mentioned. The Seligmanns were not orthodox; the triplets had no god.

"Does he love me?" Natica mused.

Even after their marriage she never knew. Ernest avoided intimacy; she learned to do the same. After all, what was more vulgar than a "showdown"? She had a wonderful husband, faithful, considerate, gentle, amusing, stimulating. If he had a secret chamber, was it consistent with her masked role to go barging in? Particularly when she suspected that the secret chamber might be dedicated to Ernest's regret that he could not devote himself altogether to one passion, be it mathematics or the violin or even law. For that, she divined, was what was wrong—or right—with him. It was not his passion for her, but an oddly puritanical sense of duty, that had kept his eye fixed on the great world. His father had persuaded him that he must become a public servant.

"Do I love him?" she would ask.

The answer was usually that she did. Precisely because of the secret chamber from which she was barred. And she grimly suspected, after the annunciation of his decision to teach in Durham, that he was going into that chamber and would have no further need of her.

3

Ernest and Natica agreed that he should spend the first academic semester at Durham without her. She would remain in New York with the girls.

"I have to find out what *I* can do," she pointed out to him. "You have discovered what *you* want. You selected me as the wife for one kind of life, and now you've chosen another. You say you want me in that other, but you haven't convinced me. I shouldn't be so dependent on marriage. I should have studied law. Perhaps I still may."

They were both very cool now and rational. Natica would have bitten off the tip of her tongue rather than admit how much she cared for him. "I suppose we can meet on weekends," she added. "You'll want to see the girls anyway."

"Oh, of course, there'll be weekends." He accepted her plan much too quickly.

Natica closed her eyes and thought of Ernest in poses that she loved: in long waders in the Canadian woods, attaching his leader to a trout fly, reading in bed as he listened with one ear to her gossip, pretending solemnly to criticize the girls for outrageous conduct while they squealed in a delight of nerves and laughter. Then she opened her eyes and saw his apprehension.

"It's all right," she said casually. "I was just thinking it out. I'm going to work for Harold Ainsworth."

Ainsworth, now a widower, was senior partner of a large law firm with offices in Wall Street and in Hartford. She worked in the former, as his personal assistant, helping him with his mail and the speeches that he was constantly called to make. Their old congeniality was intensified, and the social world, taking its cue from the triplets, began asking them to dinner parties together. Ainsworth, however, preferred the evenings when they dined alone. He had a partiality for the best French restaurants, and he would watch Natica, smiling, as he sipped his fine wine and she told him funny stories about the Winthrop girls that even he didn't know. He liked to philosophize, in semicomic vein, on their role in history.

"When archeologists dig up jewelry that must have belonged to elegant women, they call it evidence of a high civilization. Yet these same pedants are the first to sneer at society ladies in their own time. When their successors dig up your mother's things, a thousand years hence, they'll talk about Helen of Troy, and they'll be right, too!"

The impersonality behind which Natica had so long sought shelter was an asset again. The great man felt relaxed and secure dining and chatting with his beautiful companion. He talked frankly about his dislike of the exhausting traveling and handshaking that a major candidacy requires, yet confessed to the disgust that he felt when persons of less intellect and capability went blithely after the goals that he had eschewed.

"Suppose you were to divorce Ernest and marry me," he suggested, only half-playfully, one night. "It might be enough to tempt me to try for anything. Even the White House. You'd make such an ideal first lady."

"A divorced woman?"

"Remember Rachel Jackson. Besides, who minds divorce today?"

Natica looked about the bright little oblong room with its blown-up photographs of the Place de la Concorde and its scarlet, looped curtains. Did these distinguished-looking people recognize them? Probably. Did they know they were talking about the highest of positions? Probably. She felt a little movement of something like happiness in her heart.

"Are you serious?"

"Why on earth not? We get on immensely. We laugh at the

world, but we both care, quite passionately, about it. We like to see things done well, if done at all."

"You say your emotional life is over," she pointed out. "Is what you propose what they call a *mariage blanc?*"

"Only if you wanted it that way, my dear," he responded with a chuckle. "You would find me up to the other thing still. But I don't forget that I could be your father. It would be up to you to call the tune. And if you chose to have an interlude with some younger man, I know I could count on you to be discreet."

"And you? With a still younger woman?"

"No, I should be faithful," he said more seriously. "It's my style."

She pondered it for a moment. "I think I would enjoy being married to you."

"Once in, you'd be stuck, I warn you. By your sense of duty, not mine. I'd want you to feel free, but you wouldn't."

"I don't seem so stuck to Ernest."

"Ah, but that's different. With Ernest there were vows and illusions and young love. It's almost irresistible not to try to smash such things. But between you and me it would be a *mariage raisonné*. You'd be too much of a lady to back out."

Natica had a talk with her mother later that week. She was sure that Harold had not spoken to Lila, but of course the latter knew all. Natica had come early to one of her mother's dinners and sat with her now in her dressing room while Lila made up her face. It was not one of the least of the Winthrop skills that they knew how to take advantage of even the briefest interludes for intimate communication.

"I think it's time you settled things between you and Ernest, darling," Lila said between dabs of powder. "We all know that separations never end in reconciliation. That may seem hard, but it's true."

"I know it's true."

"Which leaves you with a life to get on with. Divorces always take time to work out, no matter how friendly the parties are. I think you ought to get started on yours." Lila turned around in sudden contrition to embrace her silent daughter. "Forgive me, pet. You know it's for your good."

"I know you mean it well."

"Mean it well? How else could I mean it?"

"You want me to be unencumbered in case other chances come along. But I'm not sure I want to marry again. I may go to law school."

"Why not do both?"

"You think Harold would like his wife in law school?"

Lila looked at her daughter's grave reflection in the mirror and burst into a cheerful laugh. "Bless you, I'm sure he wouldn't mind. But why should you want to go? As Mrs. Ainsworth you'd have the greatest firm in the country at your beck and call."

"You can't imagine, can you, Ma, the satisfaction of having one's own profession? Of doing one's own thing? No matter how small or unimportant?"

"Of course, I can, you goose. But we're talking about *you*. You have seen the bigger stakes. You wouldn't be happy as a clerk."

"You think I'm cold and ambitious, don't you? You think I may as well marry Harold and get my kicks out of power?"

Lila rose now and rang for her maid. "At your age, dear, you should be over trying to put your ma in the wrong."

Natica nodded ruefully. "That's quite true. Only one wishes it weren't. The question is—what is *me?*"

4

Natica was waiting for Harold at the Concorde when she saw her mother-in-law at a corner table, also alone. Elesina Seligmann was a tall, thin woman with beautiful curled silver hair and a brown crinkled skin. Her eyes were pale tan and shimmered with the apprehensiveness of one who is not afraid, but who is accustomed to disaster. She was less intellectual than her spare, bony handsomeness implied, but more affectionate. Why, Natica wondered, had such a good woman met with so much misfortune? Her daughter had committed suicide, and Ernest's brother was a drug addict. As she watched her now, Natica felt her heart go out to Elesina. She had a sudden sense that all her mother-in-law wanted was to love and be loved by her own family. She caught her eye and went over.

"How are you, dear Natica?" Elesina was always friendly, although it was hardly conceivable that she should like her son's worldly wife. "Did you know that Ernest was here?"

"Here?" Natica sat down in the empty chair beside her, astonished. "What brings him down?"

Elesina fixed those worried eyes on Natica's and then suddenly placed her long thin fingers, on which were several large, loose diamond rings, on the hand that Natica rested on the tablecloth. "He has come for tests. Oh, Natica, he made me swear not to tell you, but I don't care. He has some mysterious muscular disease. The doctors don't understand it. That is why he took the law school job. It's a debilitating thing, but slow, very slow. It rules out any active life—at least for a while."

Natica felt that all her being had shriveled up into her eyeballs, that she existed only in the cold, fascinated stare that she could not avert from the drawn agony of Elesina's face. "And he wouldn't tell me," she half whispered.

"He wouldn't have told *me* if he hadn't needed my help with the doctors. His father, you know, is on the board of Mount Sinai. No, Ernest is like that wounded animal we always talk about. He goes to his hole."

"Is it . . . fatal?"

"They don't know. Anyway, it's so slow that they may find a new drug before it's too much worse."

"Is it painful?"

"At times. It was yesterday. It's better today."

"May I come? Now? After lunch, I mean."

"May you? Darling, of course. You know, it's the wish of my life to get you two together again."

Natica rose and looked down at her mother-in-law. "I'll be in at three, if that's all right." When Elesina simply nodded, big tears like her diamonds now standing in her eyes, Natica leaned down and kissed her.

"I love you."

"Why, Natica! I thought . . ." She stopped.

"You thought I didn't love anybody."

When she returned to her own table, Harold was there. She saw him wave to Elesina, whom he knew well.

"Your ma-in-law looks unusually sad," he observed as Natica slipped into her seat. "She's even more Modigliani than usual. Has anything happened?"

"Only that she hates seeing me lunching with other men."

"But I'm not other men. I'm the boss."

"Let's not talk about Ernest's mother." Natica picked up the cocktail that she had ordered earlier. She took several quick sips. "I'd rather, as always, talk about mine. Should I marry you because she wants it so?"

Harold laughed in sheer pleasure. "No! Unless, of course, you want it too. But you don't." He studied her intent expression for a careful moment. "What on earth has happened to you, Natica?

Have you had some wonderful news? I've never seen you looking so happy!"

She stared back at him in horror. At last she burst into a shrill laugh. "Harold, you're a fiend! You're too intelligent to live!"

At three o'clock she was admitted to her mother-in-law's apartment and then directed to the library where Ernest was waiting for her. He was dressed in a gray flannel suit, and the only sign of invalidism was that he was wearing no tie. But that was a lot for Ernest.

"Of course, Mother had to blab the whole story," he began sullenly.

"Thank God she did."

"Why?"

"Because now I can come back. Now I can be where I belong."

"You mean you want to take care of me?"

"Yes, Ernest, I do."

"Have you considered that I might not want that?" It seemed to her that his face was contracted now, as if his thoughts and emotions had all been swirled into a knot. She was struck by her sudden sense of his utter weariness.

"I'm considering it *now*. You may be sure of that."

"You're not, after all, a trained nurse, are you?"

"No, but couldn't I find them and supervise them?"

"No doubt. And I can perfectly see what there is in this for you. It's a way of life, isn't it? To be a nurse to me in a long illness—obviously, it solves everything. It lets you out of your ambition. It satisfies your remorseless conscience. It kills time—oodles of time. But forgive me, my dear, if I ask you what there is in it for *me?*"

Natica turned away in pain and walked to the window. It was perhaps the justification of all her years of mask-wearing that she could still think so clearly. What she faced now was not only the fact of her pain. It was her dislike of him for causing it. "There's nothing in it for you," she said at last wearily. "It's just a final sacrifice that I was asking."

"If I were well, I would grant it. But you see, an illness like this is a very private thing. Once death is allowed as a possibility—and it is, despite what they told Mother—death is now. It justifies selfishness. A man ought to be allowed to die his own way. Condemned criminals used to be given anything they wanted for a last meal."

Natica was ashamed of herself, for she began to sob. Her tears caught her by surprise, and her shame almost became anger. "I'm a selfish bitch. It's so dreadful of me to try to find redemption in your illness."

"On the contrary, it's perfectly natural. Why shouldn't one get something out of a disease? Why should it all be negative? But here you run into *my* selfishness. I have always been selfish. I picked you in the beginning with every deliberation. I wanted the perfect consort. I wanted someone who would give me what I wanted in bed and at the dinner table and at the political rally. I wanted the minimum of interruptions from female temperament. I got exactly what I wanted. Had I asked a genie for the wife I described, I could not have had the prescription more perfectly filled."

"I see," she said bitterly. "It was like a fairy story. You got everything and nothing."

"I got what I deserved. And now I've got a disease in which you can't play a role. The perfect wife must resume her liberty. You must go back to the world where you belong."

Natica dried her eyes. "You can reject me, Ernest, but you can't tell me what to do with my life."

"I suppose that's fair."

"Of course, it's fair!" She felt a sudden little quiver of disgust at his illness, the illness that he would not let her share. It seemed a base reaction, but as she paused to evaluate it, turning away from his calm, irritating gaze, she was conscious of a tugging in her heart of some strong, unfamiliar sensation. Good God, could it be joy? She stared back at Ernest. Joy that it was *he* who was sick and not she? Joy at simply being alive? "Oh, Ernest, have I just *tried* to love you?"

Ah, he didn't like it! He didn't like it at all. "I think maybe I've had enough of this for today."

"Of course. I can come back."

"Yes. Come back."

She found her mother-in-law waiting for her, spectrally, in the hall.

"He sent you away," Elesina murmured. "Why can nothing ever be right for me?"

"The only important thing is to do what helps him."

"But do we know what helps him? Does he?"

Natica shook her head. "It doesn't matter. We must do as he wishes."

"Oh, Natica," her mother-in-law wailed, "if you'd only gone with him to Durham when he first went!"

"Oh, no, I don't regret that at all!" Natica exclaimed, as if trying to ward off some blow of ill fortune. "He didn't want what I was.

And he doesn't know what I am. It's far better to make a fresh start. Can't you see that?"

"One can never make a fresh start in life," her mother-in-law opined gloomily.

Natica put her hand on the knob of the front door. "Only, perhaps, if one has never made a beginning."

And with what the triplets would have regarded as a charming curtain line, Natica closed the door behind her, banging it in her mind as Ibsen's Nora had banged hers, upon a host of phantoms. If she could learn not to blame them for her plight—well, it might be a beginning. She would give up the mask, at any rate, even if that was all she had left from the Winthrops. Without it she might expose herself as a cipher to the world. But perhaps to be a cipher was better than to be a pose. So long as the tablet was blank, there was no reason to assume that one could not write on it. At any rate, she would have given up the mission, or the burden of seeming to have one. From henceforth the mission would be only to herself.

(IX)

The Penultimate Puritan

Here beginneth the first chapter of the gospel according to Althea Stevens Gardiner—dedicated to thee, my dear son, to be read, if at all, by the light of some dim Stockholm bar where you sit nightly in the company of your fellow war protesters.

Your sister has made me write this. Christine believes that even so shabby a status seeker as your poor mother, even so faded an anachronism as a woman who could see no weapon available to her sex but sex itself, might still, as a *ci-devant* poetess of the Edna St. Vincent Millay school, be capable of putting together a document that might make you at least consider coming home and giving yourself up. She argues that you see your father as a kind of antichrist and that I am the only person who can correct the record. "Some evangelist!" I can hear you exclaim. Who, after all, contributed more to your conception of the satanic quality of John Winthrop Gardiner than your long disillusioned and even longer complaining mother? But that is precisely the reason, according to Christine. The one who created the exaggeration should be the one to tone it down. I can hear you sneer: "Will you take the 'anti' off the antichrist?" Well, why not? As you can be counted on to take care of the Christ, that should leave your poor father where he belongs—a man. There —I have fooled you already, Jonathan! You thought I was going to say a "poor, forked animal," didn't you? But even were I in a mood for clichés, I shouldn't use that one. Your father is not a poor animal.

I know that you have said you would never forgive him for talking you out of evading the draft while all the while he was promoting illegal and secret warfare in Indochina. To you such arrant hypocrisy was the unpardonable sin. I am not asking you to forgive him. I am not even sure that I can forgive him myself. Had he kept his mouth shut, after all, you would have evaded the draft, and not now be guilty of desertion. But I am asking you to try to comprehend him. Life, in the long run, is too short for illusions, especially those which we hug to our bosoms. Think how you and I have enjoyed hating your father!

You will remember from your sacred studies at Farmingdale that in the first century Christians believed that Christ would come again to judge the world in only a few years time. They also believed that this second and final coming would be preceded by a false one, that of an antichrist, who would spread fire and destruction along with his false doctrine. Your generation believes only in the false coming. You see the future as terminated by a hypocrite with a hydrogen bomb. Your father sees only the bomb.

When he left me last month to move in with that chit of a girl, I reacted with all the violence and vindictiveness of a woman of my generation confronted with such a crisis. What I could not bear was that she and John were in love. A man of fifty-six and a girl thirty years his junior! You have never met Alison Brady. She is not only blond and beautiful; she is cool, calm, efficient. Everyone in the Central Intelligence Agency agrees that she's a first-class agent, though one never knows what they judge that on. I could see, the very first time that she dined with us in Georgetown, that she was in love with John. Not that I minded that. I was too used to girls falling in love with your father. But when I saw that he responded to her, that he was looking younger—as lean and brown and twinkling and crispy gray as an aging, still beloved movie star—I could have killed them both. They seemed so right for each other—even age-wise. That was the unforgivable thing.

Before retaining my own lawyer, I went up to Boston to confer with Sherman Gardiner in his State Street office. I know you haven't seen your uncle for years, but he's just the same. He never had your father's looks, but he suggests him: an older, tougher, sharper Yankee, with the same steely gray hair. Sherman has always been the family counsel, and in Boston this makes him what the family minister might have been a century ago. The Back Bay lawyers of his generation have thrown off that hang-up of the old Brahmins, the need to secure a front pew in a divinely ordained hierarchy, and they have accepted the facts of Irish political rule, but they have lost none of their aptitudes and precious little of their cash. That is why they still play a much bigger role than the scions of old families in other cities.

Sherman listened to my arguments, puffing vigorously at his pipe as if he were clearing the room of my hot air. His office was filled with big things, some dark, some gleaming, some ugly, some very fine. I noted a Whistler Venetian etching.

"Go on, go on," he said brusquely when I paused. "Get it off your chest."

"So it seems only fair, if I've given your brother half my life, that I should have half his property. And I don't mean in one of those trusts that stop if I remarry."

"Have you anyone in mind?"

"I do not. But do you think I'd tell you if I had? I'm the wronged wife, Sherman!"

"Which entitles you to a settlement of two million dollars? You're dreaming, Althea. Dreaming that you're back in the nineteen-thirties when every middle-aged society woman could hope to convert her sexual frustration into a fortune. Wake up. This is 1973!"

"There's no need to be abusive, Sherman."

"But there's a need to be frank. Listen to me. I'm against many of the new ideas, but there's one I'm all for: disappointment in love should not be the basis for a large cash settlement."

"You sound as if you approved of what John is up to!"

"No, approval is something else again. But I confess that I don't see why you're so much to be pitied. What about Harvey Price? Have you forgotten him?"

"Not with you to remind me. But that was the time John had his little walk-out with Daphne Photis."

"So it was a stand-off. How can you expect an unreconstructed baked bean like myself to take seriously the self-pity of a wife who freely admits that she's broken the Seventh Commandment?"

"Fifteen years ago, Sherman!"

Sherman shrugged. "Maybe the opportunities have diminished."

"Don't be a cad. But very well, I'll change my grounds. What I'm asking for is not compensation. It's my price for John's freedom."

"What does he need his freedom for? Alison is already living with him. She's a modern woman, Althea. She hasn't learned the fine ethics of gold digging. You had better face the facts. Your children are grown, so you can't use the custody wedge. And John is perfectly happy with his present arrangement. Indeed, I shouldn't be surprised if he actually preferred it . . ."

"So like him!" I interrupted hotly. "He ought to marry her!"

At this Sherman roared with laughter, and, after a moment of sputtering indignation, I couldn't help joining him.

"I tell you what," he said at last. "Leave the whole thing to me. If you hire some shyster, you'll end up with a small settlement and a big fee. I can get you something decent for nothing. There are situations in life when a girl does better to say: 'Pretty please.' "

"I suppose you *want* to see John married to this girl."

"I admit it. I think she really loves him. That's something I've never been able to get over about my kid brother: the fact that none of his girls really loved him. And he's always struck me as having just about everything: looks, charm, brains, ability, background, money. Why has it taken him until now to find a girl who loves him for himself?"

"Because he's an egoist."

"Unlike thee and me."

"Well, people forgive us because we're not as attractive as John. What they resent about him is the way he sympathizes with their envy."

"I've never envied him. I've been quite happy in my comparative shadow. But I'm going to say something that may surprise you, Althea. I consider my brother a thoroughly good man."

"Ah, but Sherman, I know what you consider good."

Sherman chuckled as he rose to conclude the interview. "Come out to Dedham tonight and dine with Priscilla and me."

Which I did. Sherman had that quality found in many closely knit families of being able to take one attitude to an in-law outside, and a totally different one inside, his home. No one hearing him talk to me that night would have guessed that he had practically called me a whore that morning. And Priscilla, plain, dowdy Priscilla, to whom I had always rather condescended—how did *she* treat me? I might have been one of the unfortunates in her settlement house. She was all kindness and smiles. Jock, I think she pitied me!

Her pity, anyway, was almost preferable to your sister's optimism. I went to the Boston Legal Aid office the next day to pick up Christine for lunch. She seems stouter and ruddier than ever, the very image of your grandmother Gardiner, and the only reason that she did not inundate me with hard-luck stories about her wretched clients was that I, for the moment, seemed to have become one of them.

"Look, Ma," she said eagerly, "this may be the making of you.

Don't take a penny from Dad. Stand on your own feet. Lead your own life. Go back to your poetry."

"Do you realize, Christine, that I haven't written a poem since I was eighteen years old?"

"How do you know the talent's not still there? Buried underneath?"

That's your sister all over. The Pollyanna in her has survived the most gruesome encounters with disease and poverty. She's an old-fashioned liberal, a throw-back to the New Deal. She has that bright eye that never clouds, even when the haggard skeleton of want is imprinted upon its pupil. The steel of Eleanor Roosevelt is in her soul. You and I, Jock, want to tear down the Establishment because we loathe and resent it—not because we give a damn about the great unwashed. We're like Byron's Lara:

> "What cared he for the freedom of the crowd?
> He raised the humble but to bend the proud."

But Christine will never entertain a thought that conflicts with her rosy view of an imminent socialist future. Her entire education is in events that took place after my birth. In Sarah Lawrence she studied the Russian Revolution and sociology. She's never read a novelist before Mailer or a poet before Cummings. Do you wonder that we don't "communicate"?

"You don't understand about poets," I tried to explain to her. "They burn out young. The passionate ones, anyway. And I was a passionate one."

"But that doesn't mean you can't still write," Christine pointed out in her labored way. "Why don't you work for Legal Aid? I'm doing a piece right now for the *Boston Bar Bulletin* on bail which I know you could improve."

"Thank you, dear," I replied faintly, "but I don't think I'm reduced to that quite yet."

"Well, then, write something else. Write about you and Dad and send it to Jock. Make him see that we're all in the same boat. That's it!" Christine clapped her hands. "It may make him less bitter. Don't they say that understanding is forgiving?"

"Do they?"

So here, Jock, is my gospel.

2

Parents get blamed for everything, and perhaps correctly so, but Christine is right about one thing. Children (even grown-up children) should try to remember that parents had parents, too. You, Jock, can remember Grandma Stevens, but she had become innocuous then, thanks to a premature onslaught of arteriosclerosis. At only seventy she thought she was a seagull, which was a good deal better than thinking, as she had at fifty, that she was a society queen.

One thing that is never understood by those who are outside the charmed circle of "society"—or by many within—is that a good social manner, or "tone," has often little to do with breeding. My mother, born a Gladwin and married to a Stevens, brought up on Fifth Avenue and in Newport, a graduate of Miss Spence's School, was indubitably a "lady," both by birth and environment. Yet what did all that count against the innate vulgarity of her nature, passed down from some primordial ape? Mother's stupidity and worldliness combined to make her a comic figure. With tightly curled, gold-dyed hair over a square face and small popping eyes, presiding over a small, pompous, shabby house with an oversized marble stairwell and a lot of gilded furniture, she might have been a parvenu in a Charles Dana Gibson cartoon. I had laughed at her, when I did not weep, as far back as I could remember.

Papa, much older than his spouse, was always somewhat inebriated. Stout and at times almost unkempt, with sloppy gray hair over a huge, blank brow, he yet had a trace, in the ruin of fine features, of a lost distinction. I liked to fancy that I could trace my own pale dark looks and romantic nature in a miniature of him as a boy in the eighteen-eighties. I have never known what made him spend his days in the library with his brandy bottles. He would dress in the evening for Mother's ghastly dinner parties and fall asleep with the men afterwards. He had lost a small inheritance, and we lived off remittances from Grandma Gladwin which came irregularly, with the result that the house was always understaffed and such servants as we had, rude and surly. I remember my mortification at a children's party when Mother, who was very greedy, asked the butler with a simpering air if she couldn't have "just one more scoop of that *irresistible* ice cream" only to be told that there was not enough for a first helping.

Had my parents had stronger personalities, I might have reacted against them in anger. I might have rebelled. This would have been much healthier than what did happen: I ignored them. I found my solace in Papa's library, which had belonged to his father, who must have been a more or less literate person, for it contained all the English nineteenth-century poets. I developed an early adoration for romantic narrative verse. I devoured Byron and sped on to Shelley and Keats, then Browning and Tennyson. As I look back, it seemed to me that I must have been somewhat lacking in discrimination; but that hardly mattered. I was on fire. I would read aloud passages to my poor father who was kind enough never to say that he wanted his library for himself and his solitary drinking. I learned long poems by heart, and at Grandma Gladwin's Christmas party I had to be stopped when I wanted to recite all of "Oenone." I wrote dramatic monologues in which I would speak nostalgically from a prison cell, reviewing my former glory and my sad mishaps, a Lady Jane Grey, a Marie Antoinette, a Ruth Snyder. The latter was a New York murderess whose execution at the time had much moved me. But by sixteen I was already ashamed of my historical effusions. I had discovered love and Swinburne.

It was all too much for Mother. I was sent off to a boarding school in Maryland where horses were supposed to cure passion and where one was considered a bluestocking if caught reading a detective story. But one blessed day after a full year in which no tuition money had been received, I was sent home. Grandma was bullied into paying for a cheaper school in New York, a Miss Hornor's, not renowned for its social exclusivity, where, for the first time, I met girls who actually liked to read and listen to music, including Daphne Photis who was the daughter of a magazine editor. She and I became passionate friends. We read aloud together; we walked in Central Park with arms intertwined; we went to the movies and fell in love with Ramon Novarro. And then suddenly it happened. The miracle happened. I began to write poetry.

It seemed to pour out of me, leaving behind a joy that I have never known since, a joy that made love itself seem a banality. I wrote sonnets about mundane Manhattan futilities, little dry lyrics about love, little bittersweet ironies of the transiency of pleasure, full of the spirit of *carpe diem*, ballads about troubadors and jesters, mad kings and doomed maidens. And Daphne's father actually published some of them! I made a sudden little name for myself, and everyone —even my stunned mother—suddenly considered me a genius. I visualized my future as a great poetess, with many lovers and a wonderful early tragic death at the height of my fame.

Of course, I made a great point of refusing to come out. I wanted to go to Paris and study at the Sorbonne. The only person who could possibly stake me to this was Grandma Gladwin, who regarded Paris as widows of her generation were wont to regard Paris. While the matter was under negotiation, Mother and I entered into a pragmatic sanction pursuant to which I reluctantly agreed to allow her to give me an occasional small dinner party before a supper dance. It was thus that I met your father. The debutante of the evening was a Gardiner cousin, and in good Boston fashion he had been sent down to represent the family.

He was a junior at Harvard, which made him seem very old and sophisticated to me, at seventeen, and he was certainly the handsomest thing I have ever seen, before or since. It was not that his appearance was unusual. He had thick curly dark hair and bold, regular, classical features. His slim, muscular body moved with an awesome grace. But that was just the beginning. That was banal. What was my undoing was the rich, pearl-like quality of his skin and the dampness of his soft brown eyes. For all his finely-fitting clothes, his pearl studs and the air of arrogance that I assumed *had* to emanate from him, he nonetheless struck me as both gentle and sensitive. And even kind. God! I was done for.

He was full of questions, however, from the very beginning. Not for John was the role, however it might have become him, of the silent or moody romantic. He wanted to know if I was coming out. No? Why not? Didn't I approve of it? Did I think it a shocking extravagance in a time of depression? What would I do with my time instead? Would I work for a settlement house? Oh, Boston, Boston!

"I am a poet," I announced firmly.

"A poet!" There was nothing but astonishment in those damp brown eyes. "Why would a beautiful girl want to be a poet?"

Enchanted as I was with the compliment, I was taken aback by the question. "Don't you associate poetry with beauty? With truth?"

"I can't say I do. We had a poetess in the family. Cousin Amy Lowell. Do you know about her?"

"She weighed three hundred pounds and smoked cigars!" I cried with a shriek of laughter. "I see what your indoctrination has been. But I emulate a different model, Miss Millay. She lives down in the Village and goes in for love, oodles of love."

"Is that what you go in for?"

"Just in my poems. I am a kind of vestal virgin."

"You mean, a guy has no chance?"

I stared. "Well, I wouldn't say he has to give up before he's even started."

"Shouldn't he consider the risk to you?"

"Are you speaking of the dangers of compromise, Mr. Puritan?"

"To a liberated New York poetess? Hardly. But a vestal virgin caught with a lover was buried alive."

His eyes were grave; he might have been sparing me the actual fate. I shivered with pleasure. "Maybe it was worth it. Anyway, that was *her* decision."

"Can I read your poems?" he demanded.

"Of course you can read them. What do you think I publish them for?"

"I mean now. Tonight."

"You mean here? At table?"

"After dinner, when the men tell dirty stories and damn Mr. Roosevelt."

"Are you a New Dealer?"

"Passionate!"

"You shall have my poems, sir. *With* your brandy. If Daddy didn't drink it all up this afternoon."

No sooner had we risen from table than I hurried up to my room and quickly selected copies of six of my better pieces. When I came downstairs the men were already in the library, but I beckoned John from the doorway, and he stepped over immediately to take the clippings. It amused me to see him go straight to a corner, without so much as a nod of apology to his host or the others, and sit down to immerse himself in my work.

Later, as my guests were leaving for the dance, I felt a firm grip on my elbow, and, before I quite knew what was happening, I was alone in a taxi with John.

"Those poems are great," he said emphatically. "I had no idea when my mother sent me down to a deb party that I'd meet a literary genius! And a girl who knows about life, too! What do you say that we skip the silly dance and go to a nightclub? How about El Morocco?"

"I'd adore it. Mother will be furious, but that's of no consequence. How about yours, though? Aren't parents rather more thought of, up in Boston?"

"Oh, yes, there'll be hell to pay, but that's for tomorrow."

I think that was the happiest night of my life. It seemed unbelievable that instead of being pinched and pushed around the floor by college freshmen and callow sixth formers from prep schools, I should be drinking champagne at a nightclub with the handsomest of men, of whose very existence I had been unaware a few hours before. Because we were not at a party where we should have been, because nobody in the world knew where we were, because he would be going back in the morning to Boston and Cambridge, unknown entities in my life, which might swallow him up forever, I had a heady sense of isolated excitement, of suspended ecstasy, which, even at the time, struck me as a kind of emotional capital on which I might be able to draw dividends for a long time to come. And in some ways I am still drawing them.

John's curiosity about life in New York was unremitting. I began to see that he had a very literal mind. I think that even then, on that first evening, I was already conscious of a wispy ghost of disappointment, stealing up inside my brain, that he was not going to be all that I so passionately wanted him to be. Why do fools say that love is blind? Would that it were! Yet I had soon to reckon with the fact that, if John's mind was literal, it was big enough to take in an infinity of detail.

My poems were of interest to him more in what they revealed of my life than of my heart.

"Do you always do just what you want?" he asked.

"I don't know yet. Because I don't know yet what I want. But I think, when I know it, I'll do it!"

He raised his glass to this. "I think you will, too. Maybe you'll teach me how."

"You? A man? Surely you must do what you want."

"Well, I thought I did. When I was at Farmingdale, I was a terrible Christer. I took communion every Sunday morning. I spent my summers working at the school camp for poor kids from South Boston. But my trouble was that my family approved so much that I got mixed up between what they wanted for me and what I wanted for myself."

"You mean you don't care about the poor kids any more? I thought you said you were a New Dealer."

"Oh, sure I care. But without the uplift. Without God and Company. I gave up God sophomore year."

I was not altogether sure that I liked this. I never thought about God myself, having a most terrestrial and unreligious nature, but I had a vague notion that the deity would go well with John, like a sports jacket or a sailboat.

"And what did you put in his place?"

"Life. At least I've tried to. But that's what an artist like you could teach me. That's what your poems are full of."

"But surely people must live, even up in Boston."

"Well, they're not very good at it. I used to believe that people like my parents lived for high ideals, but they don't. They live for pleasure, only they're too stupid to find it."

"I wonder if that's what my parents live for. If it is, they certainly don't find it, either."

But John wasn't interested in my parents, either then or afterwards. How right he was! "Ma and Pa are very outdoorsy people," he continued. "They sail and they fish and they shoot. They have the most expensive equipment for the destruction of wildlife and for their own provision in the wilderness. Yet their whole activity is permeated with a kind of frowzy virtuousness. They race because the Gardiners have always raced. They fish because the Gardiners have always fished. And when they kill, they say they're doing it for a museum."

I was perfectly able to deduce from this that Mr. and Mrs. Gardiner were much sounder persons than my own mother and father. If you have really ridiculous parents, you learn early to spot unfairness in your friends' criticism of their own. But I didn't have to tell John this. All I had to do was listen, smile and sip champagne. When he took me home at four in the morning before catching the milk train to Boston, he had promised to return the next weekend and the one after that. I found Mother asleep on the couch on the second-floor landing and quelled her awakening snort of anger at once.

"I've been out with John Gardiner. He likes liberated New York girls, and I'm *not* going to Paris."

"Oh, Althea. John Winthrop Gardiner." Mother blinking, half-awake, was still capable of reverence. "Does that mean you might come out, after all?"

Mother's inanely one-track mind had for once hit the jackpot. It was precisely what I should do! I stared at her as if she were a fount of wisdom. "Do you know I just might? It could be the very thing. A glamorous, ultra-sophisticated New York debutante." I started to strut slowly about the landing. "Oh, I begin to *see* it! World-weary and worldly-wise. In a daring, dashing quest for thrills!"

Mother still blinked. "We'll get the money out of Grandma. You'll see, we'll do it somehow!"

That was how it started. You will ask what made me so suddenly and wildly susceptible to the first handsome man in my life. Why had it not happened before? Why did it last? How could John take me over like that, without even trying, without even really wanting to? I can only suppose that he filled a vacuum that had not previously been exposed to his kind of air. My life had been bare of any real love, or even of much affection. I suppose I had liked Daphne Photis well enough, but that had been a schoolgirl's crush. And I admit that I had had some hot feelings for the boys with whom I had necked in taxis going to and from dances, but these pimpled youths had fallen lamentably short of my Byronic ideal. The love of which I constantly dreamed was quite unreal, except insofar as it had been realized in my poetry. Everything in me that pretended to passion must have been waiting for John.

Grandma Gladwin, a stingy little black beetle of a widow who closed her house in Maine every year on the same day in September and spent more money in one season keeping her artifacts in good condition than they were worth altogether, had been so alarmed at the prospect of my going alone to Paris that she was finally prevailed upon to furnish the minimum sum needed for a small dinner dance in a recognized hotel. Mother and I were late getting started, but the party was still manageable, and I now accepted all invitations. Once one puts one's whole heart into anything, even into something as frivolous as becoming a debutante, it can be fun. I began to take an interest in what today would be called my "image."

On the following Saturday night, when John took me out, I pretended that I had reluctantly allowed my parents to prevail in the matter of a coming-out party.

"What do you do," I asked with a hopeless shrug, "when your mother says you've spoiled her whole life? And weeps and wails?"

"But I thought in New York mothers didn't matter," my literal friend pointed out.

"One can still throw them an occasional crumb."

"I think it's very good of you to go through all this for her."

"Do you? Then help me. Promise you'll come to my ghastly party."

"How could I miss it?"

"And remember, too," I continued, glancing at him sideways,

"you're a tiny bit responsible yourself. How can I show you a debutante season if I'm not a debutante myself?"

"Did I say I wanted to see a debutante season?"

"You said you wanted to see life. And pleasure. Let us start with where people think it is. We can go on from there!"

I had divined that what would attract John would be a debutante as different as possible from her opposite number in Boston. It would behoove me to cultivate an air of being wearied by the banal and mildly excited by the exotic. I should have to appear avid for "kicks" and to affect a pallor of unhealthiness, as if from an indulgence in all kinds of forbidden things. John must think I had been to the very brink of hell in my desperate pursuit of sensation.

I began at once the task of developing a reputation for quixotic behavior. I passed up the best party of the month to go to the circus in Philadelphia. I arrived at the Ritz with an escort on a bicycle built for two. I carried a small New Testament in French in my purse and would sometimes read it at the supper table. But best of all was the deal I made with "Styvie Stuyvesant," the pen name of a society reporter who was actually one Digory Dice from Queens, a fat, lazy homosexual of forty who saw in me the opportunity to reduce his task of covering a social season of some two hundred debutantes to that of concentrating on one. By building me up he would have his weekly story: "Althea Stevens at the races"; "Althea Stevens' new beau"; "Althea Stevens shocks her grandmother." Styvie perfectly understood my family's shabbiness and that it need never be known.

"You see, my dear, a society article is the opposite of life. We are taught in life that labels are nothing, that we must be the thing itself. Quite true. But in a newspaper the label is everything. Your mother becomes what her background is by the mere fact of being mentioned in my column. Just you wait! You and I are going to have a lark!"

Grandma was shocked when the articles began to appear and cut back on some of the promised cash, but she was on the hook for the party, and I had no further need of her for clothes. Styvie had shown me how my newspaper reputation could be cashed in for commodities up and down Fifth Avenue. It was, as he had put it, a lark, though one little casualty to the season seemed to be my poetry. For months I did not write a line, and when, later in the season, I tried again, it was to discover that my betrayed muse had fled. I thought at the time that she would return, so I did not worry unduly. But she never did. She never has.

John Gardiner came down frequently from Boston. I was never coy with him and made myself frankly available when he called, ruthlessly canceling any other appointments. So far as my "image" was concerned, I appeared to have guessed his reaction correctly. He was enchanted to be able to take out one of the more publicized debutantes of the season (for I must note here that I was not the only one with complacencies for the press) and he cross-examined me with relentless enthusiasm on my philosophy of pleasure. But we did not seem to become any more intimate. We were friends, close friends—there was *nothing* we did not tell each other about our poor parents—but he never made a pass at me. He never even seemed to think of it.

This was not quite so strange as it may seem today. It was even part of an old sexual game that we used to play: the jaded New York girl and the Bostonian Sir Lancelot. Those games could be great fun and very sexy if not protracted too long. I was beginning to think that John was protracting it too long. And then, on top of this, came the fiasco of my dinner dance.

Everything went wrong. Tommy Dean sent his third-class orchestra, and the champagne was warm and flat. Mother's slowness in advance payments and her refusal to tip made ravages in the service. Half the guests left immediately after dessert to go on to a big party. But what was worst of all, much the worst, was that John did not show up until after dinner, and he had been seated on my right! In those days that was the greatest compliment that a debutante could pay a man, and it was his duty, after a roll of drums, to rise and propose her health. The man on her left then toasted her parents, or whoever was giving the party. On that ghastly night, because I had refused, even at the last moment, to put anyone in John's place, taking a masochistic glee in exposing my gaping wound to the multitude, the man on my left, my languid, sarcastic, older cousin, Langdon Stevens, had to make both toasts, which he was mean enough to do in two separate ceremonies instead of trying to save my face by combining them. He even went so far as to refer to the "late Mr. Gardiner," for he had always been envious of John's looks and wealth.

When John finally did arrive, at half past ten, he had the gall not to seem mortified. His grandfather had had a stroke, and he had not been able to leave Boston until his mother had obtained a satisfactory report from the doctor. He had not telephoned, he explained, because he had not "dreamed" that he would be seated so prominently. He appeared to consider this answer quite satisfactory and to be surprised when I bluntly refused to go on to the big dance with him. But he stayed with me. He stayed until my little party was over and even Mother had gone home. As we sat alone in a corner with a last bottle of the flat champagne, watching the waiters clear off, I surrendered to the sullen temptation to smash the best thing in my life. Giving in to it had the agonizing luxury of dipping one's body slowly into a scalding bath.

"I'm sick and tired of our masquerade," I snarled. "I'm sick and tired of pretending to be something I'm not just to impress *you*. What the hell type of stupid goon are you anyway, that you can't see anything straight? Where did you get your crazy notion that I'm a glamour girl and that a glamour girl is better than what you have up in Boston? Don't you know that I'd give every one of my false eyelashes to be a Miss Codfish from Bean Street? Just so long as I had a Codfish fortune?"

John's eyes glittered with amusement. "Go on, go on. I've never heard you this way."

"You probably think it's another ploy in a desperate girl's technique. Try candor when all else fails. But it's not. I'm genuinely disgusted. With my family, with my life, with myself. And with you, too! For being such a bloody ass. This horrible party, do you know what it means? That we can't go away for the summer for at least three years. Europe, college, they're simply *out*. Mother's so bust she'll accuse a maid of stealing so as not to pay her wages. And Daddy cheats at cards. He does! Everyone knows it. Nobody good will play with him. And even Granny, who's supposed to be so conservative, is secretly blowing her capital. After her the deluge! The guy who's lucky enough to receive my fair hand in marriage will receive with it a string of debts. Count on it, Boston!"

"But, Althea, the way you live, the clothes you wear . . ."

"Don't you really know how that's done?" I interrupted him. "I get my lunches free at Emile's if I take my crowd there. I get my clothes free at Le Tellier's if I drag my friends in. But everyone knows about me now, and the shops are tired of me. I shall have to sell something else, and there's only one thing I've got left."

"Honey, I love you!"

In the taxi going home, he damn near raped me. I had never known necking like that before. But at our door, as if not trusting his bestial instincts, he hurried down the stoop and watched me from the window of his cab until I was safely in. I was so hot and frustrated that I tossed all night. He, as I learned after we were married, had gone straight to a cat house. It was the other side of the coin of our New York–Boston game. He repeated the maneuver many times in the year of our engagement.

There was one remaining advantage to me, however, in the game. It enabled me to convince him that the very natural dislike on the part of his parents for me and mine was mere prejudice. I played my part very cleverly in the first weekend that I spent with the Gardiners in Manchester. I made a point of neither smoking nor drinking, but I was not such a fool, with my record, as to pretend that I never did. I simply stated airily that I smoked only in months with an "a" and drank only in those with an "e." I then managed to infuriate Mr. Gardiner, while keeping quite cool myself, in a discussion in which I maintained that FDR was a greater man than Lincoln, and outraged his wife, in the same manner, by arguing in favor of companionate marriage. When they carried their expostulations in private fury to John, they of course wildly overstated their cases and dished themselves as hopeless mossbacks.

When John at last proposed to me, suggesting that we should marry right after his graduation from Harvard, it came as the least bit of an anti-climax. Of course, I accepted him. There was never any question about that. By this time I had invested my whole emotional life in John Winthrop Gardiner. I had become a debutante, I had become a "personality," I had given up poetry, for John Winthrop Gardiner. How could I go back on all that? Nor did I want to. I yearned to sleep with John Winthrop Gardiner, and indeed I was never to find any disappointment in *that* side of marriage. But above all I *wanted* to be in love with John Winthrop Gardiner, to be in love with him always, because I already suspected what has since turned out to be true: that I should never again experience anything like the joy that I had felt that first night when he came to dinner and read my poems. I suppose I must have hoped that I could build a whole life on that memory. It seemed to me that it would remain fresher if I were married to him.

I can just hear what your uncle would say to that. "Was my brother to blame because that ridiculous woman expected the impossible of him?" No. It was not John's fault that he aroused the hope of the impossible. But some human beings are so fortunately situated in life and endowed with such charm and beauty that they cannot help but enchant their observers with a romantic vision. Maybe the significant thing about this girl, Alison Brady, is that she is the first woman to see John without illusions. That may be the advantage of his present age. That she can love him, really love him. Perhaps she *is* the first to do that! Daphne Photis and the others were basically like me.

3

I am glad I have called this a gospel, because it allows me to follow the gospel form of leaping ahead. In the true gospels we see Jesus born in a manger and then—bang—he is thirty years old and preaching. That is the way most lives are. In marriage you can skip over a decade without a significant change, and when that change comes, it may be simply your discovery that all along you've had a basic misconception of your mate.

The first ten years of my marriage were the dreary story of my turning into a bitch. I did not have far to go. When I first really took it in that I was never going to be able to change anything in my husband—his opinions, his enthusiasms, his loyalties—that I was going to have less imprint on the granite of his personality than even the generations of pilgrims who had at least partially eroded Saint Peter's toe with their kisses, I felt justified in adopting a settled attitude of mocking denigration. I suppose it gratified my ego to see the look of surprise on the faces of John's friends and relations when I derided the husband whom everyone thought I had had the Devil's own luck to catch. I felt that marriage had cut me in two, like an amoeba in fission, and that one of my selves had been absorbed into a grinning, self-sufficient John Gardiner while the other, with all my faults, my frustrations and my shallow bitternesses—the real me—was left to contemplate the superiority of my supposedly equal partner.

The first big shock came when John, in the September following our marriage, abruptly converted himself into a grinding Harvard law student. I was told that this was a common process with the young bloods of the era. Like the conditioned sexagenarians in Aldous Huxley's *Brave New World*, they presented themselves to the gas chambers of law school with a complete acceptance. The holiday of college was over; now they settled down to work. Statutes and cases marked the beginning of the serious life, the life of the responsible male, the male who cared about "getting on." It made sense, of course, in an ordered, class society, but it still bewildered me that John should cast aside quite so lightly his old epicureanism, his living for the brave minute, his scorn of the Gardiner values. Such things, apparently, were purely seasonal, as ephemeral as the silly hats and jackets that men wore on college reunions, the sight of which would be as welcome as a hangover the following Monday morning. And John not only worked hard; he worked successfully. In his third year he was editor-in-chief of the *Law Review*, and after graduation he became clerk to U.S. Supreme Court Justice Mitchell and thereafter an associate in the great New York Wall Street law firm of Abbott & Sinclair. Five years after that he was a partner. Wow!

What I could never understand about John or his Boston friends was how they managed to have their cake and eat it. When I married him, he had no religion at all, at least that I could ever discover. He always refused to be drawn into any discussion of the spirit, so I could not be absolutely sure, but he never went to church, and I am sure that he never prayed. Then, too, he was a Democrat and a New Dealer, a collector of abstract paintings, a vigorous critic of all forms of social and ethnic discrimination and an active supporter of boys' clubs. Yet his life seemed perfectly consistent, whether we lived in Boston, New York or Washington, with that of the smartest and most frivolous society in each of those cities. He never, as so many of my rich New York friends did, seemed to feel the smallest need to apologize for his wealth or background. To him there was no necessary inconsistency between what he was and what he thought. He was even able to make his parents proud of him. After their early row about me, John and Mr. and Mrs. Gardiner settled back into a harmonious love and amity that confused as much as it irritated me. Couldn't the old folks *see* that he was a threat to the arrogant caste system of which they were symbols? No. They couldn't.

My own relations with John were controlled by his own self-control. He allowed me my small victories with a shrug. I was always shrilly pointing out that he ought to resign from the Patroons' Club if he was sincerely opposed to anti-semitism, or that he should not shoot with his friends in Georgia if he disapproved of the near-peonage in which they kept their Negro servants. He would rarely even argue with me, so obvious was it to him that there was nothing wrong with enjoying the substance of a social hierarchy so long as one disavowed its forms. And then, too, I suppose, he knew that I had no real principles of my own, that I was simply goading him. I think that John's love for me withered rapidly under my sniping— particularly in the preoccupying labors of law school—but that he would never admit this to anyone, including himself. Physically, he continued for years to find me satisfactory, and my querulousness could be ignored except when it became loud. There was always the moment at a party when, if I had too much to drink or raised my voice too much, John would rise silently, bring my cape into the living room, clasp it firmly about my shoulders and take me home. There was never any question, in the last analysis, as to who was boss.

The catastrophe of World War II brought me another surprising revelation about John: that an antichrist could satisfy the spiritual needs of a Boston-bred puritan even better than a Christ. What Hitler did for John and his Harvard friends was to give them their long-wanted substitute for religion. The world in which they had grown up became precious to them to the extent that it was threatened. They might not have been able to tell you, in 1939, what they did believe in, but when they looked across the Atlantic to the horrid, screaming man with the trench coat and the mustache, they knew what they did *not*. Like their abolitionist forebears of the eighteen-fifties, they received the message well in advance of other Americans. John signed up with all the interventionist groups, and it was only because of the imminent birth of Christine that he did not, like several of his friends, join the British army. By Pearl Harbor, however, he was already on active duty with the U.S. Navy, and he spent the war on aircraft carriers in the Pacific, winning the Silver Star for his conduct in a torpedoing. He remained on the bridge with his commanding officer until all hands were clear of the ship and then thwarted his skipper's desire to go down with it by seizing him by the pants, pitching him over the side and diving in after him. They remain the closest of friends to this day.

I found his patriotism rather trying. It was made worse by the fact that I could never say anything. John, on his rare leaves, beribboned and uniformed, was received by his family and friends with adulation. Mr. and Mrs. Gardiner in particular idolized him. They were even nice to *me* when I took Christine up to Boston for wartime Christmases. I was afraid, if I ventured the opinion that he was something less than a crusader and Messrs. Churchill and Roosevelt something less than divinities, that I would be turned in as a spy. And I did not really want to be in dissent. I was not against the war. It was simply that I was distrustful of the amount and quality of the emotion that the Gardiners pumped into it. I did not see that we had to be quite so hysterical.

On the other hand, I enjoyed being fussed over as an absent hero's wife. There seemed to be a pleasant general assumption that just by existing as John's wife and the mother of his baby, I was doing my bit against Hitler and Hirohito. I played this for all it was worth and confined my war work to the easy task of joining a bureau that supplied entertainment for foreign officers passing through New York. The married women on the board were expected to give dinner parties or work at the Center, helping with advice about hotels and theater tickets or playing bridge or backgammon with the officers who dropped in. But sometimes it went beyond that.

And now, Jock, I am going to show the extent of my candor by relating a little incident that I have never told anyone. Your father and your uncle believe that the affair with Harvey Price was my first. It wasn't. There was an Argentinian naval officer named Gonzalez, rather small but very cute, with lazy eyes, who laughed at everything. He came up to the apartment alone several times and gave me the sensation of being a silly debutante again. I felt nothing for him, nothing at all, but we laughed giddily together and drank a lot, and, of course, one night it happened. He was very sweet about it afterwards, very grateful and courteous and unpresuming—he even went so far as to say it had nothing to do with my essential marital fidelity —but I still hated him and refused to see him again. For the first time in my life I understood murder. I could have killed him without a qualm—if I had been assured of getting away with it. It was unspeakably aggravating to know there was a man living who could prove that my mother-in-law had been right about me from the first.

4

There has never been anyone like your father for avoiding the discussion of basic personal issues. His negative capability in this respect is equaled only by his positive ability in assembling masses of facts for the solution of small, practical questions. John could tell you what we spent on butter in 1946, but not why Christine has never married. Yet the avoidance of any direct facing of what had happened to our marriage in the years immediately following the war was as much by my wish as his. We were both, I think, averse to the idea of divorce. John did not wish to admit to Boston that he had made a mistake, and he cared deeply about the appearance of a solid home. Besides, he knew how to find his pleasures privately. And I . . . well, what did I have in my life but the pride and irritation of being John's wife? I was afraid to be alone, without that. I still am.

It helped that John was so busy. His law practice would have been more than enough to fill an ordinary life, but, in addition, he was now passionately interested in government, particularly in the Central Intelligence Agency. On three different occasions he took leaves of absence from his firm to work for it. Like so many of his friends, he had transferred all his old hatred of the Nazis and Japanese to the Russians. I suspected that it was only thus that they could preserve the unity, the excitement, the "togetherness" which they had so loved in the war. They could not bear to go back to the old spiritless days of the thirties. Antichrist had come, and antichrist had gone, but where was Christ? Communism seemed to offer them an antichrist II. Well, then, have at it! It still seems to me that there was an element of childishness in their sleuthing, a boy's need to divide the world into cops and robbers, a yearning to change a decomposing America into a tightly-knit, brightly-lit, James Bond thriller. Of course, I could be wrong. I may rue these words one day when I see that mushroom of vapor in the sky and hear that the Reds are upon us. Your father is sure that I will.

The inevitable major crisis between John and me did not erupt from the bubbling crater of our home life until 1954, when John, now aged thirty-eight, returned to the CIA under Eisenhower's administration. He was still a Democrat, but that made no difference. He was united to the soldier-president by the far deeper bond of a faith in things military. We took a beautiful yellow house in Georgetown and found ourselves in the center of the smart crowd of "appointed," as opposed to "elected," Washingtonians. It was a bit like playing lords and commons in London, except that we had a lot more power than lords. John, as usual, was intensely satisfied with his work and did not mind that nobody outside the Agency knew what he was doing. He had always been a man who cared only for the applause of the cognoscenti.

But it was different with me. I missed my New York friends and the long lunches and the cards. There was Daphne Photis, now Daphne Smythe, my old "crush" from Miss Hornor's school, whose dull, industrious husband was in the Department of Commerce (rather looked down upon by the CIA and "State") but she was far more interested in John, for whom she had always had a mash. She wanted me to feel there was something going on there, and I gratified her by treating her with the arch detachment of the suspicious wife. But I was bored with the endless government talk and the too-hard-working men, and my drinking became more of a problem. John now rationed me at parties, and when he saw me exceed my allowance—how he kept track, I have no idea, but he seemed to be able to do so even with his back turned—he would take me straight home, sometimes going back to the party himself.

My only solace was Harvey Price. He was in "State," also a lawyer, brilliant, unmarried, fortyish, a big, handsome though rather fleshy man with rolling, laughing blue eyes and a fine head of glossy brown hair. Harvey laughed too loud and, like me, drank too much, but he was amiable and kind, and, being endowed with all the snobbishness of his native Pennsylvania small town, he was much impressed by the Gardiners. I suspected that he was homosexual, and the circumstances of his subsequent murder by a psychotic youth, some years later, seemed to confirm this, but at that time he still divided his interest between the sexes. He sensed my discontent and restlessness and found my state congenial. He had come to the Department under Acheson, and he felt like an alien under Dulles.

"Why don't you quit?" I asked him. "Why don't you go back to your old firm?"

"Because I really feel I might do something for the country by staying on."

"You mean by opposing Mr. Dulles?"

"Well, no. One doesn't oppose the Secretary. But by being on the spot I might help to defuse some of his more dangerous ideas."

"What a curious form of patriotism. So unlike John's. He loves his boss."

"Well, he doesn't have a Presbyterian psalm-singer who doubles as a Wall Street lawyer."

"John says you're very prejudiced about Mr. Dulles."

"That I do not deny."

John disliked Harvey Price, but he was perfectly willing to have him around as a distraction for a troublesome wife. Harvey and I laughed at everyone together. He never seemed too busy to hear my gossip or my complaints. I would call him constantly at his office, and we would chat aimlessly for minutes on end.

"Harvey," I would hiss into the telephone, "do you know what they call Ambassador Fox in Paris? The diplomat with the closed mind and the open fly!"

His shriek, I was sure, could be heard all over the Department. And then his answering voice would be lowered.

"Have you heard what Ike said to Joe McCarthy when they met in the washroom at the Firemen's Ball . . . ?"

And so it went. At dinner parties his eye would catch mine down the table in silent merry communion. John was constantly away, in Europe or the Far East, and people took to asking me and Harvey together. But then Harvey and I, bored with dinners, took to dining alone together. And, of course, one night, very late, while John was in Berlin and I had been drinking heavily with Harvey in his flat, things ended as those things usually end. It was the Argentinian officer all over again, very fuddled and clumsy. As I dressed soberly afterwards I had the same violent reaction.

"John wouldn't believe this if I told him," I announced in a tight voice to my pale reflection in the mirror.

"John?" Harvey was still in bed, smoking. "What does John care for such carnal matters? Hasn't he found the true and only joy?"

"What do you mean by that?"

"I mean that he's never been happier," Harvey replied in the mocking tone of one who finds happiness a refuge for the less enlightened. "John positively whistles with joy."

"Why?"

"Isn't it obvious? He's a Saint George who has finally found his dragon. And such a lovely dragon, too. With shiny scales and ghastly horns and all the fire you could wish from a nostril."

"You mean communism."

"The world communist conspiracy, of course. An enemy worthy of a Winthrop or a Gardiner. An enemy that never sleeps, that lurks in every chancery the world over, hides under every bed, that . . ."

"Oh, stuff. John had equally good dragons in Hitler and Hirohito. You should have heard him in those days."

"Ah, but *were* they such good dragons? Wasn't there something in John Winthrop Gardiner of Beacon Street . . ."

"Commonwealth Avenue," I snapped. "You never get those things right."

Harvey's smile betrayed more irritation than he cared to betray. "The thoroughfare makes no matter. My point is that there must have been moments when the representative of ancient law and order in New England wondered—oh, deep down, I concede—if the savior of the German business world, that deadly and most effective opponent of Reds and radical Jews, was not, just possibly, the wrong enemy?"

"Never!" I cried in a sudden burst of anger. "That's your middle-class, John O'Hara, Pennsylvania background coming out! You cannot admit that a Gardiner could be motivated by simple patriotism.

John abominated fascism and he fought it, too, all over the Pacific, unlike certain friends of mine who sat out the war in the Pentagon."

Harvey's smile was thoroughly nasty now. He got up to comb his hair. I could hardly blame him for resenting my broadside, yet I tingled with the pleasure of my attack.

"My, my, my, don't we take fire for our naval hero? I can't imagine why you want to *tromper* him with a Pennsylvania meatball."

"No doubt the whole thing has been a mistake," I retorted. "But at least I shall have given you the satisfaction of making a cuckold of a man you deeply envy and can never possibly equal."

Harvey's laugh was too loud, too long. "So you think *that* was my motive? Isn't it more likely that it was yours?"

"Mine? What do you think you're talking about? How could it possibly have been mine?"

"I suggest that you sought my chamber only to revenge yourself on John."

"Revenge myself? Whatever for?"

"Why, for his flagrant affair with Daphne Smythe. Don't tell me you didn't know about *that*."

"I know what Daphne wants me to think."

"She wants you to think the simple truth."

I had just enough presence of mind to leave without further discussion. I walked all the way home from Harvey's apartment on Dupont Circle. It was a cold, brisk night, and I managed to convince myself that further recriminations would be simply degrading to both of us. It would be a sufficient memorial in my mind on the tombstone of our affair that he had let me walk to Georgetown alone on a winter night. I was only sorry that nothing terrible happened to me on the way.

John flew into Washington the following Monday, very grave and busy over a Berlin crisis, and spent all day and most of the night at his office. However, I waited up for him, and at midnight, over a decanter of brandy, we had a "confrontation," to use a word that was constantly on his lips those days.

"I know you're tired," I told him, "and I'm sure you want to get to bed, but first you have to tell me about you and Daphne."

He looked at me with an expression that I could interpret only as simple exasperation. "For Pete's sake, Althea, is that a subject to bring up, with the world falling apart?"

"The world falling apart? *My* world's falling apart. Bring your mind home from Berlin, John. This is your wife talking."

"My wife?" John's eyes seemed steel-rimmed glasses of repudiation. "Or Harvey Price's mistress?"

"My God, but that only just happened!" I cried in astonishment. "And it's never going to happen again. You can't be a mistress for one drunken roll in the hay!"

After the long moment of an exchanged stare between two strangers, John burst out laughing. "Well, I shall always have to give you marks for honesty, Althea. We may have reached the point where it's all we have left. But don't pretend you care about Daphne. You care as little as Daphne cares. Or as *I* care."

"About either of us?"

John at last helped himself to a glass of brandy. "Oh, why do we draw it out? Why do we labor it? Daphne's nothing to me. What are you getting at, Althea?"

"I guess I want to know what you *do* care about. Or if you care about anything at all."

"Very well." John set his jaw now as I had seen his father set his, as jaws should be set by lawmakers, bishops, Gardiners. "I care about your never seeing Harvey Price again."

"Oh?" My heart turned over in a flutter of surprise and sudden hope. Was it possible? Still possible?

"Yes. I had not planned to tell you this, because the information is strictly confidential. But as long as you tell me that it's all over between you two—sexually, I mean—then you can help me by cutting him off—socially."

"Help you?" My heart seemed to stop, and everything was gray again. No, it was impossible. Impossible.

"Help me. Harvey will be discharged this week by the State Department. Or rather he will be allowed to resign. No difficulty is expected about this. He should be tickled pink at the chance. The alternative would be a dishonorable discharge, perhaps worse. You see, we have found out about Harvey. He has been working against the Secretary by giving out classified information to a certain senator on the Foreign Relations Committee."

"Oh, but Harvey was trying to *help*," I protested. It seemed to me quite possible that John had misunderstood it all. "He doesn't believe in what Mr. Dulles is trying to do."

"Then what is he doing in the State Department?"

"Trying to prevent Mr. Dulles from hurting the country!"

John's features were rigid. "Do you know what he deserves? He deserves to be taken out before a firing squad and shot. And if there were more than two corpuscles of red blood left in the American body politic, that is what would happen."

"You can't mean it!"

"Ah, but I do mean it. And I also mean what I say about your not seeing him again. Certainly he can never cross *my* threshold again. But beyond that I should much appreciate it if you would promise me never again to be seen in the company of that giggling, party-going fag of a traitor!"

I stared up at him, as much shocked as disappointed. "Oh, John, how can you be such a stuffed shirt?" My eyes were suddenly full of tears, tears which for the first time I was ashamed of showing him. "Couldn't you ask me to give up Harvey because you were jealous? Couldn't you pretend? Just for once? I'd have loved it so! And now what can I do? Obviously, my pride requires that I see Harvey as often and as publicly as possible. But I'd have to make up with him first. And I can't. Not even to spite you, you son of a bitch!"

What did your father do? I'll give you one guess. Once again, he roared with laughter.

5

And now, Jock my dearest, I come at last to thee. You were, from the very start, the opposite of your sister. Christine, seeing early that I was the weaker vessel, tried in vain, yet for the honor of her sex, to mold me into something at least resilient. But she always recognized that her father was unchangeable and accepted him as a fair, even as a rather amiable opponent. That continues to be their relationship. "Hi, Red!" he yells at her. "Hi, Duce!" she yells back. And they love each other—in their own Gardiner way. But you decided early, for your own peculiar psychological reasons, that I had been your father's victim and that it was to be one of your principal functions to prove to the world that behind his impressive New England front beat a heart that had no warmth and ticked a mind dedicated to the main chance.

I have to admit that you could be a very provoking child. You had not then developed your present tall, gangling, rather foxy good looks. You had a furtive demeanor accentuated by long, greasy hair rubbed constantly out of eyes that seemed to snicker out a challenge to every implied tenet or premise. It was not that you were always argumentative that irked your elders and mentors; it was that snotty little smile with which you greeted all their assumptions. Your father was remarkably patient with you. Sherman Gardiner was once heard to remark that as a parent he was "a saint or a fool, probably both." John always heard you out when you were in an attacking mood, no matter how iconoclastic the onslaught, and he would nod, smiling in answer to your smile, and opine that there was undoubtedly something in what you said. It surprised everybody that a father so tolerant should make so little headway in your affections. You treated him as if he were a usurping step-parent and yourself a brooding Hamlet.

Only on the rare occasions when your father really barked did your attitude seem to change to one of grudging respect. This was always the case when he decided to make an important *moral* point—as when those two friends of yours were suspended from Farmingdale for smoking pot. It was through me, and not, as you then thought, through your faculty adviser, that your father discovered that you had been involved. I could not resist the temptation to puncture his smug satisfaction that you had *not* been.

"You mean Jock *lied?*" he demanded. "Lied to the headmaster?"

"What else could he do? Schools don't let boys plead the Fifth."

"Althea, this is no time for joking. I don't so much mind Jock's smoking pot. I don't even mind a fib in the first flush of apprehension. But to tell a lie in cold blood to get out of the punishment given his friends who had owned up—that is not the conduct of a gentleman."

"I'm weary of hearing about gentlemen. So, I'm sure, is Jock."

"Very well, then, it's not the conduct of a *man*. I shall telephone the headmaster and see that Jock shares the punishment of his friends."

"John, you can't! It's *my* secret."

Actually, your father did not telephone. He went right up to the school and had it out in front of you and Dr. Chubb. And you took it like a lamb! All during the weeks of your suspension which followed you never once reproached him. I suppose there had to be moments, when he took that authoritative tone in matters which involved *your* supposed iniquity, and not his own, that you tended, deep down, to agree with him. Ah, yes, you have a Puritan's conscience, too. How could you escape it? Your father might be full of cant when he addressed himself to the sins of the world, but when it was a question of the sins of his own son, *then* he spoke as from the mount, in raiment white and glistening! *That* was your Achilles' heel. Oh, you Gardiners!

By the time your father and I came to the last and greatest of these moral confrontations, the climactic one over your draft questionnaire, my life had ceased to be a series of small crises and recoveries and had crumbled into what seemed a perpetual slide. My drinking was now more than a social problem; I spent considerable parts of each winter in retreats. Your father accepted my condition with a patience and a gallantry that made him a sort of hero in our set. He worked harder and traveled more, dividing his time between his law firm and government posts. He had now become a relatively famous man, and I was known as his difficult wife. I could imagine those Washington hostesses on the morning telephone:

"We have the Gardiners coming tonight. No, not Defense, he's Under-Secretary of the Navy now. Oh, yes, divine, a dream of Boston's best, with just the right New York leavening. She's the problem. Of course if she doesn't come, I'm okay—and she's apt to give out at the last minute. These loyal husbands who've married too young! There ought to be a law against it."

John had been in favor of American intervention in Vietnam from the beginning. He loved LBJ; he loved McNamara; he hadn't a doubt that we were in the right. Joe Alsop was his bible. This was the time that Alison Brady made her appearance in our life. She was as dedicated to the war as he, and their martial ire seemed to drape their adultery in the stars and stripes. When you told me that you were planning to avoid the draft by pretending to be a homosexual, I am afraid that my first reaction was a horrid glee at the prospect of your father's and Alison's scandalization. Yet he was even angrier than I anticipated.

"If Jock believes the war in Vietnam is wicked, let him refuse to serve!" he cried, on the night when I waited up to tell him.

"But then he'll go to jail."

"Not if he's a conscientious objector. And, anyway, that doesn't matter. He should stand up to be counted."

I was disgusted at the ease with which he accepted the idea of prison for you. "It's just the grounds you object to," I insisted. "You can't bear to have your son say he's homosexual."

"I find that distasteful, of course. But, believe it or not, I find the most distasteful part of it that it's a lie."

"Oh, stay out of it, John. It's not your lie. It's not your generation. You're not being drafted to fight for something you believe is evil."

"Why did you tell me then?"

"Because I want you to find him a better excuse. One that won't send him to jail if they find it's not true."

"Nonsense. How can they prove a negative? The *excuse* is okay. But I shall certainly use my prerogative as a father to make it very clear to Jock what I think of his lying to his government."

I stamped my foot. "Can't you leave that decision to him?"

"The decision *is* his."

"But you know you'll influence him."

"I shall certainly try to."

"John, what faith is it that gives you such confidence in interfering in other peoples' lives?"

"My absolute faith in what a man should be."

"And what is it based on? Do you even believe in God?"

"My faith is *me*."

What more could I say? And then followed that terrible scene between him and you which ended with your complete capitulation. What I had never anticipated was that your father's victory would be so decisive as to make you throw up the idea of resisting the draft on any ground. That phrase of his about "standing up to be counted" certainly bit into your New England subconscious. The next thing I knew you were in the army, a private at Fort Dix. And it was only six months afterwards that you converted a weekend pass into a self-exile in Europe.

The letter that you wrote your father when you discovered his involvement in the illegal bombing in Cambodia was worthy of Cicero denouncing Catiline. I recall in particular this sentence: "That a man could preach to his son about lying to his government while he himself was brushing aside a Congressional mandate in order to commit mass murder makes Judas' kiss in the garden seem the expression of a genuine affection." But your father was not affected by it. He was strangely collected in our final scene. I suppose my hysteria made him colder. By this time the war was going so badly that even he no longer defended it.

"Can't you *ever* admit you're wrong?" I railed at him. "Don't you think it might do your soul a bit of good to engage in some small act of penance? Europe is covered with shrines that violent men erected to atone for bloody deeds. Don't you think you might put up a plaque in memory of the people you've killed and the son's life you've destroyed? By saving him from a lie and making him a deserter!"

John gave me a long hard look. "You have never believed in anything, Althea. And you have always resented my failure to share your emptiness. You have spent your life trying to pull me down. And now that you see the tragic finale of the war in Vietnam, you hope that this at last will convince me of my futility. But it doesn't. A lost war is not necessarily an evil one. The right side does not always win."

"You couldn't be mistaken, could you, John?" I jeered. "Anything could happen but that!"

John's lips formed a tight straight line. "I could be mistaken, of course. The war itself could have been a mistake. But couldn't it have been an honest mistake?"

"How can you call such madness, such mass slaughter, such inept tomfoolery, honest?"

"I don't say that those responsible shouldn't be shot. That's the way it would have been handled in the old days, and I'd be perfectly willing to face a firing squad. Like Erskine Childers in Ireland, I'd even shake hands with the boys who made it up. But that's not the way we do things in America. We go on. So be it. I shall go on. But I fail to see the utility of penance for honest error. Though I am sorry to deprive you of that long-awaited satisfaction."

I began at last with this to sense that the message which I was receiving was not the only one intended for me.

"And is Alison Brady to be a part of your going on?" I cried.

"Alison is to be a very definite part of my going on. An indispensable part. And don't tell me that you care. Or that Christine cares. Christine has long thought that you and I should go our separate ways. I have only held out, because I thought our marriage might help poor Jock and give him an anchor in his own rough sea. But I'm afraid this letter of his marks the end of my role in his life. That, like the war, has been a failure. Another failure that I must learn to accept. But there is no duty to be crushed by failure."

"As if anything could crush *you!*"

"Let us spare ourselves a scene, Althea. I am moving out."

Which he did. That very night.

What you and I must now face, Jock, is what your father still means to us and what we no longer mean to him. He is a force, a natural force, which has gone out of our lives. He continues to affect others, thousands, perhaps millions. Since he has become the special negotiator for the Secretary of State, his face is constantly seen in the background of those press shots showing perfunctorily grinning world leaders grasping hands or clinking glasses. He is no longer associated with war or with the Far East. John, as he proved on his carrier in World War II, was never one renowned for his loyalty to sinking ships. He is a dove now, an agent of peace, and so convincing a one that I wager he could appear on the campus of Columbia or Harvard without receiving a single boo. So much for our political memories.

You and I have perhaps been too concerned with judging him. By the time we have found him guilty and condemned him to perdition, he is off on a new career. John is like the world, at least the world to date: he survives. He leaves to us the role of the hand-wringing chorus. You have hoped to make an impression on the world by your stand on the war. You have made none. You cannot. The world is too full of people like your father. That is why it may blow itself up. That is why it may be saved.

Come home, my child. Come home and give yourself up. Your father's firm can easily get you the minimum sentence, maybe none at all. Follow my example. For I, too, am giving up. I shall consent to a divorce so that your father may marry his Alison. I hear she's having a baby.

Please come home, Jock. I need you.